**Praise for W. Bruce Cameron,
author of the beloved #1 *New York Times*
and *USA Today* bestselling novel
*A Dog's Purpose***

"Another winning tale of an extraordinary human-canine companionship full of tug-at-the-heartstrings adventure."
—*Booklist*
on *A Dog's Way Home*

"I loved the book and I could not put it down."
—Temple Grandin,
New York Times bestselling author of
Animals in Translation, on *A Dog's Purpose*

"An amazing book. I laughed and smiled and cried. Wise . . . and sure to open the hearts of all who read it."
—Alice Walker,
Pulitzer Prize–winning author of
The Color Purple, on *A Dog's Purpose*

"*Marley & Me* combined with *Tuesdays with Morrie.*"
—*Kirkus Reviews* on *A Dog's Purpose*

"Readers will devour this wonderful story and cry from beginning to end. Sweet and heartfelt, Cameron likely has another bestseller on his hands."
—*Publishers Weekly* (starred review) on
A Dog's Journey

"*The Dog Master* is a unique, vivid story of how canine companionship came to be and, in no small way, saved humanity as a species; a truly inspired read."
—*HuffPost*

BY W. Bruce Cameron

A Dog's Purpose
A Dog's Journey
The Dogs of Christmas
Emory's Gift
The Dog Master
A Dog's Way Home

Repo Madness Series

The Midnight Plan of the Repo Man
Repo Madness

8 Simple Rules for Dating My Teenage Daughter
How to Remodel a Man
8 Simple Rules for Marrying My Daughter

For Younger Readers

Ellie's Story: A Dog's Purpose Puppy Tale
Bailey's Story: A Dog's Purpose Puppy Tale
Molly's Story: A Dog's Purpose Puppy Tale
Max's Story: A Dog's Purpose Puppy Tale
Shelby's Story: A Dog's Way Home Tale

A DOG'S WAY HOME

W. Bruce Cameron

FORGE®

A Tom Doherty Associates Book
New York

This is a work of fiction. All of the characters, organizations, and events portrayed in this novel are either products of the author's imagination or are used fictitiously.

A DOG'S WAY HOME

A Forge Book
Published by Tom Doherty Associates
175 Fifth Avenue
New York, NY 10010

www.tor-forge.com

Forge® is a registered trademark of Macmillan Publishing Group, LLC.

ISBN 978-1-250-30190-1

Our books may be purchased in bulk for promotional, educational, or business use. Please contact your local bookseller or the Macmillan Corporate and Premium Sales Department at 1-800-221-7945, extension 5442, or by email at MacmillanSpecialMarkets@macmillan.com.

First Edition: May 2017
First Mass Market Edition: December 2018

Printed in the United States of America

0 9 8 7 6 5 4 3 2 1

For my nephew, William Gage Cameron

A DOG'S
WAY
HOME

One

From the beginning, I was aware of cats.

Cats everywhere.

I couldn't really see them—my eyes were open, but when the cats were nearby I registered nothing except shifting forms in the darkness. I could smell them though, as clearly as I could smell my mother as I took nourishment, or my siblings stirring next to me as I worked my way to find life-giving milk.

I didn't know they were cats, of course—I just knew they were creatures not like me, present in our den but not attempting to nurse alongside me. Later, when I came to see that they were small and fast and lithe, I realized they were not only "not dogs," but were their own distinct kind of animal.

We lived together in a cool, dark home. Dry dirt underneath my nose gave up exotic, old smells. I delighted in inhaling them, filling my nose with rich, flavorful aromas. Above, a ceiling of parched wood dropped dust into the air, the roof pressing down so low that whenever my mother stood up from the packed depression in the earth that served as our bed to leave my siblings and me—squeaking in protest and huddling against each other for reassurance—her upright tail was halfway to the beams. I did not know where my mother went when she departed, I only knew how anxious we were until she returned.

The sole source of light in the den came from a single square hole at the far end. Through this window to the world poured astounding scents of cold and alive and wet, of places and things even more intoxicating than what I could smell in the den. But even though I saw an occasional cat flicker through the hole out into the world or returning from some unknown place, my mother pushed me back whenever I tried to crawl toward the outdoors.

As my legs strengthened and my eyesight sharpened I played with the kittens as I would with my siblings. Often I singled out the same family of cats toward the back recesses of our communal home, where a pair of young kitties were particularly friendly and their mother occasionally licked me. I thought of her as Mother Cat.

After some time spent romping joyfully with the little felines, my own mother would come over and retrieve me, pulling me out of the pile of kittens by the back of my neck. My siblings all sniffed me suspiciously when my mother dropped me next to them. Their responses suggested they did not care for the residual whiff of cat.

This was my fun, wonderful life, and I had no reason to suspect it would ever change.

• • •

I was nursing drowsily, hearing the peeping sounds of my brothers and sisters as they did the same, when suddenly my mother lunged to her feet, her movements so unexpected that my legs were lifted off the ground before I dropped from the teat.

I knew instantly something bad was happening.

A panic spread through the den, rippling from cat to cat like a breeze. They stampeded toward the back of the den, the mothers carrying their mewing offspring by the backs of their necks. My siblings and I surged toward our mother, crying for her, frightened because she was frightened.

Strong beams of light swept over us, stinging my eyes. They came from the hole, as did the sounds: "Jesus! There's a million cats in the crawl space!"

I had no sense of what was making these noises, nor why the den was filled with flashing lights. The scent of an entirely new sort of creature wafted toward me from the hole. We were in danger and it was these unseen creatures that were the threat. My mother panted, ducking her head, backing away, and we all did our best to stumble after her, beseeching her with our tiny voices not to leave us.

"Let me see. Oh Christ, look at all of them!"

"Is this going to be a problem?"

"Hell yes it's a problem."

"What do you want to do?"

"We'll have to call the exterminator."

I was able to distinguish a difference between the first set of sounds and the second, a variation of pitch and tone, though I wasn't sure what it meant.

"Can't we just poison them ourselves?"

"You got something on the truck?"

"No, but I can get some."

My mother continued to deny us the comfort of her teats. Her muscles were tense, her ears back, her attention focused on the source of the sounds. I wanted to nurse, to know we were safe.

"Well, but if we do that, we're going to have all these dead cats all over the neighborhood. There's too many. If we were just talking one or two, fine, but this is a whole cat colony."

"You wanted to finish the demo by the end of June. That don't give us a lot of time to get rid of them."

"I know."

"Look, see the bowls? Somebody's actually been feeding the damn things."

The lights dipped, joining together in a burning spot of brightness on the floor just inside the hole.

"Well that's just great. What the hell is wrong with people?"

"You want me to try to find out who it is?"

"Nah. The problem goes away when the cats do. I'll call somebody."

The probing lights flickered around one last time, and then winked out. I heard dirt moving and distinct, heavy footfalls, so much louder than the quiet steps of the cats. Slowly, the presence of the new creatures faded from the hole, and gradually the kittens resumed their play, happy again. I nursed alongside my siblings, then went to see Mother Cat's kitties. As usual, when the daylight coming through the square hole dimmed, the adult cats streamed out, and during the night I would hear them return and sometimes smell the blood of the small kill they were bringing back to their respective broods.

When Mother hunted, she went no farther than the big bowls of dry food that were set just inside the square hole. I could smell the meal on her breath and it was fish and plants and meats, and I began to wonder what it would taste like.

Whatever had happened to cause the panic was over.

* * *

I was playing with Mother Cat's relentless kittens when our world shattered. This time the light wasn't a single shaft, it was a blazing explosion, turning everything bright.

The cats scattered in terror. I froze, unsure what I should do.

"Get the nets ready; when they run they're going to do it all at once!"

A sound from outside of the hole. "We're ready!"

Three large beings wriggled in behind the light. They were the first humans I had ever seen, but I had smelled others, I now realized—I just had not been able to visualize what they looked like. Something deep inside of me sparked a recognition—I felt strangely drawn to them, wanting to run to them as they crawled forward into the den. Yet the alarm crackling in the frenzied cats froze me in place.

"Got one!"

A male cat hissed and screamed.

"Jesus!"

"Watch it, a couple just escaped!"

"Well, hell!" came the response from outside.

I was separated from my mother and tried to sort out her scent from among the cats, and then went limp when I felt the sharp teeth on the nape of my neck. Mother Cat dragged me back, deep into the shadows, to a place where a large crack split the stone wall. She squeezed me through the crack into a small, tight space and set me down with her kittens, curling up with us. The cats were utterly silent, following Mother Cat's lead. I lay with them in the darkness and listened to the humans call to each other.

"There's also a litter of puppies here!"

"Are you kidding me? Hey, get that one!"

"Jesus, they're fast."

"Come on, kitty-kitty, we won't hurt you."

"There's the mother dog."

"Thing is terrified. Watch it don't bite you."

"It's okay. You'll be okay, girl. Come on."

"Gunter didn't say anything about dogs."

"He didn't say there would be so many frigging cats, either."

"Hey, you guys catching them in the nets out there?"

"This is hard as hell to do!" someone shouted from outside.

"Come on, doggie. Damn! Watch it! Here comes the mother dog!"

"Jesus! Okay, we got the dog!" called the outside voice.

"Here puppy, here puppy. They're so little!"

"And easier than the damn cats, that's for sure."

We heard these noises without comprehension as to what they might mean. Some light made its way into our space behind the wall, leaking in through the crack, but the human smells did not come any closer to our hiding place. The mingle of fear and feline on the air gradually faded, as did the sounds.

Eventually, I slept.

. . .

When I awoke, my mother was gone. My brothers and sisters were gone. The depression in the earth where we had been born and had laid nursing still smelled of our family, but the empty, vacant sense that overcame me when I sniffed for Mother brought a whimper from me, a sob in my throat I couldn't quiet.

I did not understand what had happened, but the only cats left in the space were Mother Cat and her kittens. Frantic, seeking answers and assurance, I went back to her, crying out my fear. She had brought her kittens out from behind the wall and they were gathered back on the small square of cloth I thought of as their home. Mother Cat examined me carefully with her black nose. Then she curled around me, lying down, and I followed the scent and began to nurse. The sensation on my tongue was new and strange, but the warmth and nurture were what I craved, and I fed gratefully. After a few moments, her kittens joined me.

. . .

The next morning, a few of the male cats returned. They approached Mother Cat, who hissed out a warning, and then went to their own area to sleep.

Later, when the light from the hole had been its brightest and had started to dim, I picked up a whiff of another human, a different one. Now that I understood the difference, I realized I had had this scent in my nose before.

"Kitty? Kitty?"

Mother Cat unexpectedly left us on our square of cloth. The odd flash of cold that came with her departure shocked all of us, and we turned to each other for comfort, squirming ourselves into a pile of kittens and dog. I could see her as she approached the hole, but she did not advance all the way out—just stood, faintly illuminated. The male cats were on alert, but they did not follow her to the human.

"Are you the only one left? I don't know what happened, I wasn't around to see, but there are tracks in the dirt, so I know there were trucks. Did they take all the other cats?" The human crawled in through the hole, momentarily blotting out the light. He was male—I could smell this, though I would not learn until later the distinction between man and woman. He seemed slightly larger than the first humans I'd seen.

Again, I was drawn to this special creature, an inexplicable yearning rising up inside me. But the memory of the terror of the day before kept me with my kitten siblings.

"Okay, I see you guys. Hi, how did you get away? And they took your bowls. Nice."

There was a rustling sound and the delicious smell of food wafted onto the air. "Here's a little bit for you. I'll go and get a bowl. Some water, too."

The man backed out, wriggling in the dirt. As soon as he was gone the cats surged forward, feeding ravenously on whatever was spilled on the dirt.

I alerted to the approach of the same person sooner than the cats, as if they were unable to identify his scent as it grew stronger. The males all reacted, though, when he reappeared at the hole, fleeing back to their corner. Only Mother Cat stood fast. A new bowl was shoved forward and there was a meal in it, but Mother Cat made no approach, just stood watching. I could sense her tension and knew she was ready to bolt and run if he tried to capture us like the other humans had.

"Here is some water, too. Do you have kittens? You look like you're nursing. Did they take your babies? Oh, kitty, I am so sorry. They're going to tear down these houses and put up an apartment complex. You and your family can't stay here, okay?"

Eventually the man left, and the adult cats cautiously resumed eating. I sniffed Mother Cat's mouth when she returned, but when I licked her face she turned abruptly away.

Time was marked by the shifting light pouring in from the square hole. More cats came; a few who had been living with us before, and a new female, whose arrival triggered a fight among the males that I watched with intense interest. One pair of combatants lay locked together for so long that the only way I knew they were not asleep was the way their tails flickered, not wagging in happiness but communicating a real distress. When they broke their clinch they stretched out on the ground, noses nearly touching, and made un-catlike sounds at each other. Another fight consisted of one male lying on his side and smacking another one, who was on all four feet. The standing one would tap the sprawling one on the top of the head and the one lying down would respond with a series of rapid clawings.

Why didn't they all get up on their back two legs and attack each other? This behavior, while stressful for all the animals in the den, seemed utterly pointless.

Other than Mother Cat I had no interaction with the adults, who acted as if I did not exist. I tangled with the kittens, wrestling and climbing and chasing all day. Sometimes I would growl at them, irritated with their style of play, which just seemed wrong, somehow. I wanted to climb on their backs and chew on their necks, but they couldn't seem to get the hang of this, going limp when I knocked them over or jumped on top of their tiny frames. Sometimes they wrapped their entire bodies around my snout, or batted at my face with teeny, sharp claws, pouncing on me from all angles.

At night I missed my siblings. I missed my mother. I had made a family, but I understood that the cats were different from me. I had a pack, but it was a pack of kitties, which did not seem right. I felt restless and unhappy and at times I would whimper out my anguish and Mother Cat would lick me and I would feel somewhat better, but things were just not the way they should have been.

Nearly every day, the man came and brought food. Mother Cat punished me with a swift slap on my nose when I tried to approach him, and I learned the rules of the den: we were not to be seen by humans. None of the other felines seemed at all inclined to feel the touch of a person, but for me a growing desire to be held by him made it increasingly difficult to obey the laws of the den.

When Mother Cat stopped nursing us, we had to adjust to eating the meals the man supplied, which consisted of tasty, dried morsels and then sometimes exotic, wet flesh. Once I grew accustomed to the change it was far better for me—I had been so hungry for so long it seemed a natural condition, but now I could eat my fill and lap up as much water as I could hold. I consumed more than my sibling kitties combined, and was now noticeably larger than any of them, though they all were unimpressed by my size and resolutely refused to play properly, continuing to mostly claw at my nose.

We mimicked Mother Cat and shied away from the hole when the human presence filled it, but otherwise dared to flirt with the very edge, drinking in the rich aromas from outside. Mother Cat sometimes went out at night, and I could sense that the kittens all wanted to join her. For me, it was more the daylight that lured, but I was mindful of Mother Cat and knew she would swiftly punish any attempt to stray beyond the boundary.

One day the man, whose fragrances were as familiar to me now as Mother Cat's, appeared just outside the hole, making sounds. I could sense other humans with him.

"They're usually way toward the back. The mother comes closer when I bring food, but she won't let me touch her."

"Is there another way out of the crawl space besides this window?" It was a different voice, accompanied by different smells—a woman. I unconsciously wagged my tail.

"I don't think so. How will this work?"

"We've got these big gloves to protect us, and if you'll stay here with the net, you can catch any cats that make it past us. How many are there?"

"I don't know, now. Until recently the female was obviously nursing, but if there are any kittens they don't come out in the day. A couple others, I don't know what sex. There used to be so many, but I guess the developer must have gotten them. He's going to tear down this whole row of houses and put up an apartment complex."

"He'll never get a demolition permit with feral cats living here."

"That's probably why he did it. Do you think he hurt the ones he caught?"

"Um, okay, so, there's no law against trapping and destroying cats living on your own property. I mean, he could have taken them to one of the other shelters, I guess."

"There were a lot of them. The whole property was crawling with cats."

"Thing is, I didn't hear anything about a big bunch of cats showing up anywhere. Animal rescue is a pretty tight community; we all talk to each other. If twenty cats hit the system, I would have heard about it. You okay? Hey, sorry, maybe I shouldn't have said anything."

"I'm fine. I just wish I had known it was going to happen."

"You did the right thing by calling us, though, Lucas. We'll find good homes for any cats we find. Ready?"

I had grown completely bored with the monotonous noises and was busily wrestling with the kittens when I felt Mother Cat stiffen, alarm jolting through her. Her unwinking eyes were on the hole, and her tail twitched. Her ears were flat back against her head. I regarded her curiously, ignoring the little male kitty who ran up, swatted my mouth, and darted away.

Then a light blazed and I understood her fear. Mother Cat fled toward the back wall, abandoning her young. I saw her slip soundlessly into the hidden crack just as two humans came in through the hole. The kittens milled in confusion, the male cats fled to the back of the den, and I shied away, afraid.

The light danced along the walls, then found me, blazing brightly in my face.

"Hey! There's a puppy in here!"

Two

"Hey kitty-kitty!" The woman crawled forward, reaching out. On her hands, thick cloth was redolent with traces of many different animals, mostly cats.

The kittens reacted by darting away in terror. Their flight was chaotic and without direction, and none of them ran to the crack in the wall where Mother Cat hid, though I could smell her in there, cowering and afraid. The other adult cats were little better, though they were mostly frozen, staring in dread at the approaching human. One of them broke for the hole and snarled when the woman caught him in her heavy mittens. She handed him carefully back to another pair of cloth-covered hands. Two more adults made it past her and out to freedom.

"Did you catch them?" the woman asked loudly.

"One of them!" came the answering shout. "The other one got away."

As for me: I knew what I should do. I should go be with my mother. But something in me rebelled against this reaction—instead, I felt enticed by the woman wriggling toward me, fascinated by her. A compulsion seized me: though I had never experienced human touch, I had an acute sense of how it would feel, as if remembering something from long ago. The woman gestured toward me with her hands even as the rest of the adult cats bolted out the hole behind her. "Here, puppy!" I bounded forward, straight into her arms, my little tail wagging.

"Oh my God, you're a cutie!"

"We caught two more!" shouted a voice from outside.

I licked the woman's face, wiggling and squirming.

"Lucas! I've got the puppy, can you reach in and take him?" She lifted me up and examined my tummy. "Take her, I mean. She's a girl."

The man who had been bringing us food for the bowls appeared at the hole, his familiar smell flooding in. His hands reached out and gently wrapped themselves around me, and then he brought me out into the world. My heart was pounding, not in terror, but in total joy. I could still feel the kittens behind me, sense their fright, and Mother Cat was strong in the air, but right then I just wanted to be held by the man, to chew his fingers and pounce on him when he set me down and rolled me around in the cool dirt.

"You are so silly! You are such a silly puppy!"

While we played, the woman brought out the kittens one at a time and handed them to two men who put them into cages on the back of a truck. The little kitties were mewing in distress. Their appeals saddened me, because I was their big sister, but I could do nothing to help them. I expected that our mother would soon be joining them, and knew they would feel better then.

"I think we got them all," the woman said, coming over to where I was playing with the man. "Except for the ones that ran out."

"Yeah, sorry about that. Your guys got theirs but I wasn't any good at catching them."

"It's okay. It takes a lot of practice."

"What will happen to the ones who took off?"

"Well, hopefully they won't come back right away, if the workers are going to tear down the houses." The woman knelt down to stroke my ears. Having attention from two humans at once was simply the most wonderful thing that had ever happened to me. "There weren't any other dogs. I have no idea what this little one was doing down in there."

"I never saw her before," the man said. "It's always just been cats. How old is she?"

"I don't know, maybe eight weeks? She's going to be big, you can tell that. Look at those paws."

"Is it what, a shepherd? Mastiff?"

"No, I mean, there could be some mastiff in there, but I'm seeing Staffordshire or maybe rottie in the face. Hard to tell. Probably a whole cocktail of canine DNA."

"She looks healthy. I mean, if she's been living in the hole," the man observed. He picked me up and I went limp in his hands, but when he brought me close I tried to chew his nose.

"Right, well, I doubt she's been *living* there," the woman said. "Probably just followed a kitten in, or the adult. Speaking of that, when was the last time you saw the mother cat?"

"It's been a few days."

"She wasn't in the crawl space, so we must have come at the wrong time and she's out hunting. If you see her, let me know, okay, Lucas?"

"Do you have a card or something?"

"Sure."

The man set me down and he and the woman stood up. She handed something to the man. I put my paws on his legs, wanting to sniff it. I was interested in everything the man was doing, and most of all wanted him to crouch back down and play with me some more.

"Audrey," the man said, looking at the small thing he held between his fingers.

"If I'm not there, just talk to anyone who answers. They all know about this house. We'll come out and try to catch any stragglers. Oh, I asked around, and nobody brought in a big colony of cats anywhere in Denver recently. I think we have to assume the worst."

"How can someone *do* something like that?" the man replied, anguished-sounding. I jumped on his feet so that he'd know that if he was sad he had a puppy down here to make all of his worries go away.

"I don't know. I don't understand people at all, sometimes."

"I feel really bad."

"Don't. You didn't know what he was up to. Though I don't know why they couldn't be bothered to drive the animals to a shelter somewhere. We could have found homes for some of them, and we have connections to safe places for feral cats. Some people just can't be bothered to do the right thing." The woman picked me up. "Okay, little one, are you ready to go?"

I wagged, then twisted my head so I could see the man. It was his hands, more than anyone else's, that I craved.

"Uh, Audrey?"

"Yes?"

"I feel like that's my dog. I mean, I found her, technically."

"Oh." She set me down and I went over to the man to chew on his shoes. "Well, I'm not supposed to adopt out an animal this way. There's a procedure, I mean."

"Except if it is my dog, it's not an adoption."

"Okay. Look. I don't want this to get awkward or anything. Are you even in a position to take on a puppy? Where do you live?"

"Right there, in those apartments across the street.

That's how I saw the cats; I walk past here all the time. I just decided one day to feed them."

"Do you live alone?"

Something very subtle changed in the man's manner. I looked up at him alertly, wishing he would pick me up again. I wanted to lick his face. "No, I live with my mother."

"Oh."

"No, it's not what you are thinking. She's ill. She's a soldier and when she came back from Afghanistan she developed some symptoms. So I'm going to school and working with the Veteran's Administration to try to get her the help she needs."

"I'm so sorry to hear that."

"I'm taking online classes. Pre-med. So I'm home a lot, and my mom is, too. We can give the puppy all the attention she needs. And to have a dog, I think it would be good for both of us. My mom can't hold down a job just yet."

He reached down and picked me up. Finally! He held me in his arms and I lay back and gazed at his face. Something significant was happening; I could sense it even though I was not sure what it was. The den, where I had been born and where Mother Cat still cowered, seemed like a place I was leaving behind. Now I would be with this man, wherever he took me. That was what I wanted: to be with him.

"Have you ever had a puppy? They're a lot of work," the woman asked.

"I lived with my aunt when I was growing up. She had two Yorkies."

"This one is already bigger than a Yorkie. I'm sorry, Lucas, but I can't. It's unethical. We have a vetting process— one of the reasons why we get so few returns is that our placement protocols are so stringent."

"What are you saying?"

"I'm saying no. I can't let you have her."

The man looked down at me and smiled. "Oh, puppy,

did you hear that? They want to take you away from me, do you want that?" He lowered his face to mine and I licked him and he smiled. "Puppy and I vote she stays with me. Two to one," he told the woman blandly.

"Huh," the woman replied.

"I think things happen for a reason, Audrey. There was a reason this little girl was under there, hiding with the cats, and I think that reason was for me to find her."

"I'm sorry but there are rules."

He nodded. "There are always rules, and there are always *exceptions* to the rules. This is one of those exceptions."

They stood quietly for a moment. "People win with you? Arguments, I mean," she asked finally.

He blinked. "Well, sure. Just not this one, I guess."

She shook her head and smiled. "All right, well, like you said, you found her. Will you get her in to see a veterinarian right away? Like, tomorrow? If you'll promise to do that, I'm okay with it I guess . . . Let me give you some stuff, I've got leashes and collars and puppy food."

"Hey, puppy! Want to come live with me?"

There was a bright smile on his face, but I could sense something in his voice I did not understand. He was anxious, bothered about something. Whatever was going to happen next, it worried him.

. . .

Mother Cat did not come out. I could smell her when the man carried me away from the den, and imagined her still in the tight hiding place, cowering from the humans. I didn't really understand this—what was there to be afraid of? I felt as if I had never seen anything as amazing as the man holding me, never experienced anything as wonderful as the feel of his hands on my fur.

When the people closed the door on their vehicle the sounds of my kitten brothers and sisters was abruptly cut off, and then the truck drove away, leaving only lingering traces of my feline family on the air. I wondered when I would see them again, but I did not have time to dwell on this odd separation, where my siblings went in one direction, our mother another, and me in a third. There were so many new sounds and sights, I was dizzy with it. When the man brought me into the place I would learn to call home, I smelled food and dust and chemicals and a woman. He set me down and the floor was luxuriously soft with carpet. I ran after him when he crossed the room and dove into his lap when he folded his legs and sat down to be with me.

I could sense the man's anxiety rising, it was on his skin the way Mother Cat tensed when she knew humans were approaching the hole.

"Lucas?" A woman's voice. I associated the voice with the scents of her layered on every object in the room.

"Hi, Mom."

A woman walked into the room and stopped. I ran to meet her, wagging, wanting to lick her hands. "What?" Her mouth dropped open and her eyes widened.

"It's a puppy."

She knelt and held out her hands and I went for them, rolling on my back and chewing on her fingers. "Well, I can see it is a puppy, Lucas. What is it doing here?"

"It's a she."

"That is not an answer to my question."

"The people came from the animal rescue to get the rest of the cats. Most of them, anyway. There was a litter of new kittens, and this little puppy was under the house with them," he said.

"And you brought her home because . . ."

He came over and squatted next to the woman and now I had both people touching me!

"Because look at her. Someone abandoned her and she found her way to the crawl space and probably would have starved under there."

"But you can't have a dog, Lucas."

The man's fear was gone now, but I felt something else stirring in him, a different emotion. His body was stiffer, his face drawing tight. "I knew you would say that."

"Of course I would say that. We're barely hanging on, here, Lucas. You know how expensive a dog is? Vet bills and dog food, it adds up pretty quickly," she said.

"I've got a second interview at the VA, and they said Dr. Gann is bound to approve me—I know everybody there, now. So I'll have a job. I'll have the money."

His hands were stroking me, and I felt myself relaxing, getting sleepy.

"It's not just the money. We talked about this. I really want you to focus on getting into med school."

"I *am* focused!" His voice was sharp and I snapped out of my fatigue. "Do you have a problem with my grades? If that's the issue, let's talk about it."

"Obviously not, Lucas. *Grades,* come on. That you can carry the load you've got and hold a four-point-oh is amazing to me."

"So is it that you don't want me to have a dog, or that you don't want me making such a big decision on my own?"

His tone made me anxious. I nosed him, hoping he would play with me and forget about what was making him upset.

There was a long silence. "Okay. You know what? I keep forgetting you're nearly twenty-four years old. It's just too easy to fall back into the mother-son dynamic we've always had."

"Always had." His voice was flat.

Another silence. "Yes, except for most of your childhood. You're right," she said sadly.

"I'm sorry. I don't know why I brought that up. I didn't mean anything."

"No, no, you're right. And we can talk about it as often

as you need to, and I will always agree with you, because I have made so many, many bad decisions in my life, and so many of them concern leaving you. But I'm trying to make up for that now."

"I know you are, Mom."

"You're right about the puppy. My reflex is to act as if you're still a teenager and not my adult roommate. But let's think about this, Lucas. Our lease doesn't even allow pets in the building."

"Who is going to know? Probably the only advantage of having what everyone thinks is the crummiest apartment in the complex is that the door opens onto the street instead of the courtyard. I'll pick her up and walk outside and by the time I put her down no one from the building will even know where I came from. I'll never let her out in the courtyard and I'll keep her on a leash." He flipped me over on my back and kissed my stomach.

"You've never had a dog. It's a big responsibility."

The man didn't say anything, he just kept nuzzling me. The woman laughed then, a happy, light sound. "I guess if there's anything I don't need to lecture you about, it's being *responsible*."

* * *

Over the next several days, I adjusted to my new, wonderful life. The woman was named Mom, I learned, and the man was Lucas. "Want a treat, Bella? Treat?"

I gazed up at Lucas, feeling something was expected of me, but not comprehending any of it. Then he pulled his hand out of his pocket and gave me a small chunk of meat, unleashing a flood of delicious sensations on my tongue.

Treat! Soon it was my favorite word.

I slept with Lucas, cuddled right next to him in a soft pile of blankets that I shredded a little until I understood how unhappy this made him. Lying next to him was even more comforting than being pressed up against Mother Cat. Sometimes I gently took his fingers in my mouth while he dozed, not to bite, but just to apply the gentlest of nibbles, so full of love my jaw ached with it.

He called me Bella. Several times a day, Lucas would bring out the leash, which was what he called the thing that snapped to the "collar." He would use the leash to drag me in the direction he wanted to go. At first I hated the thing, because it made no sense to me that I was pulled by the neck in one direction when I smelled wonderful things in another. But then I learned that when the leash was un-hooked from its place by the door we would be going for a "walk," and did I delight in doing that! I also loved when we came home and Mom would be there and I would run to her for hugs, and I loved when Lucas put food in my bowl or when he would sit so that I could play with his feet.

I loved wrestling with him and the way he would hold me in his lap. I loved *him*. My world had Lucas at its center and when my eyes were open or my nose was active I was seeking him. Every day brought new joys, new things to do with my Lucas, my person.

"Bella, you are the best little puppy in the world," he told me often, kissing me.

My name was Bella. Soon that's how I thought of my-self: Bella.

At least once a day we would go to the den. There were several houses in a row with no people living in them, but only one had cats. They were walled off by a mesh fence, but Lucas would pull at the wires where they were affixed to a pole and then we would be inside.

The smell of Mother Cat was still strong in the den, though the signs of the kittens were fading from the area. I also knew some of the male cats had returned. Lucas would put food and water down but I wasn't allowed to eat it. Nor was I allowed to go into the den to see my mother.

"See her? See the kitty? She's just there, watching us, Bella. You can barely make her out in the shadows," Lucas would say softly.

I loved hearing my name. I could sense a question in Lucas's voice but it did not lead to any treats for me. I might not understand what he was saying, but I was with Lucas, so nothing else mattered.

One afternoon I was lying on Lucas's foot, where I had collapsed after a particularly vicious game of attack-the-shoes. I was not comfortable, lying there, but was too exhausted to move, so my head was much lower than the rest of my body.

I heard a noisy rumble, getting louder, and eventually Lucas shifted in a way that suggested he had heard it, too.

"What's that, Bella?"

I struggled to my feet. Walk? Treat? Lucas went to the window and looked out.

"Mom!" he shouted in alarm.

Mom came out of her room. "What is it?"

"They're unloading a backhoe! They're going to knock down the house, and there are still cats living in there!" He went to a drawer and yanked it open while Mom went to the window. "Okay, look. Here's the card. Call the rescue. Ask for Audrey, but if she's not there, just tell them that the developer is going to tear down the house and the cats will be killed!"

I could clearly feel the fear pouring off of Lucas as he went to get the leash. He snapped it onto me. I shook, fully awake.

"I'll call. What are you going to do?" Mom asked.

"I have to stop them." He opened the door.

"Lucas!"

"I have to stop them!"

Together, we ran outside.

Three

Lucas ran out the door, pulling me along behind him. We dashed across the street. The fence had been partially taken down. Some men were clustered around the den and there was a large, growly machine. The noise it made was startlingly deep and loud. I squatted to pee and one of the men broke away from the group and came over to us. He had shoes from which wafted fascinating tangs of oils and other sharp fragrances I had never encountered.

"There are still cats living under there," Lucas told the man as he approached. Lucas was panting and his heart was pounding when he picked me up and held me against his chest.

"What are you talking about?" the man asked, frowning.

"Cats. There are cats living in the crawl space. You can't tear down the house; it will kill them. You can do the others, but this one has animals."

The man chewed his lip. He looked back over at his

friends, and then at me. "Nice puppy." His hand was roughly textured when it rubbed my head, and I smelled chemicals and soils, both strong and faint on his skin.

Lucas took a deep breath. "Thanks."

"What is she, a daniff?"

"What?"

"Your puppy. Friend of mine has a daniff, a dane-mastiff. Looked a lot like this when he was just a little guy. I like dogs."

"That's great. Maybe, I don't know what breed she is. Actually, she was rescued from the crawl space under the house you're getting ready to demolish. There were all kinds of cats, and many of them are still there. That's what I am trying to explain, that not all the animals were caught. So you can't legally tear down a house with feral cats living under it."

From the hole that led to the den I could smell Mother Cat, and knew she had cautiously come closer. I wiggled, wanting to go see her, but Lucas's hand stopped me. I loved to be held by him but sometimes it frustrated me when it was time to play.

"Legally," the man repeated thoughtfully. "Yeah, well, I've got the demolition permit. It's posted right there, see? So actually it *is* legal. I got nothing against cats, except that maybe my girlfriend's got a couple too many. But I have to do my job. Understand? It's not personal."

"It is personal. It's personal to the cats. It's personal to me," Lucas declared. "They are all alone in the world. Abandoned. I'm all they've got."

"Okay, well, I'm not going to debate on this."

"We called the animal rescue people."

"Not my concern. We can't wait for them."

"No!" Lucas strode over and stood in front of the big machine and I followed, keeping the leash limp between us. "You can't do this."

I stared up at the huge thing, not comprehending.

"You're starting to piss me off here, pal. Get out of the way. You're trespassing."

"I'm not moving." Lucas picked me up and held me to his chest.

The man stepped closer to us, staring at Lucas. They were the same height, eye-to-eye. Lucas and I stared back. I wagged.

"You really want to get into this?" the man asked softly.

"Mind if I set my dog down first?"

The man looked away in disgust. "Momma said there'd be days like this," he muttered.

"Hey, Dale!" one of the other men yelled. "I just talked to Gunter. He says he'll be right here."

"Okay. Good. He can deal with the protester, then." The man turned and walked back to be with his friends. I wondered if the rest of them would come over to pet me. I would like that.

Soon a big, dark car pulled up and a man stood up out of it. He went over and talked to the other men, who all looked over at me because I was the only dog there. Then the man came over to see me. He was taller than Lucas and bigger around. When he came close I could smell smoke and some meats and something sweet on his clothing and his breath. "So what's this about?" he asked Lucas.

"There are still some cats living under the house. I know you wouldn't want to risk hurting them," Lucas replied.

The man shook his head. "There are no cats. We got all the cats."

"No, you didn't. There are still some under there. At least three."

"Well, you're wrong and I don't have time for this. We're already behind schedule because of the damn cats, and I'm not losing another day on it. I've got apartments to build."

"What did you do? With all the cats that were here? Some of them were little kittens!"

"That is not your business. *None* of this is your business."

"Yes, it is. I live right across the street. I see the cats come and go."

"Good for you. What's your name?"

"Lucas. Lucas Ray."

"I'm Gunter Beckenbauer." The man reached out and gripped Lucas's hand for a moment, but then let go. When Lucas's hand returned to holding me, there was meat and smoke on his skin. I sniffed carefully.

"You the one been rolling back my fence? I've sent guys to fix it three times already."

Lucas didn't say anything. Lying in his arms, I was beginning to feel drowsy.

"And it's you feeding the cats, that's obvious. Which isn't exactly helping the situation, you know?"

"You're saying you'd want them to starve?"

"They're *cats*. They kill birds and mice, or maybe you didn't know that. So they don't *starve*."

"That's not true. They way over-reproduce. If they aren't caught and sterilized, they have litters and most of the kittens die of hunger or disease brought on by malnutrition."

"And that's *my* fault?"

"No. Look. All I'm asking is that you give people time to deal with this humanely. There are organizations dedicated to this, to rescuing animals who, through no fault of their own, are abandoned and living treacherous lives. We called one and they are on their way out here now. Let them do their job, and then you can do yours."

The smoky-meat man had listened to Lucas but was still shaking his head. "Okay, that sounds like you're quoting from a Web site or something, but it's not what we're talking about now. You got any idea how hard it is to get anything built these days, Lucas? There's about a dozen agencies you have to work with. I finally got my demo permit after a year delay. A *year*. So I have to get working, now."

"I'm not moving."

"You're seriously going to stand in front of a backhoe while it knocks down a house? You could get killed."

"Fine."

"You know what? I was going to do this the easy way, but you're forcing my hand. I'm calling the cops."

"Fine."

"Anybody ever tell you you're a stubborn little bastard?"

"Stubborn, maybe," Lucas replied. "No one ever says I'm little."

"Huh. You are a real piece of work."

The man walked away without petting me, which was very unusual. We stood still for a long moment. The big machine went silent, and when the rumble quieted my body felt different, as if something had been squeezing me and now had stopped. Lucas put me down and I sniffed carefully at the dirt. I wanted to play but Lucas just wanted to stand there, and the leash did not give me much room to run around.

I wagged when more people showed up. There was a woman and a man, and they got out of yet another car. They were both wearing dark clothing and had metal objects on their hips.

"Police," Lucas observed quietly. "Well, Bella, let's see what happens now that the police are here."

The two people in dark clothes went over and spoke to the man with the smoky meat fingers. Lucas seemed a little uneasy, but we did not move. I yawned, then wagged excitedly when the two people came over to see me. I could smell a dog on the woman, but not on the man.

"Oh my God, that's a cute puppy," the woman said warmly.

"This is Bella," Lucas greeted. I loved that they were talking about me!

The woman was smiling at me. "What's your name?"

"Lucas. Lucas Ray."

"Okay, Lucas. Why don't you tell us what is going on," her male friend said.

The man spoke to Lucas while the woman knelt and played with me. I jumped on her hand. Now that I could sniff her I realized she actually had the scent of two separate dogs on her fingers. I licked them and could taste the dogs. The metal objects at her side rattled.

When the woman stood up I looked back to Lucas.

"But who is supposed to protect the cats, then, if not the police?" Lucas asked. It was the second time he had used that word "police." I could tell he was upset and went to sit at his feet, hoping to help him be happy.

"You don't have a role to play here. Understand?" The man in dark clothes gestured to the big machine. "I get why this bothers you, but you can't interfere with a construction project. If you don't leave we're going to have to take you in."

The woman with the two-dog smells touched Lucas on the arm. "The best thing for you and your puppy is to go home now."

"Will you at least shine your flashlight in the crawl space?" Lucas asked. "You'll see what I'm talking about."

"I'm not sure that would make any difference," the woman replied.

I watched as another car pulled up. This one was redolent with dogs and cats and even other animals. I lifted my nose in the air, sorting it all out.

The new vehicle contained a woman and a man. The man reached into the backseat and pulled out something big and set it on his shoulder. I could not smell what it was. He touched it and a strong light came from

it, reminding me of the time when lights flooded in from
the hole and flashed on the cats as they ran from it in
the den.

I knew the woman. She was the person who had climbed
under the house the day I met Lucas. I wagged at both the
newcomers, happy to see them. There were so many people
here!

"Hi, Audrey," Lucas greeted.

"Hi, Lucas."

I wanted to go see the woman, who I decided was named
Audrey, but she and her friend stopped short of coming up
to us. The light tracked across Lucas's face and then settled on the dirt in front of the hole to the den.

The man with the smoky meat smells strode over. His
footsteps were heavy and he gestured with his hands like
a man throwing a toy for a dog. "Hey! There's no filming
here."

Audrey moved closer to the man with the thing on his
shoulder. "We're filming you because you're tearing down
a dwelling that is home to feral cats!"

The smoky-meat man shook his head. "There are no
cats here anymore!"

I tensed—Mother Cat! She paused for a moment at the
edge of the hole, assessing her situation, and then streaked
out into the open, running right past us and vanishing into
some bushes at the back fence. I forgot I was on the leash
when I tried to chase after her, pulling up short. Frustrated,
I sat and yelped.

"Did you get that?" Audrey asked her friend.

"I got it," replied the man with the thing on his shoulder.

"So, no cats?" Lucas said to the smoky-meat man.

"I want you to arrest those people," the man shouted at
the people in dark clothes.

"They're standing on the sidewalk," the man in the dark
clothes observed calmly. "No law against that."

"We're not going to arrest anyone for filming," the woman with the two-dog smell added. "And you did tell us there were no cats."

"I'm with animal rescue," Audrey said from where she stood. "We've already put in a call to the building commission. They are pulling the demolition permit because of the presence of feral cats. Officers, if he tears down this house, it will be an illegal act."

"That's impossible," smoky-meat man sneered. "They don't move that fast. They don't even answer the damn phone that fast."

"They do when one of our board members calls. She's a county commissioner," Audrey replied.

The two people in dark clothes looked at each other. "This is so not our department," the man said.

"But you saw the cat. Animal welfare *is* your department," Audrey said. I wondered why she didn't come over, but she stood by where the cars were parked. I wanted her to play with us!

"This is costing me money while everyone stands around! I expect the police to do their job and get these people the hell out of here!" the man with the smoky meat smell said angrily.

Police—people who wore dark clothes and had objects on their hips were police. Both of them stiffened. "Sir," the woman said to Lucas, "would you please take your dog and move to the sidewalk?"

"Not if he is going to pull a house down on top of a bunch of helpless cats," Lucas responded stubbornly.

"Jesus Christ!" the smoky-meat man shouted.

The man and the woman in dark clothes looked at each other. "Lucas. If I have to ask you again I'm going to cuff you and put you in the back of our unit," the woman police said.

Lucas stood quietly for a moment, and then he and I

went over so that Audrey could pet me. I was so happy to see her! And I was glad, too, that smoky-meat man and the police followed so we could all be together.

Smoky-meat man took a deep breath. "There were a couple dozen cats here, but not anymore. The cat we just saw could have been in there checking things out—it doesn't mean it *lives* there."

"I see her every day," Lucas told them. A piece of paper fluttered past in the wind and I strained to get at it, but the leash held me back. "She does so live there. A couple others, too."

"About all those cats. What shelter did you take them to? I can't find them in the system anywhere," Audrey asked pointedly.

"Okay, first, this guy Lucas has been cutting my fence, officers. He's been *feeding* the cats! And second, she's right, we brought in an outside company to humanely trap them. I don't know what they did with them. Probably found them all good homes."

"So he's been feeding the cats that you say aren't here anymore." The woman in dark clothing nodded.

Everyone stood quietly for a moment. I yawned.

"Hey, Gunter!" one of the dusty men called. "I got Mandy on the phone. She says it's about your permit."

* * *

Eventually most of the people left. Audrey knelt and played with me in the sparse grass while her friend put the thing with the light back in her car.

"That was genius, showing up with a news camera," Lucas said.

Audrey laughed. "That was a complete accident. I was driving my brother around shooting B roll. He's in film school at CU Boulder. When your mom called we came right over and we thought it would be a great idea to make it look like Fox 31 or something." She picked me up and kissed my nose and I licked her. "You are such a sweetie." She put me back down.

"Her name is Bella."

I looked up at Lucas at the sound of my name.

"Bella!" Audrey said happily. I put my paws on her knees, trying to climb up to her face. "You are going to be such a big doggie when you grow up!"

"Hey, uh, Audrey?" Lucas made a small coughing sound in his throat, and I glanced up, sensing a rising tension. Audrey smiled up at him. "I was thinking it would be fun if you and I went out. And look, Bella agrees."

"Oh." Audrey stood up abruptly. I wandered over to attack Lucas's shoes. "That's sweet, Lucas. Actually, though, I just moved in with my boyfriend. It's pretty serious. We're serious, I mean."

"Sure. No, of course."

"Hey, Audrey! Can we get going? I want to get out to Golden before magic hour," the man yelled out the car window. Sleepy, I yawned and spread out on the grass, thinking it was a good time for a nap. I closed my eyes and didn't open them when Lucas picked me up.

• • •

Later I was playing with Lucas on the soft floor of the big room of the house, what they called the living room. He was pulling a string and I would jump on it and run away with it, but it would slip out of my mouth and, laughing, he would pull it along the floor again until I could pounce. I was so content to be with him, so happy to hear his laughter, that I could have played that game all night.

There was a knock at the door and Lucas became still for a moment, and then went over to it. I followed him. He put his eye to the door while I smelled the scent of a man on the colder air seeping through the bottom crack. It was the man from before, the one who smelled like smoke and meat.

Lucas went rigid. The man knocked again. Finally Lucas opened the door, sweeping me away with his foot as he did so.

"You and me need to talk," the man said to Lucas.

Four

"T alk about what?" Lucas asked.

"Can I come in, or do you want to stand here in the doorway?"

"You can come in." Lucas backed away from the door and the man entered, glancing around. Lucas shut the door even though it meant choking off the glorious wave of outdoor odors that had been flooding in.

The man sat down on the couch. "Cute puppy." He extended his fingers for me to sniff. "He a pit bull?"

"It's a she. We don't know. She was living under the house across the street."

The man went still for a moment and I watched him curiously. Then he sat back. "Yeah, about that. So am I right about you feeding the cat over there?"

"That was me."

"Okay, so that's the irony here, don't you think? I got a problem you caused. You put out bowls of cat food, you get cats. It's a law of nature. And I'm right about you cutting my fence as well, aren't I?"

Lucas didn't reply.

"Look, I came here to talk reason with you. There's a bigger picture I don't think you get."

I was impatient with them just sitting around. I attacked a fuzzy squeaky ball that was lying out on the floor. I couldn't get my mouth around it, and when I tried it rolled away, so I dove on it, wrestling it into submission. I growled, feeling fierce and triumphant.

"I'm sorry Mr. uh . . ."

"Just call me Gunter. I'm trying to be friendly here."

"Okay, Gunter," Lucas agreed.

The smoky-meat man was Gunter.

"Well, I'm sorry, but no one on your crew cared when I told them there were cats under the house," Lucas continued. "They were just going to tear the place down, even if it killed innocent animals."

"Right, and then you called the animal revenge squad and they called the county and now my permit's suspended. Which means it could be a couple of weeks before it is reinstated. Weeks, hell, they don't do anything that doesn't take more than a month—we're looking at the end of the summer, now, probably longer. So I'm paying interest on my loan and I'm paying my crew and I've got equipment and it's all costing me a ton. All of this for a damn *cat*. Which you know there's no law says I can't shoot the thing if I want."

"There's more than one cat. You really want to shoot them? That's good publicity?"

"That's why I'm here. I don't want to do that. But you know damn well that the minute we start tearing down the place those cats are going to take off for the hills. No need to kill them. I just need you to not call the woman with the TV camera. Okay? They don't care what the truth is, it'll be all over the news that we got kittens dying, which is just stupid."

"There won't be any way to know they've all escaped.

We need to catch them and then seal off the entrance," Lucas said.

"No. What? That could take *weeks*. We need an immediate solution." Gunter was silent for a moment. "Maybe we're looking at this from the wrong angle. These units I'm building, they're going to be real nice. Upscale counters, nice appliances. I'll reserve one for you, two bedrooms. What are you here, one bed one bath? I know this complex, it was built in the seventies. No central air, window units only, cheap electric stovetop. Whole thing probably going to be torn down—everybody's building, now that the new hospital is for sure going in."

"We have two bedrooms. And our rent is subsidized. We can't move."

"That's what I'm saying; I'll subsidize you."

"I don't think that would work. It's all tied into my mom's VA benefits."

"Dammit, kid, can you just help me out here? Okay, I'll keep it simple. I'll give you a thousand bucks, you stop talking to the animal rights people. Deal?"

"A thousand dollars to look away while you bring a house down on a family of cats."

"Sometimes life's like that. You got to look at cost benefit. Think of all the good you can do for Save the Cats or Greenpeace or whatever with a thousand dollars, versus the lives of a couple disease-ridden cats that'll probably die this winter anyway."

I yawned and scratched my ear. It didn't matter if there were toys to chase and chew; people usually preferred to just *sit*.

"Five thousand," Lucas said after a moment.

"What?" The man twisted suddenly, making a noise on the couch. I watched him curiously. "You're seriously bargaining with me?"

"I'm just listening to you. You're worried about months

of delay. It could cost you a lot of money. Five thousand seems pretty cheap. Ten thousand, even."

The man was silent for a minute, then laughed out loud. There was a harshness in his voice. "What do you do for a living, kid?"

"Mostly I'm a student. Next week I start a job at the VA hospital as an administrative assistant. It's a good deal, because that's where my mom gets treatment."

I sprawled on the floor, bored.

"Well hooray for you. No, I offered you a good deal and you insulted me by extorting from me. So here's what you get, a good lesson for you. Nothing. You could have had a grand. You think you can get by in this world as a contractor without making a few friends in the government? All I have to do is find an animal control officer who is willing to sign something saying no cats under the house. He'll probably be a lot cheaper than a thousand dollars—I was trying to help you out. You clearly could use the money."

"Actually, you insulted me first by telling me I should compromise for a few pieces of silver. We both know I wouldn't take your money," Lucas replied evenly. "And now you're implying something about our standard of living."

Gunter stood up. "You stay off my land. I catch you over there, I'll have you arrested for trespassing."

"Appreciate you stopping by," Lucas said dryly.

Sometimes people hug or briefly touch hands when they leave, but Gunter and Lucas did not do either.

"I'm not going to let them hurt the cats, Bella," Lucas told me. I heard my name and wondered if it was time for dinner.

* * *

Sometimes Lucas and Mom left me alone. The first time this happened I was very upset and chewed things I knew

I shouldn't—papers and shoes, items that I was not given by Lucas's hand and that were always snagged out of my mouth when I was caught with them. Mom and Lucas were angry when they got home. They shook a shoe in my face and yelled "No!"

I knew the word "no" and was learning not to like it. The next time they left me I chewed my toys and just one shoe. I understood they were angry again but I did not understand why they left me alone. That seemed to me to be the important issue.

When I was with Lucas the world was a wonderful place and when he was gone it was like hiding with my mother in the crack in the back wall of the den, where everything was dark and frightening. I did not understand what I had done and just needed Lucas to come home and reassure me he still loved me. Whenever he said "No!" I cowered and waited for him to stop being angry over whatever the problem was.

My favorite thing to do was go with Lucas to feed the cats. I was always thrilled at the sound and fragrances of the bag of food, though so far he had not let me have any. We would cross the street and Lucas would push through the flap in the fence. I wanted very badly to follow him to the den so I could play, but Lucas would tie me to a tree on the street side of the fence so that I couldn't. I could smell three felines in there, now. Mother Cat never came close enough to the hole to be seen, but the other two sometimes were in the light.

"I can't be here all the time, I have a job now," Lucas said to the cats as he stood at the hole. "I'll try to protect you, but if the machines come you're going to have to run away." Sometimes Lucas would wriggle into the den and I would whimper in distress until he returned.

One night we returned home and Mom and Lucas sat at the table and ate chicken! I sat patiently, waiting for a little morsel, and wasn't disappointed—Lucas's hand came down with a tiny piece of skin that I quickly took from his fingers. I loved chicken and anything else that came from his hand. "There are at least three of them now, maybe four. It's hard to tell."

"How do they get past the fence?" Mom wanted to know.

"Oh, there are plenty of places where a cat could squeeze through. Bella spends a lot of time sniffing at a gap in the back under the bottom frame—I think maybe that's where they are getting in and out."

I looked at him expectantly when he said my name. Treat? Go for a walk? More chicken?

"Any chance of luring them out?" Mom asked.

"No, they're pretty spooked. Especially the black female—she's oddly the most brave and will walk right up to the hole, but I can tell she'll never come out while I'm there."

"What about the woman from animal rescue? Wendy?"

"Audrey. Yeah, I talked to her. She says they'll try to come back out, but they're really swamped right now," Lucas replied.

"She was cute."

"She has a boyfriend."

"Well . . . sometimes they'll say that, but . . ."

"Mom."

She laughed. "Okay. So what is the plan?"

"We're at an impasse until Audrey can come. But I'm not going to let him kill the cats."

"What if he sets out poison?"

"I've been watching for that. He hasn't tried it yet. I think he's trying to find somebody to bribe at the sheriff's department to say the cats have all left."

Mom was quiet for a moment. "Lucas . . ."

"Yeah?"

"Why is this so important to you? Not that I don't love animals, but for you it seems, I don't know, more than that."

Lucas shifted in his chair. "I guess it's because they're all alone in the world."

I glanced over at Mom as she sat back, crossing her ankles. "You feel like you need to protect them because they're abandoned. The way you once felt you, yourself, needed to be protected, when *you* were abandoned."

"Your group therapy is making it almost impossible to have a normal conversation with you."

"I'm serious."

"Couldn't it just be that I feel responsible for them?"

"Why? Why do you feel responsible for everything all the time? It's as if you've been a grown-up since you were five years old. Is it . . ."

They were quiet for a moment. I sniffed carefully at the floor in front of his feet, hoping for a morsel I might have missed.

"Is it what?"

"You're the only child of an alcoholic."

"Can you let this one go, Mom? Sometimes I do things for no reason I can name, okay?"

"I just think it would be a good idea to take a look at it."

"Mom, they're cats. Can we just maybe say that's all there is to it? I honestly don't go through life blaming you every day, or thinking about all the things that happened. I know that's important for you, but I'm just glad things are finally back to normal. All right? And I think it's *normal* to want to stop some builder from bringing a house down on some helpless cats."

"Okay, Lucas. Okay."

• • •

Lucas and I played and played. He liked to say, "Do your business." This meant that when we were outside he would sometimes give me a treat, but most of the time not. He also could put his fingers in his mouth and let loose with a shrill, piercing noise that scared me at first but then became a signal to run to him for a little snack of some kind, so that I became excited whenever he raised his hands to his mouth.

My least favorite item in the house was the "crate." Mom and Lucas sounded very excited when they introduced me to the thing, but it was built from thin metal bars and was not chewable. They put a soft pillow in it and taught me "Go to Your Crate," which meant that I would go inside it and lie on the pillow and they would give me a treat. Then they suddenly changed the game: we did Go to Your Crate and they gave me a treat and then left me alone in the house!

There was nothing to chew but the pillow. Once I had shredded that (it was not too tasty) I was very lonely. I missed Lucas so much I barked the whole time he was gone.

Lucas was very upset that he had left me alone all day, though I was in such a frenzy of joy when he returned I raced around the living room, jumping on the furniture and rolling on the carpet and licking his face. He seemed unhappy that I had strewn pillow stuffing all over the place, but what else was there to do with it? He didn't taste it himself and did not know how unappetizing it was. I certainly wasn't going to eat it.

"I have an old towel you can put in there," Mom said.

"You shouldn't rip up your dog bed, Bella," Lucas told me.

I wagged.

"Maybe put her ball in with her next time," Mom observed.

I stared at her alertly. Ball? I knew that word—the ball was the most wonderful toy in the house. When Lucas threw it, it would bounce away and I would chase it and catch it and bring it back to do it again.

Sometimes Lucas took the ball with us on a walk. There was a wide open place with grass where Lucas would let me off the leash—a "park"—and he would toss the ball over and over again. The ball never got away from me.

I loved chasing the ball and I loved bringing it back and I loved when Lucas told me I was a good dog. Sometimes there were other dogs and they chased other balls, pretending they didn't wish they were chasing a ball thrown by Lucas.

He was my person. I wanted nothing more in life than to be with him every day. Well, that and treats. "Do your business," he'd say. Treat! Then, "Do your business." No treat. It was not the best game.

Then I understood: Do Your Business referred to squatting and peeing, which I had come to prefer to do outside. Lucas radiated such approval, giving me a treat when we were in the grass, that I realized what Do Your Business was all about. We went to the park and I did Do Your Business and got a treat and Lucas was so excited he threw the ball and it bounced over to where children sometimes played on swings. I was right behind it, gaining ground, and when it bounced onto a plastic ramp and rolled to the top I followed, my nails digging for purchase on the slippery surface. At the top of the ramp the ball kept going and so did I, jumping off and catching the ball after it hit the ground and bounded up to mouth-level.

"Bella!" Lucas called. "You ran up the slide! Good dog, Bella!"

Lucas was pleased with me. He led me over to the ramp. "Okay, chase the ball up the slide, Bella!"

We played that game over and over. The ball went up the "slide" and I jumped off after it and caught it and took it back to him. Sometimes I caught the ball in the air on the other side of the slide, right after it bounced off the ground. Lucas would laugh in delight when I did this.

Later he gave me water and we sprawled in the grass. The air was cool and the sun was bright in the sky. I put my head on his legs and he stroked my head. Whenever his hand stopped I nuzzled it, wanting more.

"I am so sorry I have to leave you for work. I love my job, though. I have a desk but I'm hardly ever there; mostly I'm running all over the place assisting my managers with their cases. It's fun but I do miss you, Bella."

I loved it when he said my name.

"Did you hear Mom walking around last night? She's back to not sleeping. I don't know what to do if she is going back into one of her cycles. God, I wish they could just fix her."

A sad feeling came off of him, so I climbed on his chest. That worked: he laughed and pushed me off. "You are such a silly dog, Bella!"

Any time I was with Lucas, I was happy. I loved Mom, but what I felt toward Lucas was as compelling as hunger, and often when I was sleeping I would dream that he and I were together, feeding the cats or playing ball-up-the-slide.

I did not like the phrase "go to work" because when Lucas said it, he meant he was going to leave me for a long, long time. "I'm going to go to work," he would say to Mom, and then I would be alone with her. I could not imagine why he would do Go to Work. Wasn't I a good dog?

Mom would play with me during the day, and take me for short walks on the leash, but we did not feed the cats and did not go to the park.

When it was time for Lucas to stop doing Go to Work I could feel him coming home. I knew without smelling him that he was walking down the street toward the house, and I would go to the door and sit, waiting for him. When I felt him right there, I would start wagging, and a moment later I would smell him and hear his steps on the walk.

"I don't know how, but she knows when you're coming

home," Mom told Lucas. "She goes to the door and whimpers."

"She probably just has my schedule memorized."

"Honey, *you* don't have your schedule memorized. You get out of work at a different time every day. No, she has a sixth sense about it."

"Bella, the psychic dog of Denver," Lucas said. I looked at him but saw no sign that him saying my name was going to lead to any treats.

• • •

Lucas was doing Go to Work and Mom was resting on the couch. Some days she moved around and took me for walks, and she would sing, her voice rising and falling in a way that was entirely different from talking. Recently, though, she did not do much more than lie on the couch. I would cuddle with her, feeling her love, but also some sadness.

I heard someone come up the front steps, though I smelled that it wasn't anyone I had ever met. I could tell it was a man. I barked.

"No, Bella!" Mom scolded.

No? I did not understand the use of that word in this context.

I heard the high, clear chime of the bell that rang when someone was on the front porch. My job was to alert everyone that I had heard it, so I barked again.

"Bella! No! Bad dog."

I regarded her in guilty dismay. Bad dog? What had I done?

Mom opened the door slightly and I pressed my nose to the crack, sniffing and wagging my tail.

"Hey, babe." A large man stood on the steps. His breath smelled of a strong chemical that stung my eyes a little, plus there was a nice bread odor clinging to his clothing.

I sensed Mom feeling unhappy, so I stopped wagging my tail so enthusiastically.

"How did you find me?" Mom asked.

"You going to ask me in, Terri?"

"Okay, but I was just headed out."

"Whoa, big dog! What's his name?"

"She. Her name is Bella."

"Hey, Bella!" He squatted and almost stumbled as he reached for me, putting one hand on the carpet. His hand rubbed the top of my head.

Mom's arms were folded. "I'm not sure why you're here."

"I'm spontaneit-ous."

"Are you drunk or something, Brad? Something *else*?"

"What? Nah."

"Look at me."

The man stood up.

Mom shook her head, looking disgusted. "You're stoned out of your mind."

"Maybe a little." The man laughed. He shambled into the living room, glancing around. Mom watched him coldly. "Look," he began, "I've been thinking a lot about us. I feel like we made a mistake. I miss you, babe. I think we should give it another shot. Neither one of us are any younger."

"I'm not talking to you when you're like this. Ever."

"Like what? Like *what*?"

The man had raised his voice and I flinched from it. Mom put her hands on her hips. "Don't start. I don't want to fight. I just need you to leave."

"I'm not leaving until you give me one good reason why you dumped me."

"Oh, God."

"You look good, Terri. Come here." He smiled.

"No." Mom started to back away from the man.

"I mean it. Do you know how often I think about us? We were good together, babe. Do you remember, that time, we checked into that hotel in Memphis . . ."

"No. Stop." Mom shook her head. "We were *not* good together. I was not myself with you."

"You were never more yourself than with me."

"That's ridiculous."

"Okay, I came here to tell you these compliments and you're acting like a bitch."

"Please leave."

He looked around the room. "Not bad. Looks like your son's back to living with you?" He squinted his eyes. "Maybe he needs a man-to-man talk about growing up and not depending on his mommy for everything."

Mom sighed. "Oh, Brad, what you're suggesting is so wrong in so many ways."

"Really? You want him to wind up like his father? Dead behind a liquor store somewhere? Yeah, you probably don't remember telling me that. You forget what bad shape you were in when I found you," he said with a leer. "You owe me."

"That's what you think? I owe you nothing. You *are* nothing, nothing to me, nothing to the world."

"I don't feel respected here. You know what I'm saying? You got no right to treat me with disrespect. Not after what we done together. What I *know*."

"You have to leave *now*!" Mom's voice was loud and angry. I lowered my eyes, hoping she wasn't mad at me, but then looked up in alarm when the man reached out and grabbed Mom by her arms.

Five

"S top it!" Mom yelled, her voice so harsh I barked. I was terrified. She and the man stumbled against the wall together and something fell with the crash of breaking glass. I cowered away from it.

I heard a thud and the man grunted and backed away, bent over, and Mom went after him, her hands making dull sounds as they struck his face. She whirled and kicked him and he staggered. "You bitch!" he screamed at her. He flailed and she grabbed his arm and twisted it and stomped his legs and he toppled to the floor. I stopped barking. "God, Terri," he wheezed. He was radiating fury and pain. He held his wrist in his hand. I smelled his blood and a trickle of it leaked from his lip and down his jaw.

"No, don't try to stand up, if you stand up I will hurt you," Mom warned angrily.

The man stared at her.

"You need to leave," Mom told him.

"You broke my *wrist*."

"No, I didn't. I could have, but I didn't."

"I'm going to kill you."

"No, you're in my house and if you ever come near me again, *I* will kill *you*," she said furiously. "Now get out. No, I said don't stand up! Crawl. Go on. Do it before I change my mind."

I watched, baffled, as the man made his way on his hands and knees to the front door. I went to sniff him, but Mom snapped, "No, Bella!" so I cringed and sat down. I knew I had done something to make her mad at me.

"I'm going to vomit," the man choked.

"Not here. Get going."

The man reached the front door and opened it, lurching to his feet as he did so. He turned back and started to say things to Mom, but she went to the door and shoved it closed. I could hear him fall on the front steps, but then he was weaving across the yard, and his smell drifted away.

Mom stood at the door for what seemed like a long time. She was so sad. I went to nuzzle her hand, which was wet from wiping her eyes. I was sorry if I had been a bad dog. "Oh, Bella, why can't I ever do even one thing right?"

When she sat on the couch I jumped up to be with her and I put my head in her lap. I could feel some of the tension and sadness leave her. I was giving Mom comfort. This was more important than going for walks, more important than helping feed the cats—it was the most important job I had. I knew I should sit with Mom for as long as she needed me.

She stroked my fur. "You're a good dog, Bella. A good, good dog."

One of the house items I had learned to identify was the "phone." It was metal and not the sort of thing I would ever want to play with, but Mom and Lucas talked about it a lot. Sometimes they held the phone to their faces and talked to me, though I never knew what meaning I was supposed to get out of that, and it never led to a treat of any kind.

While I lay cuddling with Mom, she put the phone to her cheek. "Lucas, can you talk?" she asked. I glanced up at his name. "I just . . . Brad was just here. No, I'm fine. I don't know, it isn't as if we moved here in secret, he could have found out from anybody. I had to get a little rough with him. He was . . . I'm not sure what he was on. Tequila for sure. And he does love the pipe. No, don't come home, I'm okay here with Bella."

I wagged.

"I just wanted to tell you that I was always afraid, if I saw him again, that his world would look good to me. That I'd want to go back to him, to that life. Like part of me doesn't believe I'm really in recovery. But when he walked in I realized right then and there I will *never* do that again. Not to me and not to you. I almost lost you—no, listen—I know what I put you through, and I am just saying you don't have to worry about me. Never again. Okay?" Mom listened for a while. "Yes, I'll go up for a meeting tonight. I love you, too, honey."

Mom put the phone down, still anxious. I climbed into her lap. Gradually, the tension left both of us.

. . .

The next time Lucas took me to feed the cats, I could smell there was another one hiding in there with the others, a new female. She did not come out. Cats, I realized, did not like people very much.

"So I talked to Audrey and she said they can't do anything now because of all the NO TRESPASSING signs Gunter put up," Lucas told his mother.

"I would think he would be happy they're willing to try to rescue the ones remaining under there. It's a win-win."

"I don't know what he's thinking." Lucas sighed.

"Do you need me to help with the nets she dropped off?"

"Honestly, no, I'd rather have you sitting on the porch keeping an eye out for Gunter."

Lucas snapped the leash into my collar. Walk! We went across the street but did not have any food with us. He pushed at the fence and squeezed through a gap, then clapped his hands for me to follow, lifting me over and letting the fence flap back into place. "Ugh, you're getting so heavy." Lucas grunted.

He had me sit and watch while he picked up some thin blankets with little blocks of wood sewn into them. They smelled faintly of cat, and I could see his hands through the material. "Okay, are you ready, Bella?"

I wagged. Lucas unclipped my leash. "Okay, here's your chance. Go ahead, Bella! Go!"

Lucas picked up the blankets and gestured with them. I tensed. What was I supposed to do? "I know you want to do this. Go ahead! Go see the cats!"

There was not a word in any of it I understood. I sat, trying to be a good dog.

He laughed, and I felt the love coming off him and wagged. "You can't believe I'm letting you, can you? Okay, here." Lucas released one handful of blanket and seized my collar. He pulled me over to the hole to the den. I could smell several cats in there, and one of them was Mother Cat. She was not close, though. I remembered the crack in the wall and wondered if she had slithered into that small hiding place.

Lucas pushed my head in the hole. I did not know what he was doing but I did not think I was a bad dog. The cats smelled afraid.

I decided to go see my mother. I sank down to my belly and squirmed through the hole, which had gotten much smaller. When I was in the den I shook myself, wagging.

A familiar panic shot through the adult cats, who acted as if they saw me as a threat. *Me!* As I made my way back to the hiding place they bolted as a pack, streaking for the hole.

"Ahh!" I heard Lucas yell.

I shoved my nose into the crack but could not fit myself into the hiding place. I breathed: Mother Cat was right there in the darkness. I wagged. I heard her ease forward, and then her nose briefly touched mine. She purred.

"Bella! Come!"

I turned away. I wanted my mother to come with me, but I knew she would not.

When I squeezed back out into daylight, Lucas was happy. He held the blankets off the ground, and two very surly male cats glowered at him from inside them. "Netted two of them!" he told me, grinning. I was happy because he was happy.

Back home, Lucas put the two cats in a box. They were moaning in there, their fear loud in their voices. I sniffed curiously at the lid, and when I did so, they stopped making any noise at all.

"You'd like to chase them up a tree, wouldn't you, Bella?"

I wagged, thinking he might let me play with them. Maybe that would make them less grouchy.

Right before dinner the bell rang. I barked like I was supposed to and clearly Lucas was upset at the ringing. "Stop! Don't bark!" he shouted, probably to warn the person to go away. I barked again. "Hey!" he snapped. He swatted my rump and I stared at him in disbelief. We were all yelling and barking because the bell rang, why was he suddenly upset at *me*?

I wagged when I smelled the woman on the doorstep. It was Audrey! She was happy to see me and told me I was a good dog and a big dog and then she carried the box of cats away. I thought probably she was going to take them back to the den. If that were the case, I would see them the next time Lucas let me in there.

The remnants of cats in the box were still in the air when Lucas said, "I'm going to go read," and he and I went to lie in his bed. He had a plate next to him with such glorious fragrances I was nearly dizzy. "You want some cheese, you silly dog?" He held out a delectable morsel between his fingers and I froze, watching it intently. "Oh my God, you're hilarious—it's such a tiny piece of cheese!"

• • •

The next afternoon Mom had just brought me in from outside and was unclipping my leash when I sensed there was something wrong with her. A new emotion came off her, accompanied by a sharp change in the tang of sweat on her skin. I sniffed her anxiously. "Good dog, Bella," she whispered, but she wasn't looking at me, she was staring off in the distance. "Wow, I feel really weird."

Eventually she sat down to do Watch TV. Watch TV was where Lucas and Mom would sit on the couch and pet me, so I normally loved it. This time was different, though, because Mom was different. The bad smell was still there, and when she put her hand on me it felt shaky and tense. I was so apprehensive I jumped down and curled up at her feet, but a moment later was back up. Panting, I got down again and went to drink some water. When I came back, I sat and anxiously nosed her leg. Whatever was wrong with her, I could sense it was getting worse.

"What is it, Bella? Do you need to Do Your Business? We just went out."

She went into the kitchen and pulled out the treat box. I loved the sound of that box coming out of the cupboard, but when Mom walked to the basement steps and opened the door, I was unhappy. She and Lucas liked to toss treats down there and have me run down and back up. Usually

one of them said "good exercise." I did not know what that
meant and did not see why, if they wanted to give me a
treat, they couldn't just hand it to me or let me have the
whole box. This time, though, I did not feel good about
leaving her alone at the top of the steps when she pitched
a couple of morsels down the steps.

"Bella? What are you doing? Don't you want a treat?"

Even her voice alarmed me. I whined.

"Bella, go! Get your treat!"

Her meaning seemed clear, and those snacks at the
bottom of the steps were luring me with their tantalizing
odors. I ran down, needing Lucas. Whenever things were
wrong Lucas would make them right.

As I gobbled the treats as quickly as I could, I heard a
loud crash from overhead, a percussion that seemed to lin-
ger in the air.

Terrified, I dashed back upstairs. Mom was lying curled
up on the floor. She was making small sounds and her
hands were up by her face and were shaking.

I did not know what to do. I tried putting my head on
her shoulder to give comfort, but her shoulder was rigid
and did not relax.

I barked and barked. Mom stopped shaking as much after a moment, but her lips were moving and she made low
groaning noises.

I was never more glad to realize, in that instant, that I
could feel Lucas coming. He would soon be home. I was
frantically waiting for him when his smell finally blos-
somed and the door swung open. "Bella? Why were you
barking? You can't bark in here! Mom? Hello?"

I ran from Lucas around the corner to where Mom lay.
When he didn't follow I ran back. He had gone into the
kitchen and was pulling open drawers. "Your treats are
out, did Mom give you a treat? Is she taking a nap?"

I barked.

"Hey! No, Bella!"

I ran back to Mom. Lucas was still in the kitchen. I stood over Mom and barked.

"Bella! Be quiet!" Lucas came around the corner. "Mom!" He ran to Mom and felt her neck. Then he stood up. I nuzzled Mom's cheek. Lucas picked up his phone and after a moment was talking loudly, his voice full of fear. "Please hurry!" he shouted.

Not long after that, men and women came into our home. I could smell them, but Lucas had locked me in his room, so I couldn't see them. There was a lot of noise at first, and then the front door closed and everything was completely quiet.

I was alone and frightened. I needed Lucas, but I could tell that he had left with all the other people. I did not understand what was happening, but I knew Lucas had been afraid and Mom would not wake up when he touched her. I put my fear into my voice, crying and whimpering, scratching the bedroom door, and then barked, so that people would know I was abandoned and frightened and needed a person to come help me.

No one came.

• • •

I missed Lucas so much I could think of nothing but feeling his hands on my fur. I would not be safe until he came home and let me out of the bedroom. The light filtering in the window had faded and I had smelled the change as the day turned into night and it seemed so very long ago. Now it was the time of night when only the quiet animals rustled in the grasses, and the birds were silent, and the cars going past were solitary and whispering, their lights briefly glowing in the curtains. Where was Lucas?

I was a bad dog. I had learned not to squat in the house, to do Do Your Business outside, but I now had no choice, and went to the corner and made a pile there. I knew Lucas would come home and shout "No!" at me. On the floor by the bed I found a long chewy thing with his smell on it and was gnawing it to bits when I at last felt his approaching presence and heard the unmistakable sound of his feet as he came toward the house. I was leaping frantically, yipping, when he opened the front door and finally, finally came down the hall to me.

"Oh, Bella, I'm so sorry." He put his face down to mine so I could lick it. I cringed when he got papers and water to clean up the mess I'd left in the corner, but he did not yell at me. He picked up the chewy thing. "Well, I never liked that belt anyway. Come on, Bella, let's go for a walk."

Walk! The sky was starting to grow brighter and I heard birds and smelled Mother Cat and other dogs and people as we strolled down the street.

I hoped we were going to the park. I wanted to scamper joyously after squirrels, to run up the slide, to play and play.

"It was another grand mal seizure," Lucas said. "She's not had one of those for a long time. We thought the medication had it under control. I'm really worried, Bella. The doctors aren't even sure what is wrong with her."

I sensed his sadness but didn't understand. How could anyone be unhappy on a walk?

Mom did not come home that day, nor the next. When Lucas did Go to Work I was left in the crate and barked out my frustration and fear at what was happening. Why did Lucas have to leave? Why wasn't Mom home? Was she ever coming back? Was Lucas ever coming back? I needed my person. I would be a good dog and do Sit and provide comfort if everyone would just come back and let me out of the crate.

• • •

I was overjoyed the day Mom and Lucas entered the house together. I barked and whimpered, desperate to be let out of my crate. When Lucas opened the crate door I barely gave his face a swipe with my tongue before I ran into the living room and jumped on the couch where Mom was lying. She laughed as I licked her cheeks.

"Down, Bella," Lucas told me.

I did not like "down." When he clapped his hands, though, I knew that he was going to be angry, so I reluctantly jumped to the floor. Mom reached out to stroke my head, which was almost as good as lying with her on the couch.

"So what does the notice say?" Mom asked.

"Basically, because we have a dog, we're in violation of our lease. We've got three days before they call animal control and start eviction proceedings." Lucas sounded gloomy. I wanted to go to him to provide comfort but I also wanted to remain so Mom would keep petting me.

Mom put her hands on her hips. "I've seen other dogs here."

"Right. You can have a dog *visit,* but I guess somebody told them Bella's been barking a lot for a couple of weeks."

"Who?"

"They didn't say."

"I don't know why, if we're all trying to be good neighbors, they didn't just come to talk to us."

"Well, you can be a little intimidating sometimes, Mom."

They were silent for a moment. I nuzzled her hand when it stopped stroking me. "We can't move, Lucas," Mom said softly.

"I know."

"It's perfect that you can walk to work here. And to switch my housing benefit, that's not something we can do in just a few days. Plus this was the only place we found that we could remotely afford. Where would we even get the money for a security deposit?"

"That was before I got a job, though. Maybe we could afford to pay a higher rent."

"I want you saving that money for college," she replied.

"I am. I am saving. But this is what savings are for—emergencies."

"I can't believe this is happening."

They were quiet again. I went over to Lucas—I could sense that he was troubled, though I did not know why since we were all home together at last. I curled up at his feet.

"What are we going to do, Lucas?"

"I'll think of something," Lucas said.

• • •

The day after Mom came home, she pressed the phone to her cheek while Lucas watched and I chewed a rubber stick called a "bone." There were other things called bones that I liked a lot better.

"That's what I am trying to tell you. This notice is a mistake. I do not have a dog," she said.

I looked up at the word "dog." What was she trying to tell me? I looked to Lucas, but he was still focused on Mom.

"I had a puppy visiting but I do not personally own a dog." I looked back at Mom at the word "dog." "That's correct. Yes. Thanks very much. No, I appreciate it." She put the phone down. "I didn't lie. I don't personally own a dog. Bella is *your* dog."

I brought the bone to Mom, thinking she was saying she wanted to throw it down the stairs for me to do Good Exercise.

Lucas grinned. "It's an excellent legal argument."

Mom made no move to take the bone.

"But that's not going to make our problem go away. Sooner or later they're going to catch us."

"Maybe not. I'll take Bella out only before dawn or after sunset. There's no staff working at those hours. I'm sure the neighbors don't care as long as she's quiet. And once we hit the street, who is to say I live in the complex? I could just as easily be walking my dog past the building as coming from it."

I did not know what they were saying, but I liked the repetition of my name and the word "dog."

"But what if I have to go in to the clinic? You can't take off work every time that happens. I can do my meetings at night, but that's it."

"Maybe we could send Bella with a dog sitter."

"And give up what, food?"

"Mom."

"I'm just saying we can't afford that."

"Okay."

I sighed with contentment.

"I'm sorry. I just don't know how this is going to work. One of these days, probably pretty soon, she's going to have to be left alone, and when she is, she'll bark."

Six

O ver the next several days, we played two new games. One was "no barks." My job had always been to alert everyone whenever I detected there was a person at the door. Under the right circumstances, I would hear or smell someone even before the bell rang, and would bark out my knowledge to the benefit of everyone who was home. Sometimes Lucas or Mom would join their voices with mine, shouting their own warnings. "Stop it!" they would yell. "Quiet!" But with No Barks, Lucas would stand in the open doorway and reach outside and the bell would ring and then he would sternly say "No Barks" and hold my snout. I did not like this game, but we played it over and over again. Then Mom went outside and Lucas sat in the living room and Mom rapped her knuckles on the door, which was outside the pattern but Lucas *still* said No Barks. It was as if they didn't want me to do my job!

No Barks was a lot like Stay, another game I did not like. When Lucas said "Stay," I was to sit and not move until he came back and said "okay!" Sometimes he gave me a treat and said "good Stay," and I liked that part, but otherwise Stay took concentration and was fatiguing and boring. Humans seem to have no sense of the passage of time, of how much fun they are missing when a dog is doing Stay and has to sit and sit and not play. The same thing was true of No Barks: Lucas expected that once he told me No Barks, I was only a good dog if I remembered it as something like a permanent state of being. When someone rang the bell and I did No Barks Lucas might give me a treat, or he might not. It was exhausting. I kept hoping he would forget all about No Barks, but he repeated it constantly, and so did Mom.

Much, *much* more fun was "Go Home." Go Home meant Lucas would unsnap my leash and I was to run back to our house and curl up by the front door. Lucas was very particular about where I was supposed to lie down. "No, you have to be here, Bella. Here, where no one from the street can see you. Okay?" He patted on the cement until I lay down and then he gave me a treat. When we did Go Home, I was a good dog who was given food. When we did No Barks, I did not feel like a good dog, even if he gave me a treat.

"She picked right up on it. If I ever need her to, she will just come right home and lie by the wall under the hedge, completely hidden from view," Lucas told Mom.

Mom petted my head. "She's a good dog."

I wagged.

"Still having trouble with No Barks, though," Lucas said.

I groaned.

I craved nothing more than having Lucas tell me I was a good dog—that, and "Tiny Piece of Cheese," which meant Lucas loved me and gave me a wonderful treat.

Several times Lucas put me in my crate and set his phone down in front of it. I had no interest in the phone.

"No Barks," he said crossly. Then he and Mom went out the door. I got lonely and barked and Lucas came running in the house, which was what I had wanted! But he was angry at me and told me "No Barks" several times without letting me out or even petting me, despite how overjoyed I was to see him.

I decided No Barks was even less fun when it involved the crate.

"I don't think she's getting it," Lucas told Mom one night. We had gone to the park and played ball and I was deliciously drowsy.

"She doesn't bark at the doorbell anymore," Mom replied.

"No, that's true. Bella's a good dog for the doorbell now."

I sleepily thumped my tail. Yes, I was a good dog.

"I have my appointment with the neurologist tomorrow," Mom said.

"Maybe I'll call in sick. We can't risk leaving her here."

"No. You can't do that, Lucas."

I wagged my tail at the word "Lucas," easing to my feet in case a walk was coming.

"I don't know what the alternatives are," he said somberly. "You can't miss that appointment; the waiting times are impossible."

I sat up and gazed at Lucas, my person, coming alert despite my fatigue. Something was going on—he and Mom were very, very tense.

I did Sit, being a good dog doing No Barks, but it didn't seem to help.

• • •

Early the next morning, right around the time that Lucas normally would do Go to Work, the three of us took a walk. I loved when we all walked together!

We crossed the street the moment we were out the front door, just as we always did. I smelled Mother Cat in the den.

"See?" Lucas said. "It's a new fence. Now there's this nylon draping on both sides. No way for me to get a foothold. And the links are heavy gauge and connect directly to the posts. It would take a pair of industrial bolt cutters to get through them."

Mom frowned. "Wait, you've been cutting the fence?"

"No. Gunter said I did, but I never had to. I just used pliers to unwind the loops of wire."

"I'm glad to hear that. How about if you leapt up and grabbed the top rail, could you haul yourself over?"

"Maybe." Lucas nodded. "But Bella would still be on the street side of the fence. I need her to go into the crawl space to flush the cats into my net."

"What if you went in yourself, could you catch them in the net?"

"Possibly. I could try."

"What if I went with you?"

Lucas grinned at Mom. "It's pretty disgusting under there."

"Oh, I imagine I've seen worse," she said.

"Probably have."

"Can the cats even get out of the yard?" Mom felt the cloth that was on the fence. "I guess they could climb this."

"I guess they could, but in the back they dug out the dirt under the frame where the old fence was bent, so they've probably been getting in and out through that hole."

"Why did he put up the new fence, do you suppose?" Mom asked.

"Honestly, I think he wants to prevent me from catching the rest of the cats. He's making a point—he can do this and I can't stop him."

"What a nice guy."

We went up the street together. Soon we came to a road

where there were a lot of cars driving quickly past. Each one dragged different scents in its wake, and there were wonderful fragrances on the lawns and bushes I kept pausing to appreciate. A white dog barked at me from behind a fence and I wanted to go sniff him but I was on the leash.

At a big building, Mom walked away in a different direction. I kept stopping and turning to look at her, but she continued going without glancing back. It was very distressing. What had started as a wonderful family walk had somehow broken apart. I did not understand. We were supposed to be together! A nervous whine rose in my throat.

"Come on, Bella. She's just going to her appointment. She'll come find you once she's finished. I have to go to work."

I was confused that he was talking about Go to Work, which was when he left me at home alone with Mom. We were out on a *walk*.

Lucas led me to a door that beeped when he opened it. He stepped in, looked cautiously around, and then pulled me after him. The floor was very slick and smelled of chemicals and *a lot* of different people, though I couldn't see anyone. This was a fun new place, especially when Lucas ran me down the hall! Lucas closed us in a small room with an even stronger chemical odor. He knelt down. I wagged excitedly. "Okay, listen. You're not supposed to be here in the hospital. If they catch you, I'll be in real trouble. I could get fired. This is just for while Mom is having her appointment. I have to go to work. I can come back by here as soon as I check in for my shift. Please, No Barks, Bella. *Please*."

Not that again. He grabbed my snout and shook it. "No Barks."

I wasn't barking.

I was mystified when he walked out the door, shutting it behind him. Now what?

I wondered if this was the version of No Barks where

when I barked Lucas would open the door. Even if he were cross with me, it would be better than being left by myself in the strange place. I did not smell him standing on the other side of the door, though I could still sense that he was close by. It was similar to the growing sensation of his nearing presence when he was coming home from Go to Work. So even though he had left me, he was still in the building or close to it. But where? Where was Mom? I whimpered. They could not have meant to leave me alone in this room! Something was wrong!

I did Sit like a good dog, staring at the door, willing it to open. I could not hear anything at all on the other side of it. Finally, unable to stand it another second, I barked.

• • •

Lucas opened the door after a long, long time—a time of many, many barks. Before he did so I could smell him and another person, and when he came into the room a woman followed. She had a flowery scent combined with something nice and nutty. I was overjoyed to see Lucas and jumped on him, putting my paws on him and trying to get him to bend over so I could kiss his face. My person was back! Now we could get out of this tiny room and maybe go to the park and have treats.

"See?" Lucas said to the woman.

"You told me it was a puppy! She's full grown." The woman stooped down and held out her hand, which had a sugary residue on it. I licked it tenderly, liking her immensely for having such sweet fingers.

"No, she's still a puppy, maybe eight months old. The vet says she was born sometime in March or early April."

The woman rubbed behind my ears. "You know, having a puppy really works on chicks." I leaned into her hand.

"I've heard that."

The woman stood up. "Not on me though."

"Really? Because the whole reason I adopted Bella was to impress Olivia from the maintenance department."

"That seems to be your motivation for everything lately, I've noticed."

"Must be working if you've been doing all this *noticing*."

"I also noticed that the trash chute is backed up again. That's kind of my biggest priority, in the noticing department."

"Good to know where I stand."

"So what's your plan? You know if you get caught with a dog in here you'll be fired. Dr. Gann's e-mail of the two zillion things employees must never do kind of had take-your-dog-to-work day near the top of the list."

"I was thinking, you're in maintenance, this is a maintenance closet, maybe you could clean it up or something for an hour. Just to keep Bella company so she won't bark."

"Really. And why do I owe you any favors at all?"

"Not me. Do it for the dog."

"Bella," the woman said, stroking my head, "your daddy is such a dork."

"You called me a nerd. I don't think you can have it both ways."

"Oh, they make an exception for people like you."

"So now you're calling me exceptional?"

The woman laughed. "There is absolutely nothing about you I find exceptional. Or surprising. Or interesting."

"That's where you're wrong, because I'm actually very surprising."

"Really."

"I promise."

"Tell me one thing about you that I might be surprised by."

"Okay." Lucas was silent for a moment.

"See?"

"Okay, how about this: I live across the street from a cat house."

"*What?*" the woman laughed.

"Told you. Full of surprises."

"Right, well, I still can't spend an hour in here. I'm not like you; I don't have a job where I run around doing nothing all the time. I have a boss and she's probably wondering where I am right now."

"But that was the bet! I surprise you, and you watch my dog."

"There was no bet. I don't bet."

"Please?"

"No. Anyway, if I get caught with a dog, we'll *both* be fired."

There was a knock on the door. These seemed like circumstances where No Barks did not apply, so I let Lucas know there was someone there. He and the woman stood staring at each other.

* * *

When Lucas opened the door there was a thin man standing there. His shoes smelled of dirt and grass, and he had long hair and a hairy face. I pressed forward to greet him, but was blocked by Lucas, who moved in front of me.

"Hope I'm not interrupting something," the man said wryly.

"He wishes," the woman replied. "It's all he thinks about."

Lucas laughed. "Hi, Ty. Olivia pulled me into the closet. You came just in time to save me."

"So what's this I hear about barking down this hallway?" The man squatted and I went to him, wagging. "Could there be a *dog* in the VA hospital? Surely not." His hands were gentle and smelled of people and coffee.

Lucas raised his hands and then let them drop. "We

can't leave her home alone. She barks, and the leasing company said if they catch us with a dog they'll evict us and send Bella to the pound. I know it's against the rules, but I didn't know what else to do."

"So his big plan was for me to babysit Bella in this closet," the woman added.

"Just until my mother is finished with her appointment."

"He panics a lot," the woman said. "He's two years older but I'm the mature one."

"Well, I think I've got a solution to our little problem, here," the man declared. "I'll just take Bella to the ward with me."

"What if Dr. Gann hears about it?" Lucas asked anxiously.

"Dr. Gann is running this whole hospital on a reduced budget and doesn't have time to hunt down a visiting dog. Besides, I imagine we'll be able to keep Bella under wraps for a couple of hours."

The man took my leash and led me to some new rooms. The floor here had a firm carpet and several chairs with people sitting in them. I could smell people and chemicals and food in that carpet, but no dogs. I did not like being away from Lucas, but everyone loved me and petted me and called out my name. Many of the people were old, but not every one of them, and all were glad to see me. The chairs were soft when I put my head on them so that people could stroke my ears.

I learned that the man who took me was named Ty. He was very nice to me and fed me some chicken and some bread and some egg. One woman, Layla, had trembling hands as she smoothed down the fur on my head. "Good dog," she murmured into my ear.

A man gave me a spoonful of gravy so delicious it made me want to wriggle on the floor. "Don't feed her pudding, Steve," Ty said.

The man dug for another helping. "It's vanilla." The gravy was in a small plastic container on a table next to his soft chair, and a lamp on that table heated the food so that a sweet odor rose into the air. I watched his hand as intently as I would focus on a Tiny Piece of Cheese. The spoon descended and I licked my lips, holding myself back until I could gently take it from him.

Ty tapped a finger on the man's chair. "Okay, that's the last one, Steve."

The gravy man was Steve. "This one reminds me of a bulldog mix I had when I was a kid. You can come back any time you want, Bella." I licked his fingers.

Ty shrugged. "Not sure about that. Dr. Gann learns about Bella being here he's going to throw a fit."

"Let him." Steve's voice was harsh, and his hand clenched my fur. I looked up at him, not sure what was happening. "He's got no idea what we're going through."

Ty reached out to stroke my head. "No, listen, he's a good man, Steve. He's just got a lot on his plate and a lot of rules coming down on him all the time."

Steve relaxed his grip. "Sure. Fine. Then I say, don't tell him."

"Huh." Ty rubbed his chin.

"One more spoonful." Steve turned in his chair and picked up his spoon and I focused on him without blinking.

"No. We gotta go." Ty pulled on my leash and I reluctantly followed him, glancing mournfully back at Steve. "You're a good dog, Bella. There's someone I want you to meet."

Ty led me over to where a man sat in a big, wide chair by a window. His name was Mack. He had no hair on his head and his hands were soft when he ran them over my ears. His skin was very dark and his fingers smelled mostly of soap and faintly of bacon.

Mack was sad, sad in the way Mom was sometimes sad—an ache tinged with fear and despair. I remembered lying next to Mom to provide comfort when she felt like this, so I put my front paws on Mack's chair and then climbed up to be with him.

"Whoa!" Ty laughed.

Dust rose from the cushions and I inhaled it deeply. Mack hugged me long and hard.

"How you doing, Mack? Holding it together?"

"Yeah," Mack said. It was the only word he spoke. As he clutched me, though, I could feel the pain loosen its grip on him. I was a good dog, doing my job and providing comfort to Mack. I felt sure Lucas would approve.

Eventually Mom came into the room. She hugged several of the people.

"You need to bring Bella back here. She's a big hit," Ty told her.

"Well . . . we'll see," Mom said.

"I mean it, Terri. You should have seen Mack perk up."

"Mack? Really?"

"Talk to you for a minute?" Ty asked her softly.

Mom and Ty went to a corner so they could be alone with me.

"You know why most of these guys are here every day?" Ty asked.

Mom looked at the people sitting in their chairs. "To hang out with people like themselves."

"Sure, yeah, that's part of it. Also, they don't really have any other place to go. They're not like you, they don't have a son to take care of."

"Take care of," Mom replied slowly. "I'm not sure that's how I would define it. More like the other way around."

"Copy that. I'm just saying that when they found out you smuggled the dog in here, it gave them a real sense of purpose. You know? Let them win at something. They're warriors, it feels good to be back in a fight, even if all we're doing is rebelling against a dumb dog rule. Why don't you bring her back tomorrow?"

"Oh. I don't think that's a good idea, Ty. If Dr. Gann finds out, Lucas's position would be—"

"Dr. Gann *won't* find out," Ty interrupted. "We'll hide Bella from him and anybody else who might care. Okay? Let's do this, Terri."

• • •

The next day, when Lucas left to do Go to Work, Mom and I went with him! I was taken back to see my friends in the big room with the chairs, and Mom sat there and talked to people, too. Everyone was happy to see me.

The man named Steve did not have any astoundingly sweet gravy. "Want some cake?"

It was wonderful. I liked Steve. I liked Marty, who got on the floor to wrestle with me. I liked Drew, who did not have any legs but who took me for a car ride in his chair. I sat in his lap and wagged as people laughed. Though the smells were different from a real car ride, I liked being able to press up against Drew as he drove. I wondered if for my next car ride Lucas would let me sit in his lap.

It was a wonderful day. Everyone cuddled me and fed me treats and love.

I was doing Sit for Jordan, who was feeding me little pieces of hamburger a morsel at a time, when Layla said, "Dr. Gann is coming!" and then Ty picked me up and ran me over to sit on a couch with Mack.

"Lie down, Bella!" Ty told me. Mack reached out with his hands and held me and I lay against him to provide comfort. Someone covered me with a blanket. I did not understand the game, but when I moved even a little, Mack put his hand on me and held me still. His heart was pounding.

"Dr. Gann!" I heard Ty boom. "Can we talk about getting some cable in here besides The Weather Channel?"

There were other voices. I lay still against Mack. "Good dog," he praised in a voice so quiet I almost couldn't hear him.

When the blanket was lifted off of me people clapped and told me good dog and I wagged in joyous excitement.

Later I learned the woman from the closet was called Olivia. She came to see me and gave me small snacks and then stood and talked to Mom.

That night Mom said her name a couple of times.

"Why don't you ask her out?" Mom asked Lucas.

I had brought the ball out and was staring at it now, hoping Lucas would roll it across the floor.

"Oh, I don't know. Because she hates me?"

"If she hated you she would ignore you instead of taunting you."

"She's not *taunting* me. We're just different people. She's sort of Goth. She calls me White Bread Boy and says I'm a cure for her insomnia."

Mom was silent for a moment. "It's not because of me, is it?"

"What do you mean?"

"You can't watch me all the time, and even if you could, I would hate that. Being a burden to your child is the worst thing for a mother. If you put everything on hold because of me it means my life has all been for nothing."

"Don't talk like that!"

"No, I'm not having dark thoughts, I'm speaking the truth. You know there's nothing I regret more than the times I abandoned you. I abandoned you when I joined the army and I nearly abandoned you when I tried to take my life. But I am past that now, Lucas. I won't leave you, and want only for you to have a future. Please believe me—nothing is more important."

"Okay, then believe me, Mom. I do have a future. I have a *great* future. I promise I won't let anything get in the way of that."

A little later Mom left and Lucas and I went to feed the cats. Instead of going to the den, Lucas led me around to the back, where a rut was dug under the base of the fence.

The dirt and the fence there smelled of several felines, and I knew that even more of them were living in the den now. I could tell that Mother Cat was in there, too. Lucas poured food from a bag into a bowl and then shoved it under the fence. "That will have to do it," he said resignedly. "I can't get any closer." I waited for Lucas to push open the fence, but he did not. Instead, he walked me around to the front and then stood with his hand on his hips, staring at something white on the dark fabric covering the fence.

"It's a notice of demolition, Bella. I guess he got his permit."

I sensed Lucas's distress and looked at him curiously. We ran back to our door and went inside. Mom was not home. Lucas went to his closet and pulled out the thin, cat-smelling blankets with the wood blocks in the corners. Then he grabbed his phone and my leash.

"Ready, Bella?"

We ran back across the street. "Huh," Lucas said. "This isn't going to work. Even if I could climb up there holding onto you, I don't know how I would get you down the other side without hurting you." He petted my head. "Okay. Let's do this, instead." He unclipped my leash from my collar. I wagged. "Good practice. Ready? Go Home, Bella!"

I knew what to do. I dashed across the street and then curled up in the right spot. This was fun!

I heard Lucas banging on something. I lifted my head, knowing I should be doing Go Home but unable to help myself. Lucas was on top of the fence, wobbling, and as I watched he vanished on the other side.

We had never done this as part of Go Home before. Normally, he came to me and gave me a treat, or Mom opened the door and gave me a treat. The point of Go Home was for someone to give me a treat.

I whined. I did not understand.

And then Mother Cat came dashing from around the

corner! She ran down the street. This was entirely new and seemed to mean Go Home no longer applied.

My mother had vanished into the shadows, but I could easily track her scent.

I joyously ran after her.

Seven

I tracked Mother Cat up a slope to where a row of houses all had wooden decks jutting out over the lip of the hill. I found her presence strongest under one of these decks—way in the back, where the dirt rose up to meet the boards, she had found a place to hide. I was only able to squirm a little way under the deck before the gap was too narrow for me to fit. I thrust my nose forward and breathed her in. Did she know I was there? Would she come out?

After a moment her scent strengthened and then I saw her. She regarded me for a moment with unblinking eyes. I pulled my head back, crawling to where I could stand up, and she followed and rubbed her head against my neck, purring.

Mother. When I was little, I roughhoused with her, wrestling and tumbling in the den, and even though this place, with its low, wooden ceiling, was so similar to where I was born, I did not feel that trying to play would be the right thing now. I was too big and she was too frail.

Mother Cat was from a time before Lucas. Smelling her, I was reminded of when my world contained no people and no dogs but many cats. I now only dimly remembered what life was like in the den, but her purring now made me feel safe and protected. The scents and sounds came back to me as strongly as if I were nestled up to her side, my kitten brothers and sisters lying next to me.

On her breath I could smell the food that Lucas had been providing her. I understood this, that Lucas did Feed the Cats and gave her food that was not for me. Lucas took care of Mother Cat. Caring for cats was our job.

Mother Cat did not understand how wonderful life could be with a person like Lucas. She was afraid of humans. I knew that even if I tried I could not provide her enough comfort to make her trust his hand, even when he brought food. Cats are different from dogs.

Thinking of Lucas made me feel a bit like a bad dog. I had run off without him, instead of remaining in my spot next to the wall, though it was true that he had changed everything by scaling the fence.

I decided I needed to do Go Home, that if I did Go Home I would be a good dog. I hesitated to leave Mother Cat, because if she remained here I did not know how Lucas would find her to feed her. I wanted her to follow me, but as I turned away from her I knew she would not. I went down the hill and then looked up at her. She was watching me from the crest of the slope, her tail up and lazily twitching.

I wondered if I would ever see my mother again.

* * *

I did Go Home. Lucas opened the door when I curled up in my special spot. I ran to him, elated, jumping up to be loved, but he was stern with me and called me a bad dog. I did not know what I had done, but I could tell he was very angry with me.

"You can never run off, Bella! You must always Go Home."

I heard my name and knew I had done the right thing to do Go Home, but he was still angry, for some reason. I went to my dog bed and flopped down there, aching inside because I had made Lucas unhappy.

When Mom came home I jumped up and wagged and she told me I was a good dog, so I figured whatever had happened was past and everyone loved me now.

"How was group?" Lucas asked her.

"Good. Good group tonight. Everyone asked me about Bella—she's the best thing that's ever happened to that place. She seems to have formed a special relationship with every single person. What happened with the cats?"

"I didn't catch any except on video. I also took a shot of the demolition permit and sent it to Audrey at the rescue."

"Good idea. Maybe she can do something with it."

"Maybe."

"Would you e-mail me a copy?"

"Sure. Oh, and Bella ran away."

I looked up at my name.

"She did?" Mom gasped. "Bella, you *ran away*?"

I lowered my eyes. Now I felt like a bad dog again, though I had no idea what I had just done.

"I thought it would be a good idea to have her go home and hide on the front porch while I scaled the fence. I was anxious to get started trying to net a cat and didn't take the time to bring her home first. It was my fault. When I finally gave up on trying to corral the cats in the crawl space and came home, she was nowhere to be found."

"Where did you go, Bella?" Mom asked.

I wagged. Was I forgiven? It didn't sound like Mom was angry anymore. I went to her and pushed my head under her hand and she stroked it. Yes!

"I'll try again tomorrow," Lucas said. I went to him and he petted me. There was no better feeling in the world than being a good dog to Mom and Lucas. I ran and got the ball and brought it to him to celebrate.

That night, just before bed, we did Tiny Piece of Cheese. I trembled with concentration, watching the treat, until finally he laughed and gave it to me.

I was a good dog.

The next time we did Go to Work, the ground was covered in cold, wet, wonderful stuff. "Snow!" Lucas told me. "It's snow, Bella!"

I thought snow was the most amazing thing I'd encountered since Tiny Piece of Cheese and also probably bacon. I was still wet with it when Lucas was met at the big building by Ty, who took my leash and led me to the room with the chairs so I could see all my friends. Mack reached for me and I jumped up on the couch next to him and slept pressed up against him for a little while. Mack was the saddest man I had ever met, but he always seemed happier when I saw him. I was doing my job, fulfilling my purpose, providing comfort.

Ty guided me to a room where people were sitting in chairs in a circle. One of them was my friend Drew and he did not take me for a ride, though he did tell me good dog.

Ty gently pulled my leash so we were both in the middle of the circle so that anyone who wanted to see a dog could do so. "Listen up. Anybody got a problem with Bella, you're allergic or something, tell me now. Otherwise, she's here to help. She's got this way of knowing when you're struggling to find words, you know? She'll come right over to you. Oh, and last thing before we get started—Bella's visits to the VA are unauthorized. Everybody copy?"

We spent a long time in the room, just sitting with no treats. One man cried, pressing his face into his palms, and

I put my head in his lap, trying to help, doing my job the same way I helped Mom. These were my friends and I wanted them to know they shouldn't be sad because there was a dog here to give comfort.

Later, Lucas came to visit my friends and call me good dog. As he and I were leaving, Olivia came over to see me. She had a small piece of chicken in her hand that she gave me. I really liked Olivia.

"Want to walk home with us?" Lucas asked her.

"I'll walk home with Bella. You can come along, I guess," she replied.

We slipped out the side door. Snow! I jumped in it, lying on my back with my legs in the air.

"You are so silly, Bella," Olivia told me.

Lucas pulled gently on the leash. "Okay, enough. Let's go, Bella." I got to my feet, shaking the water from my fur.

"How is it going with hiding Bella from Dr. Gann?" Olivia asked. I looked at her, hoping that the reason she said my name was that she was going to feed me more chicken, even though I could smell that she didn't have any in her pockets. Humans can always find chicken and cookies and fish, if they want.

"Ty has got a whole operation. When they have their twelve-step meeting, she stays with them. When Bella's on the floor with the patients, Ty posts lookouts. They run it like it's a POW camp and they're fooling the guards. I think the nurses know but the doctors are clueless. Ty says if Bella gets caught, he'll say she's his dog. They're not going to kick out Ty; all the vets look up to him and he kind of runs the group therapy they have in the evenings."

As we walked we found a squirrel! It lay flattened on the pavement and gave off amazing odors. The snow around it had melted. I inhaled carefully. It was dead. I knew death; it was a knowledge I had somehow acquired without ever encountering it, the way I knew to lick Lucas when he bent down to talk to me, or the way I knew that what I should do now was roll my shoulder into the squirrel.

"Bella! No!" Lucas yanked on my leash. I looked at him, startled. No? What had I done?

"You don't want that yucky smell on you, Bella," Olivia told me. We walked away and I glanced back in regret, wanting that perfume on my fur.

"Things still dicey with the landlord?" Olivia asked.

"Honestly I think they are doing a don't-ask, don't-tell. As long as Bella doesn't bark, no one is going to complain, and we have a system where I check left and right and then take her right to the street. If none of the other tenants officially notifies them, I think we're okay. Bella does a good job of No Barks."

I glanced up, startled. No Barks? What did that mean in this context?

"So, I had fun the other night," Olivia observed after a moment.

Lucas smiled. "Me, too. It was like a date, with insults."

"You're the one who made fun of my driving."

"I didn't make fun of it, I just noted that I didn't expect to run over so many pedestrians."

"You know, this is America. You could buy a car and then I could sit in the passenger seat and scream while *you* drive."

"Stop, I didn't scream, I was too terrified to make a sound. Anyway I'm finding public transportation to be more than adequate. It's good for the environment; maybe you should try it."

"I just am amazed to find myself dating the bus boy."

"Dating? So we're *dating*. Like, officially."

"I just made a serious error."

"No, this will be good for you. You'll finally be dating

a guy who doesn't have to put in a once-a-week call to a parole officer."

"We've had one date, don't pick out your china pattern just yet," Olivia said.

"I'm changing my Facebook status."

"Oh, God."

"I'm going to go to med school next fall. I don't need a car until then—my mom and I can walk to the VA and the stores, and Denver's got a great bus system. Plus, the woman I'm *dating* has a car."

"This is the worst day of my life." When we turned up our street, Olivia put a hand out to touch his arm. "What's with all the police?"

· · ·

I had heard the word "police" before, and associated it with the people with the dark clothes and the metal things on their hips.

"I don't know. Looks like somebody called the cops for something," Lucas said. "It's not my mom, though; they're all across the street from our place."

"It's a protest. See?" Olivia pointed.

We were stopped, which frustrated me because I wanted to go see everyone who was standing on the sidewalk in front of the den. Some were holding large sheets of paper on sticks, waving them in the air.

"I took video of the cats and of the demolition permit. Someone put it on Facebook or something." Lucas was tapping on his phone. Then he held it out for Olivia to look at. I yawned. Phones are boring. "Perfect! Look, my mom cut in the shot of the backhoe pulling up on the trailer and the rest is the video I took in the crawl space. She tagged every animal activist in the city with it."

"That's awesome. I love your mom; she's a rebel. Unlike some people I could mention," Olivia said.

"See the guy who looks so angry? That's Gunter. He's the one who wants to tear down the place. I think *he'd* call me a rebel. He told me he was going to bribe an animal control officer to certify there were no cats."

"He *told* you that? Not real bright."

"He pretty much feels he can do whatever he wants in the world."

"That's a news van." Olivia pointed again. "Looks like you're going to be famous."

"I won't forget you or any of the little people who made this possible."

"Oh, I know you'll never forget *me*."

Lucas left me with Olivia. He talked to some of the people, including someone I had smelled before, the woman named Audrey. There were several people in dark clothes, and they stood in the street and waved at cars. At one point someone put a bright light on Lucas's face while Olivia held my leash.

Her hand still smelled a little like the chicken.

* * *

I was glad to see Mom when we finally turned away and went home. Then Lucas and Olivia left, which upset me until Mom put food in my bowl.

I heard the loud chime and did No Barks. Mom went to the door, blocking me with her legs, and it was the smoky-meat man, Gunter. "Is your son home, ma'am?"

"No, he's out."

"My name is Gunter Beckenbauer."

"Yes, I know who you are," Mom replied coolly.

"Do you know what your son did tonight?"

"Yes."

"He had a bunch of his friends stage a phony protest on my property. Why is he doing this to me? What the hell did I ever do to either one of you?"

"I think he is just trying to save some innocent animals."

"My website got all these death threats. I could sue your asses."

Mom was apparently not going to let me get any closer to Gunter to sniff him, though I was really interested by the meaty fragrance on his clothing. I sat down.

"Let me ask you something," Mom said. "Why don't you just let the rescue people go in there and capture the remaining cats? That would solve everything."

"Those houses are condemned. They're falling apart. Someone gets hurt under there, it's a huge liability."

"So, they'd sign a release. Absolve you of liability."

"Look, you know what this is about? That's my property, and your son has been breaking and entering and feeding the damn cats, which is the only reason they are even there! Now it's *winter*. You know how much more expensive construction is when it's below freezing? He created this problem, it's his fault, and if a bunch of cats get squished it's on him. Post *that* to your social website." Gunter was pointing his smoky meat finger at Mom's face. He sounded very angry, and I felt the fur rising on the back of my neck. A growl grew inside me, but I didn't make a sound. Did No Barks mean I wasn't supposed to growl?

Mom gazed at Gunter without any expression on her face. "Are you through?"

"You do *not* want to go to war with me, lady."

"War." Mom took a step toward the man, staring at him. I could feel strong emotions coming off her. "You think this is war? You don't know anything about war."

The man shifted his gaze. "Dog's getting pretty big. What is that, a pit bull? How can you have a dog here? I know the management, isn't a dog against your lease?"

"Is there anything else I can do for you, Mr. Beckenbauer?"

"I just want it on the record that I tried to work things out on a friendly basis."

"The record shows you came over here to say we're going to war. Good night." Mom shut the door. As she did, the tension left her muscles, but she seemed tired. "Oh, Bella," she said softly, "I have a really bad feeling about this."

• • •

Lucas started leaving home without me a lot. When he came back, he smelled like Olivia. I wondered why he would be with our friend Olivia and not take me, his dog.

There were so many things I did not understand. I liked going to the vet, who was a nice lady, but one time we went and I fell asleep and when I woke up I was home with a stiff plastic collar around my neck. The thing was uncomfortable and ridiculous. I couldn't lick myself anywhere.

"You're spayed now, Bella," Lucas told me. I flicked my tail at my name, because he did not seem to be cross with me, but he still punished me with the odd collar for several days.

Long after the collar came off, Mom and I were home alone because Lucas had done Go to Work so that he could see Olivia. Mom seemed tired and unhappy. Several times she put her hand to her face.

Then a sharp and sour scent filled the air. It was familiar: the last time it happened, Mom got sick and I was left alone in the house all night. I whined anxiously, but she didn't look at me.

So I barked.

"Bella! No Barks!" Mom scolded loudly.

I panted, anxious and frightened. When Lucas came home I jumped up on him, whimpering. "What is it? What's wrong with you, Bella?"

"She's been acting strangely for the past half an hour," Mom said, coming into the living room. "Oh, I need to lie down for a few minutes." She collapsed on the couch.

"You okay?" Lucas asked, concerned.

"Give me a minute."

The tang from her turned sharper and I couldn't help myself. I barked again.

"Bella! No Barks!" Lucas told me.

I barked.

"Hey!" He swatted my rear. "No Barks, Bella! You just . . . Mom? Mom!"

Mom was making small peeping sounds, her hands curled up as they batted at the air. Lucas ran to where she lay on the couch. "Mom, Mom," he whispered, his fear potent and raw. He pulled out his phone. "My mother is having a seizure," he said into it. "Hurry."

Then he curled up on the couch to give her comfort. I jumped up next to him and laid my head on his shoulder, trying to help. "You'll be okay. Please be okay, Mom."

Soon there were two women and a man in our house. They lifted Mom onto a bed and wheeled her out the door. Lucas took me to my crate and closed me in. "You're a good dog, Bella," he told me. "You stay."

I did not feel like a good dog because I had been left alone. I did No Barks all night, missing Lucas. I was afraid he might never come home.

I did not understand what was happening.

. . .

Lucas returned while it was still dark outside, fed me and walked me and then lay down on the bed with me. We did Tiny Piece of Cheese, but he seemed distracted and didn't laugh. I snuggled against his side, feeling some fear in him, loving being so close to my Lucas, helping him by pressing up to him. When he left that morning it was more normal, and I waited patiently for his return.

Mom, Lucas, and Olivia all came home together. I spun around in circles, so excited to see all of them.

"Thank you so much for the ride," Mom told Olivia. "It wasn't necessary; I felt fine to walk."

"No, it's okay. Lucas thinks I'm his personal Uber now anyway," Olivia replied.

That night, after Olivia left, Lucas sat at the table and played with his phone. "It says that fifteen percent of dogs can sense seizures."

"That's amazing. It sure did seem like she knew what was going on," Mom replied.

"You are one amazing dog, Bella," he praised.

I wagged, hearing approval in the way he said my name. I was happy we were all home together, and knew that soon Lucas would do Tiny Piece of Cheese.

There was a knock at the door. I fought down my urges and did No Barks. "Hang onto Bella," Mom said.

Lucas grabbed my collar. "We need to make sure it isn't someone from the building, Bella," he said softly. "Just No Barks." I loved the feel of his hand on my fur and the way he made gentle noises and said my name.

I smelled a man on the doorstep whose scent was sometimes on the air near our house. Mom spoke to him briefly, then closed the door. Lucas released me and I went to her because she felt sad and angry.

"What is it?" Lucas asked.

"Eviction notice."

"What?"

"I had gotten complacent. It seemed like we were going to get away with it." Mom sat heavily in her chair.

"Bella's been so good!" Lucas sat down, too. "She's never barked once. How did they even find out?"

"Oh," Mom replied, "I know how."

Eight

The next day I did Go to Work with Lucas, which was my favorite thing to do except Tiny Piece of Cheese. I spent time seeing Ty and my other friends. Many of them now carried little treats because I was such a good dog. Steve gave me a cold and delicious bite of something tasting like milk, but much sweeter. Marty gave me bacon. Their affection for me was obvious in their pats and words and cuddles. One old man liked to kiss me on my nose but could not bend over very well so I had learned to go to his chair and put my paws on his chest and lick his face. He laughed when I did this. His name was Wylie and he called me Keeper instead of Bella.

"This one is a keeper," he told Ty every time.

Normally when I went to visit my friends I spent most of the day with them, providing comfort, eating treats, and playing "Dr. Gann," which was the game where I lay on the couch between two people and they covered me with a blanket and petted me gently until someone called "Okay!" It was like Stay only much more fun. This day,

Lucas and Ty took me to a different part of the hospital. We stood for a while and listened to bells, and I did No Barks, and then a door slid open and we went into a small room that hummed and shook. I felt a sensation in my stomach similar to a car ride. When the door opened, the smells had changed and I knew somehow we were somewhere else. It was like a car ride without a car!

Following the two men down a slick hallway, I smelled along the walls, picking up the scent of many people and chemicals. Ty and Lucas seemed nervous and we were moving very quickly so I was unable to drink in all the odors properly. We turned a few corners and then Lucas knocked on an open door and poked in his head. "Dr. Sterling? It's Lucas Ray. I called you this morning?"

"Come in," a man greeted. His hands smelled strongly of chemicals as he grasped fingers with Lucas, changed his mind and grabbed Ty's hand, then changed it again and dropped his arm. "So is this the dog?"

"This is Bella."

I wagged. He leaned over and rubbed my head. I liked this man despite the sharp tang wafting from his palms. "You'd better shut the door, Ty."

Everyone sat down, so I did, too. There was nothing much to smell in the room. I could tell the open bin by his desk had some potatoes in it, though.

"So," the man began, "I looked into it. Yes, there are seizure dogs. Most of them are trained to do what you say Bella does naturally, which is to signal. Some people claim they've saved lives, though naturally there are naysayers. And by law you have to be allowed to have a seizure dog if a doctor prescribes it. Doesn't matter if you're in a no-pet building, they have to make an exception. I talked to our house counsel and he says the Fair Housing Act, the FHA, is very clear on the matter."

"Thank God," Lucas murmured.

The man held up one of his stinky hands. "Well, wait a

88 W. Bruce Cameron

minute, it's not that simple. There's a whole procedure to go through. Bella would have to be certified. Right now, she's just a pet."

"But I told you, she's barked both times recently when my Mom has been going into a seizure. If we understood what was going on, we could have prepared for it!"

I felt my person's agitation and looked at him anxiously. What was wrong?

"I do understand that, son," the man replied. "But having the innate ability is a far cry from obtaining a legal certification."

"How long will that take?" Lucas asked.

"I don't really know, but it looks like an involved process." The man shrugged. "We don't do that here, I can tell you that much."

"We only have three days left before they start proceedings," Lucas moaned. I licked his hand.

"Doc, couldn't you give him some kind of letter about this?" Ty asked.

"I can't do that. Even if a letter would do any good, which I highly doubt—as I said, there's a clear process—I can't state she's a trained seizure-alert animal, because she's not trained, she's just a dog with innate ability."

Ty stood up. If anything, he seemed more agitated than Lucas. "Look, this is a really special dog. She comes on the ward and you can just see people's stress going away. In twelve step, the new ones are thrilled to have her there; she gives them confidence. She sits right up front and nearly everyone who wants to speak pets her first. And I know she helps Terri; she told me Bella's more effective than the antidepressants she's taking. Everyone loves her. She's doing good here, doc. That's got to count for something."

The man was quiet for a moment. "So you do know having a dog in the VA is against the rules, right?" he finally asked.

"I know I will do what it takes to help the men and women I care about. Men and women who served this country. People who are having a tough time for a lot of reasons. And if this dog can make a difference I am damn well going to see to it she gets to come here!" Ty responded hotly.

The man held up a hand. "No, don't misunderstand me. I just was making sure you knew that if Dr. Gann, or a couple of doctors I could name, find out you've been smuggling a pet into the hospital, they'll shut you down. I personally don't have a dog in the hunt, no pun intended."

"Bella is more than just a pet," Ty stated evenly. He seemed less angry. "That's what I am telling you."

I liked hearing Ty say my name, and I wagged.

"How is your mother?" the man asked Lucas.

"She's . . . in some ways better, some ways worse. She hasn't been too depressed lately, except these seizures are a real concern. We thought they were over."

"And your dog helps her with depression?" the man asked.

"Yes. Absolutely."

"Tell me about that."

"Well, she stays with Bella all day. When I come home, she is so much better than how it used to be, before the dog, I mean. It has been a long time since she was so down she hadn't gotten out of her pajamas or had anything to eat when I got back. She takes Bella for walks and gets a lot of energy from that. And Bella seems to know when she's starting to go to a dark place and will put her head in Mom's lap."

Lucas had said my name, so I wagged again.

"I'm glad to hear she's doing better."

"She is going to meetings on a much more frequent basis." Lucas looked to Ty.

"I sort of can't confirm that, Lucas," Ty said apologetically.

"Oh right. Sorry."

"Well, here's the thing," the man said, clearing his throat. "I cannot give you anything regarding her being a seizure dog. But as I understand the FHA, all that's required for her to be considered an emotional support animal is a letter from a doctor currently treating Terri. So I'll do that right now."

"Will that . . . will the building allow us to stay if we have that letter?" Lucas asked hopefully.

"I'm not an attorney, but what I read online seems to clearly imply they have to."

"Thank you so much, Dr. Sterling. You have no idea how much this means to me and my mother."

The man was using a pencil to scratch a piece of paper. "This doesn't give you a get-out-of-jail-free card for the VA." He looked sharply at Ty. "Having her here is still against the rules. A seizure dog, that might be a different story, but emotional support animals are barred."

"Understood, doctor," Ty said.

"I'm not going to rat you out, I'm just warning you what might happen if you're discovered."

"Oh, I think we can keep Bella a secret," Ty observed dryly. "We've got good people on it."

The man handed over a piece of paper and Lucas put it in his pocket. He seemed really, really happy, but he did not celebrate with any treats.

• • •

After that, things changed at home. No longer did Lucas step outside for a moment before running with me to the sidewalk. Now we left together, and Lucas did not mind if I sniffed and dawdled around our front door.

At first, I was confused. A good dog, I had decided, learned from doing things over and over. That's how I knew No Barks meant to remain silent no matter what the provocation, and Tiny Piece of Cheese meant Lucas loved me and had a very special treat in his fingers. When he told me I was a good dog it was as good as any treat, even chicken, except of course it was always better if there was a treat as well.

But humans can change without warning, and I just accepted this as part of being with my person. So if our pattern of leaving the house was different, I couldn't begin to guess why.

When Mom took me, we did not walk as far, but sometimes we met people. "She's my therapy dog," Mom would say to them. Whatever that meant, I heard the word "dog" and I could feel the approval and affection of the people who would pet me, and knew they understood I was a good dog.

When the air warmed and the leaves waved in the breeze, Olivia took us for car rides to places high up in the hills where the smells were all different. "Let's go for a hike," Lucas would say. I always got excited when he went to his closet and brought out a sack with straps looped onto his shoulders—there were always treats in there for me.

"Fox!" Olivia blurted on one such hike. I smelled an animal I had never before encountered, and saw it up ahead on the trail. It ran a little like a cat, low to the ground.

"See the fox, Bella? The fox!" Lucas said excitedly.

A fox was different from another animal—a coyote. We sometimes saw a few of those and I growled deep in my throat at each one. The fox looked fun to chase, but something about the coyotes made them look like small, bad dogs—dogs I instinctively hated.

"Bella wants to chase it," Olivia remarked on one such occasion. Far up ahead of us, a lone coyote was staring at me as it stood insolently on the path. I growled.

"Right, well, even though they're small, they're vicious," Lucas replied. "And there might be more than one—this one's out in the open, trying to lure Bella into pursuit, while one or two more are hiding in the bushes."

"I wasn't saying you should let her do it, I was just saying she wants to."

"You're always telling me I should lighten up. I thought letting my dog chase wildlife might be part of the program."

"You're misunderstanding me. What I'm saying is that you should be a better person in general," she responded lightly.

"I like these long hikes. Gives us time for you to list all my faults," Lucas observed dryly. "Thank you for that."

Frustrated, I watched the coyote slink off. Why didn't we go deal with it?

"How's your mom?"

I glanced up at Olivia as she mentioned Mom.

"You know, really pretty good. Except for the seizures. Her mood, though, has been really great."

"Has she always struggled with depression?"

I stopped to smell the deliciously rotten skeleton of a bird until the leash tightened and drew me away.

"I don't actually know. When she enlisted, I had already gone back to living with my aunt Julie. And then things got really bad when she came back from Afghanistan. You know, drugs and alcohol. Julie got court-ordered custody and Mom just sort of vanished for a couple of years. Then she was committed, got into a program, and asked if I would let her back into my life."

"Asked you? Wow."

"Yeah."

"She sure is proud of you. Talks about your grades all the time, how responsible you are."

"Well, but you're teaching me to explore my inner risk-taker."

Olivia laughed, a short, quick sound. "Yeah, about that,"

she said after a moment. "Have you ever said it to anyone else before?" We walked steadily up a high hill, cold air sweeping down from the white-covered mountains. There was snow up there—I wondered if we were going to go roll in it.

"Said what?"

"You know what."

He kicked a stone that skittered ahead of us like a ball. "No, you're the first. Why, have you ever said it before to anyone?"

"No."

"So if next time, you tell me you love me back, it would be history making."

"You're going to say it *again*?" She laughed.

"I love you, Olivia."

"Men are always telling me that."

"I'm serious."

"Of course you're serious. You're the most serious person I've ever met."

Lucas stopped and solemnly held my head in his hands. I stared up at him. "Bella, Olivia is terrified to express her emotions."

I wagged.

Olivia knelt next to me. "Bella, Lucas feels like he has to discuss *everything*."

They leaned toward each other over me and kissed. The surge of love between the two of them drew me up on my back legs, reaching up with my forepaws. They were doing love and I wanted to be part of it.

* * *

We were on the sidewalk, returning from the park, when two trucks pulled up near us. The door to one opened and it was the smoky-meat man, Gunter.

The other vehicle smelled amazing. Dogs and cats and

other animals, some dead, had painted overlapping odors all over it. I strained on my leash to go to it for a closer examination, but Lucas held me fast.

"Animal control," Lucas said worriedly. "Come on, Bella."

"Hey, Lucas!" Gunter called. "Come here a minute."

A man got out of the front seat of the other vehicle. He smelled like dogs and cats. He was heavy, and he wore a hat. "Kid! Need to talk to you about your dog," he said.

"Go Home, Bella!" Lucas commanded, but in this variation of the game I stayed attached to the leash and when I ran, he ran with me. This was so much fun I wanted to run and run, but part of Go Home was to go to my spot and lie down. As I did so, Lucas opened the front door and pulled me inside the house.

I could feel that Mom was not home. Lucas was panting, and there was tension on his breath and on his skin. "Good dog, Bella. Good Go Home."

I wagged.

The bell rang and I did No Barks. Lucas went to it. I could smell that it was the hat-wearing man from the wonderful truck with all the animal odors. Lucas put his eye to the door for a moment, then, sighing, he opened it. "Stay, Bella," he commanded at the same time.

I had been about to greet the new guest but I knew Stay and promptly sat.

"Animal control," the hat-man informed Lucas gruffly.

"I know."

"So I understand you've got a pit bull living here."

"I . . . we don't know what breed she is, she was abandoned at birth. We found her in the crawl space where someone from your office says there are no animals living. There are still cats there. More than ever, in fact. You probably know that, though."

"I'm not sure I care for your tone," Hat-man stated softly.

"Well, I know I don't care for your ethics," Lucas responded.

I heard the rustle of cloth as Hat-man stiffened. "Pit bulls are not legal in Denver, anyone ever tell you that?"

"Bella is special. She's my mom's therapy dog. My mom is a vet; she served in Afghanistan."

"Therapy dog, huh?"

"Would you like to see the letter from her doctor?" Lucas asked politely.

"Can you call your dog over here for a minute?"

"Why?"

"I'm not going to try to take her; I can't enter a residence to do that."

"Bella." Lucas seemed reluctant, but he snapped his fingers. I went instantly to his side. I had the feeling Lucas did not like the hat-man, so I did not approach him to be petted, but remained by Lucas's leg, catching a strong whiff of all the animals on the man's clothes.

Hat-man gave an emphatic nod. "Yeah, that's a pit, all right."

"Whatever." Lucas shrugged. "We have the letter."

The man reached into his pocket and pulled out something. He thumbed it and with a small popping sound a delicious scent filled the air. He threw the treat down on the ground and I lunged for it instantly. Despite what Lucas might think, I found myself liking the hat-man.

"Next time, I'd appreciate it if you'd ask before you feed my dog," Lucas said coldly.

"Point is, she's supposed to be able to ignore a treat on the ground. She didn't, so she doesn't qualify as a therapy dog."

"That can't be true."

"I catch this animal outside of the apartment, I'm impounding it. It's an illegal breed."

"Impounding?"

"You got to pay a fine, and then we chip her and if we ever catch her again, we destroy her."

"You can't be serious."

"That's the law. I'm just doing my job."

"The way you did your job certifying there were no cats across the street? Is Gunter paying you to harass us? We've done nothing wrong!" Lucas declared hotly. I stirred uneasily.

"That's where you're incorrect. You are harboring a banned breed. Pit bulls are fierce, dangerous animals."

"Does Bella look fierce and dangerous to you?"

"Doesn't matter. She could be as gentle as a baby lamb, if the law says she's a vicious animal, she's a vicious animal. See you, pal. See you soon."

. . .

The next afternoon, when Lucas came home from Go to Work, Olivia was with him. We went for a car ride! I thrust my nose as far into the wind as I could manage and drank in the amazing mixture of scents coming at me so fast.

Soon we were in a building very similar to the one where Lucas did Go to Work to visit Olivia. We stood in a small room with some strangers in it whom I wanted to visit but was held back by my leash, a room that hummed and made my stomach lurch. This one was much quieter than the one I'd stood in with Ty and Lucas, and every time the room opened, the smells were completely different on the other side, and people would get out, perhaps upset they hadn't been allowed to play with me. I didn't understand what we were doing in the small room but I was happy to be there and happy to get out.

We walked down a quiet hallway to a place with a table and where the floor was soft with carpet. A man came in holding papers.

"I'm Mike Powell," the man greeted. I wagged.

"Thank you for seeing us. I'm Lucas Ray, and this is my . . ." He gestured to Olivia.

"Careful," she warned.

"My friend Olivia Phillips."

"I am his driver." Olivia held the man's hand briefly before deciding she didn't like doing it and letting go. "He treats me inappropriately."

The man laughed and then bent down to see me. I licked his face. "This must be Bella. What a sweetie."

They talked and talked while I searched for the softest place in the room. By a narrow table there was a rug on top of the carpet, but it wasn't quite large enough to get my whole body on it. I lay down, grunting.

I dozed off, but opened my eyes sleepily when I heard the man say my name.

"Bella's up against the government. I'm afraid the law in Denver is irrational on this subject. Did you know there's not even such a thing as a specific AKC breed called a pit bull? It's a whole class of dogs, like 'retriever.' Anyway, a couple of years ago a child was killed by what was called a pit bull in the press, so the city council passed the ban. There was lots of testimony that none of these dogs are any more dangerous than any other dogs—in fact, I think that dachshunds bite people more often than any other breed. Pits are very protective of their owners, maybe that's how this all got started. And did you know that since the ban, pit bulls are more popular than ever in Denver? Got to love Americans. Tell them they can't have something and they immediately want it so they can stick it to the man.

"Anyway, the problem isn't that Bella is a pit bull, the problem is that animal control says she is. On one officer's word alone, she can be picked up. If two more officers agree Bella is a pit, the law says she is a pit. Crazy system, but there it is."

"But what about the doctor's letter? It's not BS, Bella really does give my mom emotional support," Lucas said.

"I'm afraid the law is pretty harsh on this. Throwing down a dog treat may seem like a crude test, but it's one of several they can apply—and if she flunks one, that's it. There's no appeal."

"None? Really?" Olivia asked.

"Not in the animal shelter system. We could go to court, of course, but that would be very expensive," the man replied. "And while we worked through it, Bella would have to stay in the shelter. That could take months."

"Then what can we do?" Lucas asked desperately. "The guy says if he catches me outside with Bella he'll take her away."

The man spread his hands. "Honestly? The way the laws are written in Denver? Nothing. There's nothing you can do."

Olivia stirred. For the first time since I had met her, I felt a rising anger in her. "Animal control can come onto Lucas and Terri's property?"

"No. I didn't say that. They'd need a court order for that."

"What about the front porch?"

"Same thing. Or a driveway or a garage. If it is part of your lease, she'll be okay."

Lucas bent down to talk to me and I wagged. "That's it, then, Bella. The bad man comes, you have to Go Home and *stay in your spot*. Okay? If we do that, we'll be safe."

I tensed, not understanding. Go Home?

"I'm really worried, Lucas," Olivia murmured.

"Yeah. Me, too."

Nine

A few days later Lucas did Go to Work so he could come home smelling like Olivia, but he did not take me. I could feel him out there somewhere, though—I carried his presence with me like a scent. He was my person and we belonged together. Nothing could change that. It was as much a part of me as being a dog.

Mom snapped the leash onto my collar because we were doing Go for a Walk! I danced impatiently as she put on a coat, then took it off with a laugh. "Getting to be too warm for a jacket, Bella," she told me. I sat at the door, being as good as a dog can be, and finally we went outside. As we passed the den I smelled the cats in there but not Mother Cat.

I was excited to think we might be doing Go to Work ourselves, and that I would soon see Ty and Steve and all my other friends and Olivia and, of course, Lucas, but Mom turned in a different direction. I smelled many wonderful things as we went up a street we had never walked before—animals alive and dead, and delicious foods in plastic bins that sat lined up at the end of people's driveways. Flowers painted the air with their pollens. A dog barked at me from behind a fence, so I squatted in the green grass in front of him and politely left him notice that I had been here.

Mom rarely took long walks but today she was happy and we kept going, exploring new places. As we did so the truck with all the animal smells passed us—the odors were so intense I wanted to run up to it and sniff. When it stopped I was happy, because of the fragrances it emitted, but Mom slowed up and I sensed her unease.

There was a small dog riding in the back in a wire crate. She was a female who stared at me, but I was a good dog and did No Barks even when the dog took offense at me and yipped sharply.

The man with the hat got out of his truck, hauling up his pants as he did so. Mom halted, and I could tell she was feeling more and more alarmed. I stared at the hat-man, wondering if he was a threat. I would protect Mom because Lucas would want me to.

"I'm impounding the dog," the man called out as he shut his front door. The way he said "dog" sounded like I was being a bad dog, though I was still doing No Barks.

"No, you're not," Mom responded evenly.

"Public property. It's my job. You give me any trouble and I'll call for backup and you'll be arrested. It's the law." The hat-man reached into his truck and pulled out a long stick with a loop of rope at the end of it. I regarded it curiously as he approached. What kind of toy was that?

"You can't take Bella. She's a service animal."

"Not according to the law, she ain't." Hat-man paused, and I could sense he was worried, maybe even more worried than Mom. Whatever was happening was causing everyone to be anxious. "Look, I don't want any trouble."

"Then I suggest you don't start any."

"Let me do my job or you'll go to jail."

Mom knelt next to me, putting a hand on my face. I licked her palm. I could faintly taste some butter. She unsnapped my collar. "Bella! Go Home!"

I was startled: I only did Go Home with Lucas and did not realize Mom knew the game, too.

"Go Home!" she repeated loudly.

This was as far away from my spot at home as I had ever been, but I knew what to do. I ran.

Behind me I could hear the small dog in the crate barking, and even as the truck faded from my nostrils I was able to track it by her barks and knew it was moving, turning behind me. I dashed across yards, loving the wild feeling of my full-out galloping legs and the utter freedom. Dogs barked at me but I ignored them. I had a job to do.

When I got to the front porch I curled up in my spot by the bushes, panting. I had been a good dog.

I heard a truck pull up and instantly detected the mix of animal odors coupled with that of the one small dog, who had stopped yapping. I heard a door slam and raised my head curiously.

The hat-man stood next to the truck. He patted his pants. "Hey! Bella! Come!"

I was confused—this was not how to play Go Home. But then the man tossed something at his feet and I smelled meat. Yes! I had done Go Home and now I was being rewarded. That was how this worked. I bolted from the porch, gobbling up the treat from the sidewalk.

"*Bella!*"

It was Mom. She was turning the corner all the way at the end of the street, and was racing toward me. This was also a change; neither Lucas nor Mom ever ran calling when I finished hiding.

I wondered if I should run to her and tensed, and just as I did so I felt a collar of rope slip over my neck and then suddenly I was on the worst leash imaginable, stiff and unyielding. I twisted against it. "No, Bella," the hat-man told me.

"*Bella!*" Mom cried again, her voice filled with anguish and despair.

The man lifted me up with one arm, holding onto the stiff leash. He shoved me into a crate next to the one containing the little dog, who cowered away from me, no longer willing to challenge me now that I was this close to her. He shut the door of the crate. What were we doing? Mom needed me! I whined. When the truck rumbled and pulled into the street I was frightened and confused. I did not understand.

I was in the crate and knew to do No Barks. The truck drove away and Mom was still running, but as we turned the corner I saw her sink to her knees with her hands to her face.

· · ·

Hat-man drove his truck to a building that was powerfully redolent with cats and dogs and other animals. I could faintly hear dogs giving voice to what I felt, which was a devastating fear.

One at a time, Hat-man led the little dog and then me into the building at the end of the stiff leash. When I entered the barking was much louder and the odors much stronger. I could track where the little dog had gone, but I was led into a different room, one with big, sad, barking dogs in crates with high walls. I did not want to be here. I wanted to be with Lucas.

My collar was removed and I was put in a crate myself. It was very big compared to any other I had seen. There was a soft bed for me, and a bowl of water. I drank from it, wanting to do something normal and familiar.

The din from the other dogs was incessant, and I was pulled by it, yearning to join my voice with theirs. But I did not because I knew I needed to do No Barks. I needed to do Sit. I needed to be the very best dog I could possibly be so that Lucas would come get me and let me out.

I wasn't there long before a younger woman came to get me. She had one of those stiff leashes—I could not understand why they would want such a thing. It prevented a good dog from licking and pawing.

She took me to a room that reeked of chemicals. The hat-man was there, as well as a nice woman who touched me softly, the way the vet often did. The nice woman pressed something up against my chest. "I don't think you can call her a pit, Chuck." I wagged my tail a little, hoping when this was over Lucas would come get me.

"Me and Glenn and Alberto all say she's a pit bull. Signed and sealed," Hat-man replied.

"Alberto is on vacation," the nice woman snapped. She seemed irritated.

"I texted him a photo and he faxed in his affidavit."

"This is BS," she muttered.

"No, see, I been telling you this is how it works. Every time we bring in a pit bull you want to have the same argument."

"Because it's wrong! The three of you certify more dogs as pits than the rest of the ACOs combined."

"Because we been here long enough to see what happens when some kid gets bit by one!" Hat-man said harshly.

The woman gave a weary sigh. "This dog isn't going to bite anybody. Look, I can put my hand in her *mouth*."

Her fingers tasted of soap and chemicals and dog.

"I'm doing my job. You do yours. Get the chip in her so if we pick her up again in Denver we'll know she's a two-strike-you're-out dog."

"I know what to *do*, Chuck," she responded in clipped tones. "And I'm going to file an objection as soon as we're done here."

"Another one? I'm pissing my pants." Hat-man sneered.

Eventually I was returned to the same crate. I could not

remember ever being so miserable. The fear and despair and anxiety coming off the other dogs affected me until I was panting and pacing. All I could think about was Lucas. Lucas would come to get me. Lucas would take me home. I would be a good dog.

Every time the door opened it was someone else, someone not Lucas. Some of the dogs would charge to the door of their crates to be near these people, wagging and pawing at the wire and whining, and some would shy away in fright. I wagged but did not otherwise react. Usually someone left with a dog, or brought in a dog.

What were we all doing here?

Eventually a nice man came to get me, but not to take me to Lucas. Instead, he put a very strange leash on me, one that completely encircled my snout.

"You're a sweet dog. You're a good dog," he told me as he touched me gently. I wagged, thrilled to be leaving the crate. I hoped we were going home to my family!

The nice man led me to a steel door and then outside into a yard. The abrupt change in smells made my nostrils flare. The ground underneath my feet was hard and knotty, with limp grass lying sparsely against the dry earth. Almost every inch of yard was painted with dog smells, evident with every inhalation. "My name is Wayne," the man told me. "I'm sorry about the muzzle. Supposedly you're a vicious killer dog who will rip my limbs off."

His tone was as kind as his hands. He lifted his knuckles to my snout and I licked past the strange collar as best I could. We walked around the yard, staying on a path that ran along a high fence. It was obvious that many, many walks had been taken prior to mine. I gratefully squatted by the fence—I did not want to Do Your Business in the crate, even though it was a large enclosure and other dogs in the room had not been as clean.

The man did not pick up after me the way Mom and Lucas did. "Just another pile for me, don't worry, Bella. I have to come out in a little while and get everybody's. It's the glamor part of my job."

He was compassionate and he petted me but he did not take me to Lucas. He led me to the same crate, though I sat on the floor and resisted as he pulled my leash.

"Come on, girl," he murmured to me. "Get in your kennel."

I so did not want to go in there, but when the man pushed me I slid on the slippery floor and then I was back, curling up mournfully on the dog bed while he fastened the door. I put my nose between my paws and listened to all the bad dogs ignoring No Barks. I was heartbroken. I must have been a very, very bad dog for Lucas to have sent me to this place.

• • •

Was this my new life? I was walked in the yard a few times a day, sometimes by a nice woman named Glynnis and sometimes by the man named Wayne, and always with the uncomfortable collar that held my teeth together. Dogs barked all the time, whether it was dark or light. Sometimes Wayne came in with a hose and sprayed it and at first the smells of dog poop rose on the wet air and then the odors would fade away, which made the room with all the crates even less interesting than before.

I missed Lucas so much. I was a good dog with No Barks, but I did cry sometimes. I thought I could feel his hands on my fur when I slept, but when I awoke he was not there.

I remembered the squirrel we found in the street, the squashed one. How different it was from a living, bouncing squirrel. It was an almost-squirrel, a dead squirrel.

That's how I felt.

I did not eat. I lay on my dog bed and never moved when my door was opened for Wayne or Glynnis to walk me in the yard with the high fence. I didn't even care about all the wonderful markings left by male and female dogs out there. I just wanted Lucas.

When a new woman came and put the strange leash on my nose and led me out into a hallway, I struggled to get to my feet, feeling stiff and lethargic. I went willingly but I did not wag. My head was lowered and I registered all the dog and cat scents on the air without excitement.

She led me into a small room. "Here, Bella, let's put this back on." With a familiar tug on my neck I was wearing my collar, so that I sounded like myself again. There was a soft pad on the floor, so I went to it, circled, and lay down with a sigh. "I'll be right back," she told me. The woman left. I did not know where I was and did not care.

And then the door opened. Lucas! I scrabbled to my feet and leapt into his arms just as he entered the room. "Bella!" he cried, staggering back and sitting down.

I was sobbing and panting, trying to lick him through the stupid collar. I rubbed my head on his chest and circled in his lap, putting my paws on his chest. He put his arms around me and a feeling of well-being flooded through me. Lucas had come for me! I *was* a good dog! Lucas *did* love me! I never wanted to be apart from him again. I was so happy, so relieved, so grateful. My person was here to take me home!

The new woman was there, too. She had found Lucas for me!

"Can I take off the hockey mask?" Lucas asked.

"We're not supposed to with pit bulls, but sure, she's obviously no threat."

Lucas unsnapped the thing around my nose so I could kiss him properly.

The woman held up some papers. "Okay, I know you signed the forms, but I want to reiterate what they say. If your dog is picked up again for any reason within Denver city limits, she will be held for three days and then destroyed. It's two strikes with pit bulls. There is no process for appeal other than the courts, and I have to say, the judges pretty much defer to the ACOs. Most of the officers here are amazing human beings who are really concerned with animal welfare but the one who picked up Bella is . . . Let's just say Chuck is not my favorite, and he's got a couple poker buddies and they cover for each other on everything. Do you understand what I am saying? It's the system; it's stacked against you."

Lucas felt sad despite the fact that we were back together. "I don't know what to do."

"You have to get her out of Denver."

"I can't . . . there are reasons why I can't move right now. My mom . . . it's complicated."

"Then good luck. I don't know what else I can say."

When we left the room and went outside, Olivia was waiting! I yipped with excitement, so happy I wanted to run around and around. She dropped to her knees and gave me love, hugging me and letting me lick her face.

A man approached—it was Wayne. I wondered if we would all take a walk in that yard now.

"Lucas?" Wayne asked.

"Wayne?" They punched each other's hands, but it wasn't a fight. "Uh, Olivia, this is Wayne Getz. He and I went to high school together. Wayne, Olivia is my driver."

"I'm his girlfriend," Olivia said.

"Nice," Wayne said, grinning. "Hey, Bella's your dog? She's awesome."

I wagged.

"Thanks. Yeah, she's a good dog."

I wagged.

"So you work here?" Lucas asked.

Wayne shrugged. "I'm doing community service. I got caught shoplifting again."

"Oh."

Wayne laughed. "No, it's okay. I'm giving up walking on the wild side, I promise."

I was impatient to see Mom. I nuzzled Lucas's hand.

"So what are you doing now?" Wayne asked Lucas.

"I work at the VA hospital. I am an assistant to a couple of case managers. Olivia works there, too—she yells at people."

"Only at Lucas," Olivia said.

"You were always going to go to med school," Wayne said.

"That's still the plan." Lucas nodded. "Everything works out, I will start in the fall."

Finally—finally—they stopped talking to each other and I got into Olivia's car. I sat in the backseat and stuck my nose out the window.

I knew that I would never fully understand what had just transpired. I did not understand why I was put in the room with the crates and all the dogs, nor why Lucas waited for so long before finally coming to get me. I just knew that we were a family and that I would never leave home again.

· · ·

We were back to getting up before the sun was light, taking a walk, and then going out again after dark. "It's the only time we can be sure the dog catcher isn't out," Lucas told Mom.

"We'll move out of Denver city limits," Mom declared.

"Where? Aurora bans pits. Commerce City bans pits. Lone Tree bans pits," Lucas said bitterly.

"I am sure there is someplace we can go."

"Someplace we can afford? After we break our lease here? Where do we get the security deposit? How do we move our stuff?" Lucas demanded. "We don't even have the money to buy a car!"

"Stop it! I won't have you talking like this. The only time anyone is defeated is when they give up," Mom said sternly. "Let's start looking for an apartment *now.*"

That night when Lucas took me for a late-night walk, I could smell the truck with all the animal odors far behind us. Lucas did not turn around to see it, but I knew it was there.

Ten

The next morning when we went outside, there was wet snow on the ground and the sky was still dark. Lucas made a small chuckle. "Springtime in Denver, Bella."

The lack of people and cars made for a peaceful, hushed environment. Smells were muted, and my paws were instantly soaking. It was wonderful. The foreboding in Lucas's manner changed as he stood laughing at me rolling in the delightfully cold blanket. I was snorting and sneezing and wanted to play all day, but once I had done Do Your Business we turned around.

Mom was waiting at the door when we went up the steps to the porch. "Any sign of animal control?"

"No. They're not going to be out this early," Lucas told her. "And then tonight I'll wait until late to take her out again."

"Poor Bella. That's such a long time to wait."

"She'll be okay. I don't know what else we can do."

"I'll keep searching online for a new place."

"Okay, Mom."

"Rents have gone up so much." She sighed.

"Did you talk to your case manager?"

"Yes. It's not hopeless, just time consuming. I can submit an appeal once we've actually located a place."

"Time is the one thing we don't have," Lucas observed gravely.

"Don't look like that. We'll be fine."

Lucas made a frustrated noise. "We're never going to find a place where Bella's allowed, that's on the bus route, that we can afford, and that qualifies for your subsidy."

"Don't say never. I promise we will."

Lucas stroked my head. "You be a good dog, Bella. I have to go to work now."

Mom and I spent the day together. I was so content just to lie there, to not be in a room with barking dogs, to know that I was home and that Lucas would be back and would smell like Olivia. Outside, sun heated the air and my nose told me the snow had melted.

That night Lucas went outside without me, carrying cat food, and then returned. "No sign of the dog cops," he told Mom. He hooked my leash and I danced around in excitement. I went to the door, whimpering to get out.

I could smell that my mother was in the den on the other side of the fence, and that Lucas had given her and the other cats some food.

I could smell something else, too. One street away, that truck was back, the one with the crates on the back. My happy mood vanished—was it coming back for me? I did not want to ride the truck and go back to that building. I looked up at Lucas.

"It's okay, Bella. We're safe."

I heard the sound of the truck's distinctive rumbling as it eased onto our street. The smells became much stronger, but Lucas apparently couldn't sense them.

Lucas pulled gently on the leash. "Let's go, Bella." That

truck was moving, coming closer. I did what Lucas wanted, moving ahead of him on the leash, and then suddenly he froze. The truck roared loudly and pulled in front of us and stopped. Hat-man jumped out.

"By the authority of the city of Denver I am seizing that animal," he declared.

Lucas knelt by my side, fumbling with my collar. I tensed—time to do Go Home?

Hat-man raised a hand. "If you release that dog and I catch him off leash I will dart him."

Lucas was afraid and angry. "No, you will not." He took a step toward home.

"Don't make this difficult, kid," the hat-man said softly. "I called for backup as soon as I saw you step out on the curb. Anything you try now will just make it worse."

"Why are you doing this?"

"I am enforcing the law."

"We're moving. Isn't that what you want? What Gunter wants? We'll move away and won't be able to see him tear down the house where you said there were no cats. We just need time to find a place. Okay? You guys win. Just let us have a few days."

"Can't do it. You don't think everyone says this? If we gave everybody with a pit bull extra days, we'd never pick any of them up. Place would be overrun."

"*Please.*"

A car pulled up behind us. There were bright, flashing lights on its roof. Two people got out. They had dark suits and metal tools on their belts. Both were women. One was much taller than the other. Police.

"This is a pit bull. It's been picked up before. The owner is resisting," Hat-man greeted. "I need you to arrest him for failing to comply with a legal order."

"That's a pit bull? You sure?" one of the women, the tall one, asked.

Hat-man nodded. "Been certified by three ACOs."

"Maybe," the woman replied doubtfully.

"We don't get involved in that decision," the other woman said.

"It just doesn't look like a pit bull to me," the taller woman said.

"What you think doesn't matter," Hat-man said angrily.

Both women regarded him without expression. Then the taller one turned to Lucas. "What's your name?"

"Lucas Ray."

"Well Lucas, you do need to surrender the dog to animal control," she told him kindly.

"But they want to kill her! It's not fair. She just got out of the dog pound yesterday. That was *one day ago,*" Lucas replied. "We're going to move out of Denver, we just need time."

I yawned anxiously, feeling Lucas's distress, Hat-man's rage, and the tension in the two women.

"You couldn't give him a few days to relocate?" the taller woman asked. "Seems like a reasonable request."

"No. I am doing my job here. You need to arrest the kid for refusing to surrender the animal."

"Please do not point your finger at me," the taller woman said coldly.

Hat-man dropped his arm.

"If an arrest is called for then we'll make it. Our first concern is to defuse the situation. Your rhetoric isn't helping."

"What?" Hat-man sputtered.

I nosed Lucas for reassurance that nothing bad was happening.

The other woman had turned away and spoken quietly to her shoulder. Now she came back. "Sergeant says to wrap this up," she said to her tall friend.

The women approached us. I could feel kindness; it was

evident in the way the shorter woman touched Lucas's arm. "Maybe you can get a lawyer or something, but for now, you have to let him take the dog," she told him gently. "Otherwise, we'll have to cuff you and take you in. You don't want that."

"We can't afford a lawyer. *Please.*"

"I'm sorry, Lucas."

Lucas knelt and put his face into my fur. I licked the salty tears on his face. Waves of profound sadness came off of him. "But she won't understand. She'll think I'm abandoning her," he choked, anguished.

"Let's get this show on the road," Hat-man declared.

"You need to back off, sir," the taller woman said tersely.

"Say good-bye. You'll wish later you'd said good-bye," the shorter woman whispered softly.

Lucas bent over me. "I am so, so sorry, Bella. I can't protect you. This is my fault. I love you, Bella."

The hat-man came over, waving the oddly stiff leash. "You don't need that!" Lucas snapped, his anger flaring.

"So are you two just going to let him spout off to me like that?" the hat-man said to the two women.

"Yeah, we are. That a problem?" the shorter woman replied testily.

"Let him take his dog over and put him in the cage himself," the taller woman commanded.

Lucas led me over to one of the outside crates. The hat-man opened the door and Lucas lifted me gently inside. "I love you, Bella," he whispered. "I am so, so sorry."

I knew that whatever was happening, it was good, because Lucas was right there making sure I was safe. I wagged when he unclipped my leash. He kissed my face. My person was still so sad. I wanted to Go Home and cuddle with Lucas on the bed, like I did at Go to Work with Mack. Provide comfort. Do Tiny Piece of Cheese. He would not be as sad then.

The hat-man shut the door to the crate.

"Good-bye, Bella," Lucas said to me in a breaking voice. "I will always remember you."

When the truck pulled away, Lucas stood in the street, wiping his eyes.

I knew I should do No Barks, but I was suddenly so frightened I couldn't help myself. I thought I understood now what might be happening.

* * *

I was soon back in the room of crates and barking dogs. I was thoroughly miserable. Lucas needed me, and I needed my Lucas. Why had he sent me to this place? I did not belong here.

I curled up on the soft mat, tucking my nose into my tail, and tried to shut out the dogs who did not know No Barks. Their terror and loneliness and frustration was in their voices and their smells, and I tried not to let it affect me, but soon I was whimpering.

I was conscious of time passing. The room got brighter in the day but at night was not completely black. The dogs barked, ceaselessly. I vomited in the corner of my crate and Wayne hosed it away. I was taken for walks around the fence by him and the nice woman Glynnis, the leash strapped to my face. The dirt in the yard was packed hard with the pads of many, many dog feet.

"This sucks, Bella," Glynnis told me as she indulged me in long, careful sniffs along the fence. The scent of all those dogs was hugely distracting to me. "You are such a gentle dog. You didn't bite anybody. Most of the ACOs wouldn't give you a second look. You just got picked up by one of the bad ones. Everyone thinks Chuck is an asswipe."

She did not say the name Lucas and I did not smell his scent on her.

I was back in the same place but everything seemed worse. Glynnis was so gloomy. The dogs around me seemed especially sad.

I panted and paced and tried to lie down on my bed and then got right back up again, over and over. And I could no longer do No Barks. I barked like a bad dog, pleading, crying, mourning, questioning. All I got back in response were the similar howls from the other dogs.

The next night something curious happened. I smelled the man Wayne come into the room, though I did not see him. There was a small closet at the end of the aisle, and because it had been accessed by many people, I was familiar with the sound it made when its door was opened and closed. I heard that sound now. Then the scent of Wayne changed—it remained, but was muted, stifled. *Wayne was in that closet.* The other dogs smelled him, too—I could tell by the way they barked that they knew he was there.

No one had ever spent any time in the closet before, but now he was in there so long I grew tired of waiting. I fell into a twitchy, troubled sleep, but woke instantly when I heard the closet door cautiously open. Wayne came to my crate and eased up the catch. "Bella!" he hissed. "Come!"

The other dogs were now in a frenzy, which might have been why Wayne came to my crate and not any of theirs. He put an unfamiliar collar on my neck and snapped a leash into it—a normal leash, not the kind that clamped my mouth shut. "Come on!"

I was led past the other dogs, down the hallway, and out into the yard. I had never been taken for a walk by Wayne this late at night. I squatted quickly, but didn't even have time to finish before the leash tightened. Wayne was running and I had to gallop to keep up. It was not like with Glynnis, who knew there were scents I wanted to investigate and allowed me an opportunity to stop and sniff. He was pulling me too quickly. We ran all the way to the far end of the yard, where it was dark.

"Wayne!" I heard someone whisper. And then I smelled him: Lucas was here!

Wayne and I went right up to the fence. I clawed at it, trying to get at him, trying to lick him. Lucas and Olivia were on the other side and she put out her hand so I could kiss it. "Lift her up!" Lucas said urgently. "We put a blanket over the barbed wire."

Grunting, Wayne lifted me up off the ground. When he raised me over his head, he swayed on wobbly legs. I was intimidated and went limp. "She's really heavy!" he hissed.

"Hold the ladder!" Lucas said to Olivia. My dog blanket was on the fence and Lucas was reaching over it toward me. His hands gripped me and pulled me up and over.

"Steady, Bella. I've got you."

I licked his face as he climbed down some metal stairs, clutching me to him like he did when I was a puppy. Olivia's hands touched me, too. "Good girl, Bella!" she praised quietly.

Finally I was on the ground. I was wagging furiously, unable to keep the whimpers from escaping my throat. I wanted Lucas to lie down so I could climb on top of him. He felt my neck. "This is the wrong collar."

Wayne peered at me. "Oh, yeah. I just grabbed one off the rack."

Olivia pulled gently at my collar. "Does it matter?"

"I guess not," Lucas replied. "It had a tag with her name and my phone number is all."

Olivia stroked my ears. "We'll get you new jewelry, Bella."

I wagged.

"Hey, Lucas? I'm thinking maybe more than a hundred bucks," Wayne whispered. "I had to swipe a pass from an

ACO who is on vacation. The log will show that he's the one who opened all the doors. They're going to figure out something's up."

"You said a hundred. I've got it right here," Lucas said.

"It was a bigger risk than I thought, is what I am saying," Wayne said.

"You erased Bella's arrival from the computer?" Olivia asked.

"Yeah, that was the easy part, I just sat at the reception desk and hit delete. She's still in the system, but not this visit. Bella won't show up on anyone's schedule."

"Thank you, Wayne," Olivia replied.

"I don't have any more money." Lucas went back up the steps and retrieved my blanket. He dropped it to the ground and then landed next to it. "I only brought a hundred. That's what you said."

"I'm just thinking that if I get caught I'm in serious trouble."

"Then don't get caught. Here." Lucas pushed something through the fence and Wayne took it.

"Dude," Wayne said sadly.

"Thank you, Wayne. You saved Bella's life," Olivia said.

"Yeah, well, I don't mind sticking it to the A-hole who picked her up. Everybody hates his guts."

Lucas pulled on my leash. "Come on, Bella!"

• • •

We took a car ride in Olivia's car! I was so happy to be with them. I sat in the back and pressed my head between the seats and both of them stroked my ears.

Lucas, though, seemed sad, even though we were all back together. Whatever it was I had done wrong, I would make sure I never did it, ever. I never wanted to go to the room full of barking dogs again.

"Are you okay, babe?" Olivia asked softly. She touched the back of his neck.

"Yeah," Lucas said hoarsely.

Olivia sighed. "You know I'd take her in a second."

"Of course. But it would still be Denver."

"And you've thought of everybody? There's nobody?"

"Aunt Julie lives in London. Grandma's too frail. Pretty much all my friends live within the Denver city limits. My buddy Chase already has two dogs and his girlfriend says no more."

"I'm so sorry."

Mom was home, and when she knelt I greeted her by putting my paws on her chest and licking her face when she fell on her back. "Bella!" she laughed, but there was something unhappy in her, too.

Another friend of Lucas's was there. She smelled familiar to me but I didn't remember who she was until she reached out and stroked my face. "Hello, Bella," she greeted. The scent of cats mingled with her own fragrance, reminding me of the time when she came crawling into the den to try to catch Mother Cat, the day I met Lucas.

"Some good news. Audrey says the cats are going to be fine," Mom said.

"That's right," Audrey said. "Having one of our board members be a commissioner comes in real handy sometimes. They stalled Gunter's permits until finally he's letting us go in and do a proper job of rounding up the rest of the cats."

"That's great," Lucas replied, "but I don't think it helps with Bella."

"No, not with her in the system."

"Thanks for doing this, Audrey," Olivia said.

"No, of course. Glad to help. It happens all the time. The way the law is written, so many dogs are destroyed who would never hurt anyone. Once Bella's out of Denver, she'll be safe."

"Where are you taking her?" Olivia asked.

"Down to Durango," Audrey replied. "There's a foster family there who takes condemned pits all the time."

"As soon as we find a place outside of city limits, I'll go right down to get her," Lucas said.

"Oh. Um, do you have any idea how long that will be?" Audrey asked.

"It's not going to be quick," Mom answered. "The bureaucratic crap we have to go through is ridiculous. Plus a lot of apartments have a limit on the size of dog, which is obviously an issue here."

"I see."

Mom looked at her. "What is it?"

"Well, I guess I misunderstood your intentions. I thought we were finding a foster family in a safe location where they would take good care of her until a forever family can be found."

"Oh no," Lucas said. "We just need a safe place for her until we can move."

"I can see there's a problem. Why don't you tell us what it is?" Mom asked.

"Well, what you are saying, that's really not what this is for. When Bella moves in with her foster family, she'll be taking up room in a home that could go to another dog. We need to get our dogs adopted as quickly as possible. That's the only way to save them—the system is overwhelmed, with too many animals and too few slots. If weeks or months went by with Bella at a foster home, some other dog might be euthanized because there is no place for her to go.

"Look," Audrey continued, "I know how hard this is for you and yes, of course, if you find a place right away, you can certainly go pick her up. But please consider what is right for everyone, including Bella. From what you've told me, animal control is gunning for your dog and isn't going to give up. They are nearly all decent people who are in that line of work because they want to help animals, but the one you're dealing with has a reputation."

"She was on the final day of her last three-day hold," Lucas said.

"Then I would agree, we can't risk letting her remain another minute inside city limits. I'm surprised they processed her out of there, I've never heard of them doing that before," the woman observed.

Olivia and Lucas exchanged glances. I wished everyone would get out a ball and some treats and we could all delight in being home instead of being so tense and standing around talking.

"How long do I have?" Lucas asked quietly.

"Oh. When you put it like that . . . I'll tell the foster your plan. I'm sure we can wait at least a week. You'll keep me informed of your progress finding a new apartment?"

"I'm on it," Mom replied.

Lucas knelt on the floor and put his arms around me. "I promise you I will do my best to find a new place. I'll work two jobs if I have to. I will come get you as soon as I can, Bella. I am so, so sorry."

He and Mom and Olivia were crying, which was bewildering. I felt the urge to comfort them but did not know how.

"She won't understand. She'll think I'm abandoning her," Lucas said. His voice was anguished.

After a few more moments, Audrey snapped my leash onto my collar, and to my utter astonishment, led me out to a car. Olivia and Mom stood on the porch, hugging each other. "Bye, Bella!" they called.

Lucas put me in a crate inside the woman's car, arranging my dog blanket so that I had something soft to lie on. He leaned in and put his fingers through the grate. We were doing Tiny Piece of Cheese! Not understanding, but so, so grateful to be a good dog, I gently took the treat.

When I finished, he left his fingers there and I licked them, mystified. I could feel his grief. None of this made sense. "This might be good-bye, Bella. If it is, I am so sorry. I want you to know, in my heart, you will always be my dog. I just don't have any other way to protect you."

When he shut the door I could see his face through the glass. It was contorted, his cheeks wet, and I whimpered as the car drove away.

I felt like a bad dog again.

Eleven

Audrey was nice. She spoke to me and said Bella good dog. But she was taking me away from Lucas. I could feel him fading, becoming farther and farther away the longer the vehicle swayed and hummed. His scent was strongly infused into my blanket and I nosed it, breathing deeply, drinking him in. It was my Lucas blanket.

Another smell emerged for me as we traveled. Previously, the bouquet made up of the cars and people and smoke and all the other odors that comingled in the atmosphere near our place never seemed distinct to me, it was just the backdrop for the unique scent of our porch and door and bushes and Mom and Lucas and me. But now, as we drove, these background smells gradually coalesced into a separate, wholly disparate presence on the wind, a powerful collection of perfumes that defined itself for me as home. We passed other, similar clusters of smells, but it was easy to detect the strong palette of fragrances that was where I lived. I could even pick out my bearings when the nice lady let me out of the car so I could do Do Your

Business—that direction, I thought, pointing my nose, in that direction lies home.

That way lies Lucas. But we did not go that way.

Instead, she took me to a house where I stayed for many days with a woman named Loretta and a man named Jose and a big dog and a little white dog and two cats and a bird. The little white dog was named Rascal and he had never been taught No Barks. The big dog was named Grump and he was old and slow and a light brown color. He never barked and was very sleepy all day. Both dogs were smaller than I was. The cats ignored me and the bird stared at me when I sniffed at her cage.

I was too miserable to eat the first day, and also the second. Then I realized Lucas sent me to this place to wait for him, so I began feeding when the other dogs did. What I needed to do was be the best dog I could so Lucas would come get me.

I was given a bed imbedded with the pungent redolence of many other canines and at least one cat. I pulled my Lucas blanket into the bed with me so that I could have his essence with me while I slept.

Jose mostly sat in his big, soft chair. He liked to eat food out of a bowl and would slip me a piece of salty treat when Loretta wasn't nearby. I spent a lot of time doing Sit by Jose's chair. I knew if he gave me treats I was being good, the way I knew I was a good dog when Lucas did Tiny Piece of Cheese.

Loretta was very nice to me and told me I was a good dog. She had a big yard in the back of her house with a fence made of wood. When she let us out in the morning we would do Do Your Business and Rascal would bark at the fence and Grump would lie in the sun. When it rained Grump would barely go out in it before returning to lie on a small rug by the door and Rascal would quickly lift his leg and then stand next to Grump and bark at the door until Loretta opened it.

In the center of the backyard was an area filled with loose wood chips. I liked to do Do Your Business there. There were wooden structures of unknown purpose to me, except one was a swing and I also recognized the ramp with the steps at the high end: it was a slide.

Neither Loretta nor Jose threw the ball up the slide for me to get it as it bounced down the other side, making me miss Lucas all the more. That's what he would want to do when he came to get me. We would play in the backyard and he would toss the ball up the slide and I would catch it. "Good dog, Bella!" he would say. I could picture his smile and his hands on my fur.

For me, trips to the backyard gave me an opportunity to explore with my nose what I had learned as Audrey drove me to be with Loretta and Jose: that there were concentrations of homes and dogs and cars in the air that could easily be separated from each other, and that one of these was very distinctly the smell of home. When Jose took car rides to "town" we drove straight for one of these clusters of aromas, and that's how I came to think of those places: towns. The whole entire land was populated with towns, and one of them was my home, my hometown.

All of these things I experienced knowing that I did not live here with Jose and Loretta. I lived with Lucas and Mom, and my purpose was to do Go to Work and see all the people who loved me and provide comfort to those with pains and fears. Every morning I sniffed the outside air as soon as I was let out, hoping to pick up Lucas coming to fetch me the way he had found me at the building full of crates and barking dogs.

"I thought Bella was just staying with us a few days until her owner came to get her," Jose said one day. I had been asleep, but of course I lifted my head at the sound of my name. I eased to my feet and then did Sit like a good dog who deserved treats. "It's been two weeks."

"I know." Loretta shrugged. "Next weekend they're coming."

"Okay." Jose did not give me any salty treats then, but when Loretta went into the kitchen he snuck me a couple. Jose and I had an understanding. Sometimes, though, Loretta would catch us and say, "Don't do that!" I would slink away, but it seemed most of her unhappiness was directed at Jose. There were times it was better to be a dog.

In the backyard there was a fence and beyond it, trees and grasses. When the wind blew from one direction I smelled people and dogs and food and cars: a town. When the breeze shifted I detected plants and trees and water—like a park, but with a much more expansive breadth. Sometimes Jose and Loretta would take me for short walks on a path behind their fence and there were no other houses, though we often met people and dogs. They called our walks "hiking the trail."

"I love living right up against the state forest. Isn't it fantastic, Bella?" Loretta sometimes asked when we were doing Hike the Trail. I could sense that she was very happy, but she kept me on leash, so whatever was going on it wasn't *that* wonderful.

We only walked on nice days. I remembered being with Lucas on similar days, when flowers released their fragrances and small animals darted into the ground or up trees at my approach. Surely he would come get me now!

"I'm going to put down new wood chips in the play area," Jose told Loretta and me after the walk. "Those are getting rotten. Summer's coming, the grandkids will want to play."

"Good idea. Thank you, Jose."

Loretta left us in the backyard and returned to the house. "Let's freshen this place up, Bella," Jose declared. "Do you know your master is coming to get you tomorrow? I'll miss you, you've been good company."

I yawned, scratching myself behind the ear and contemplating a nap.

Jose pulled something out of the garage that had wheels on it. Grunting a little, he moved the swing and the slide and all of the other structures from atop the wood chips to a spot next to the fence. "Whew! Enough for today," he told me. "Come in, Bella."

I lay on the soft pillow in front of the fireplace and closed my eyes. I thought of Lucas. I thought of Olivia. I thought of Go to Work and Go Home.

Go Home.

I was a good dog, but Lucas had not come to get me. Maybe he wasn't going to come.

Maybe I needed to do Go Home.

* * *

That night Jose let me out in the backyard by myself to do Do Your Business. I could smell so many things, but I could not smell Lucas. But I knew where he was, I could feel him like a pull on the leash. That sense of him was much more faint than when he was coming up the sidewalk at the end of the day, but I knew what direction to go. To Go Home.

I could not climb the fence. It was too high to jump over. But I needed to leave the yard. Jose and Loretta took me for walks, but always on a leash.

If Lucas were there he would throw a ball for me and it would bounce up the slide and I would chase it. The slide was up against the fence. I pictured Lucas throwing the ball and it going up the ramp and over the wooden fence. I would chase it and when I caught it I would be on the other side.

I did not need a ball. I ran across the yard and up the slide and sailed over the top of the fence and landed lightly on some soft dirt.

I would now do Go Home to Lucas.

I left the houses and the dogs behind me and went toward the trees and the smell of rocks and dirt and water. I felt strong and good and alive with a purpose.

I did not sleep that night, nor in the day, either. I found a trail that smelled of many people, but when I heard anyone approaching me I turned away and trotted a good distance from the path until they had passed. There was a stream nearby that I drank from several times.

I began to feel hungry, hungry in a way that was not familiar to me. My stomach was empty and ached a little. I remembered Lucas feeding me Tiny Piece of Cheese, and my mouth became wet. I licked my lips, thinking about it.

When the day began cooling and turning dark, I was exhausted and knew I needed to sleep. I dug a hollow by a rock, thinking as I did so of Mother Cat's other den, the one under the deck.

It was then I realized I had left behind something very important, very dear: my Lucas blanket.

I curled up cold and sad and alone.

*   *   *

A shocking scream jolted me awake not long after I had closed my eyes. I jumped to my feet. Whatever had made the noise was close by.

I froze when the noise fractured the silence again. What had seemed a human voice the first time was too raw and feral, but what kind of animal would make that sort of call? When it split the air yet again, I could hear no pain, no fear, but nonetheless it frightened me. I hesitated, wondering what to do. Run? Investigate?

The next time I heard it it was harsh and loud, like a dog issuing a single bark, pausing, then barking again— though this was no dog. I wanted to find out what was doing this, shattering the gloom with the piercing sound, so I padded off to find out.

I slowed as my ears told me I was close, though the breeze was flowing away from me and I couldn't smell what I was approaching.

Then I saw it: a large fox, sitting on a boulder. Its mouth yawned open, its chest contracted, and a shrieking call filled the night. Moments later, it did it again. Then the fox whirled and stared at me.

I felt the fur rise on the back of my neck. I knew what a fox was from doing Go for a Hike with Lucas and Olivia. They were a little like squirrels—animals that ran low to the ground. Something about it, though, made me not want to chase it. We regarded each other, dog and feral animal, and I inhaled its wildness. What did it think of me, larger, a good dog with a collar who lived with people?

It leaped silently to the ground and dashed off into the trees. Watching it go, I thought about the first time I saw a fox, how confident I had been, ready to chase it if Lucas wanted. But today everything was different. Without people with me, I was in the fox's world now, not the other way around. I suddenly felt very vulnerable.

What other creatures were waiting out there in the darkening forest?

The next morning I was anxious, hungry, and a little afraid. I knew I was being a good dog to do Go Home but the path I was taking did not go directly toward where I sensed Lucas would be. If I went off the path, sometimes the footing was rocky, and sometimes it was covered with plants, making for difficult travel. It just seemed easier to stay on the trail.

After a time, the trail descended, and the people smell became stronger. I knew I should run away, but I was drawn forward by the feeling that I would soon be with humans. I remembered a similar sensation when the cats were scared and there were men and women in the den, this desire to go to them and be with them. Maybe the people would recognize me the way Ty and others always did, and they would take me to Lucas.

I heard the voices of two boys. I hesitated only a moment before I went in that direction.

* * *

I smelled the boys, the wind in my face, long before I saw them. As I trotted toward them, I heard a sudden, loud cracking bang. It sounded a little like a door slamming— but in most ways it was a noise I had never heard before. A whiff of caustic smoke reached my nose.

"Nice shot!" I heard one of the boys call.

The noise frightened me, but the pull of seeing humans was just too much to keep me away. I came over the top of a small rise and saw them standing side by side, not looking in my direction. One of them held something long, a pipe of some kind, and it was from this that the acrid odors rose. The other boy wore a sack on his back similar to the one Lucas took when we went to do Go for a Hike. They were facing some bottles on a fallen tree, and from these I could smell the faint remnants of what Jose liked to drink while he slipped me treats. My mouth watered at the thought.

With a small cloud of harsh smoke and a repeat of the loud noise, one of the bottles shattered.

"Dude!" cheered the sack-wearing boy, the one not holding the pipe. Then he glanced up and saw me. I wagged my tail. "Hey! A dog!"

The other boy turned to look. "Whoa," he said. He raised the pipe to his shoulder, and pointed it at me.

Twelve

The sack-wearing boy pushed on the pipe, forcing it up and away. "Hey! What are you doing?" he asked sharply.

The boy with the pipe pointed it at the sky. "It's a stray."

"We're not going to *shoot* it. That's illegal."

"Dude, what we're doing is *already* illegal."

"You don't shoot somebody's dog just because it's lost. You wouldn't really do that, would you?"

Something about this situation made me hesitate to approach any closer. The boys didn't sound angry but they did seem tense with each other. The pipe drooped. "What the hell, Warren. I don't know. Probably not," he mumbled.

"I mean, Jesus. We came out here to shoot bottles."

"You shot at that crow," the boy with the pipe said.

"Yeah, a crow, not a dog. And I missed."

"How do you know I wouldn't miss the dog?"

"Here, boy! Here!" The sack-boy slapped his legs.

"It's female," said the other boy. The acrid tang from his pipe was on his hands and clothing.

"Okay, I see that now, dude," Sack-boy said. "How are you, girl, huh? What are you doing way out here, are you lost?" I sniffed his hands carefully. He did not have food in his pockets, but his fingers smelled as if they had been holding pungent meat recently. I licked them for confirmation. Yes! This boy had access to good dog treats!

"So now what?" asked the boy with the pipe.

"I've got some beef jerky back at the car."

"Hang on." The boy with the pipe raised it to his shoulder and lay his head on it. I watched curiously, then jumped when a roar burst from the pipe's end, filling the air with the same caustic stench.

"It's okay, girl," Sack-boy said to me. "Hey, nice shot."

We went for a walk then, but I was off leash and ran ahead, nose to the ground as I picked up the trail of some small rodent. I heard the boys talking and treading steadily behind me on the trail. I understood that for the moment I was with them, just as I had temporarily been with Jose and Loretta. Perhaps, until I was back with Lucas, I would be with other people on a short-term basis.

The sack-boy was Warren, and the other was named Dude. Sometimes, though, Dude called Warren "Dude," which was confusing to me. We strolled through warm green grasses to a car and when Warren opened it a delicious odor floated out. We'd found the dog treats, they were in the car! "Want some beef jerky, girl?"

I was so excited I was spinning in circles, but then I sat down to show I could be a good dog. Warren handed me a chewy, smoky piece of meat that I quickly swallowed.

"She's really hungry," Dude observed. "Has to be, to eat that crap."

"I've seen you eat it," Warren said.

"I didn't eat it because it was *good,* I ate it because it was available."

"You want some now?"

"Yeah."

Both boys ate some of the dog snacks, which I found both odd and disturbing. With all the wonderful foods people can pick from, why would they take away the treats from a deserving good dog?

"What kind of dog is it, you think?" Warren asked.

"Dude, no idea," Dude replied. "So what, you have a dog now?"

"No, 'course not," Warren answered. "My mom wouldn't let me have a dog."

I glanced at Warren. Mom? Did he know Mom?

"What do we do, then?" Dude wanted to know. He squinted up at the sun.

"Well, we can't just leave her out here," Warren said. "She probably belongs to somebody. I mean, she's got a collar. She maybe got separated from her owners."

"So like what?" Dude asked. "We take her with us?"

"Maybe call somebody?"

"So you're like, 'We were on the Colorado Trail shooting at beer bottles and we found this giant dog, can you come pick her up?'"

"Okay. No."

"No which part?"

Warren grinned. "We leave out the target practice. Look, maybe there's even a reward or something. We should call it in."

"Except how long is that going to take?"

"I don't know, dude, I'm just figuring it out, here."

"Because I got to be at work at four thirty."

"I don't even know if they would send somebody out here anyway. How 'bout this? Let's just load her into the backseat and take her to the Silverton sheriff's station. They'll know what to do."

"You want *me* to voluntarily go to the sheriff's," Dude observed dryly.

Both boys laughed. My attention had become focused on the crinkly package in Warren's hand. There was still a little piece of dog snack in there. I wondered if he knew it. I was doing Sit, and now I shuffled my weight from one front paw and back to signal that such excellent behavior deserved that last fragment of meat.

"Come on, girl!" Warren called to me. He held the back door of his car open. I hesitated—I loved car rides, but this felt strange. Where was he taking me? But then Warren rustled the bag and tossed the last morsel into his car and I knew what would be the correct decision. I bounded onto the backseat and the boys climbed in the front and that was it: we were off on a car ride.

We were a long distance from Lucas. I could smell home, and it was far, far away. But maybe that was where the boys were taking me.

• • •

I lifted my nose up to the crack in the window, pulling in the clear, clean fragrances from outside. I could tell we were heading toward a town because the combination of aromas grew stronger and stronger, but I also smelled many animals, most completely foreign to me.

I was not enjoying this car ride as much as when Olivia drove. Neither of the boys had repeated Mom's name, nor had they mentioned anyone else I recognized. This was what some people did—they took dogs for car rides, because having a dog along made things more fun. But I had been driven places before, which, upon arrival, were new and not home.

"So you do know I don't have exactly the best relationship with the San Juan Sheriff's Department," Dude told Warren.

"It's not like they're going to take our fingerprints. We're just dropping off a dog."

"What if they find the rifle in the trunk?"

"Dude, why would they look in the trunk? Quit being

so paranoid. And anyway, there's no law against having a gun, it's our constitutional amendment."

"We weren't supposed to be shooting in the national forest, though," Dude said worriedly. I picked up the anxiety in his voice and glanced at him curiously.

"How would they even know about that? Gimme a break. God." Warren snorted derisively. "You think they're going to find the bottles and do forensics or something?"

"It's just we had one thing going and now we're driving to see the cops."

"You want, you can wait in the car with the dog."

We rode for a time in silence. There was a stale smell of ashes in the automobile's interior, so I kept my nose at the window. Eventually we slowed, making a few turns, and then stopped. The motor stopped running, all vibrations and noises ceasing. I went from one window to the other in the backseat, but could not see any reason for us to be parked here with a few other cars and no other dogs.

"So do we just go in with her?" Dude asked.

"I dunno. No, let's go in and tell them, see what they say. Maybe there's a reward's been posted," Warren said.

"Right. You said that."

"Stranger things have happened."

The window suddenly slid down, so that I could stick my entire head out!

"Why did you do that?" Dude demanded.

"Because it's sunny. Obviously we're not going to bring a deputy out here and the dog is all closed up in a car," Warren said patiently. "That's like known animal abuse. Even on a cool day like this, they can overheat." Warren reached over and rubbed my head and I licked the meaty taste off his palm. "Okay, girl. You stay here, okay? You'll be okay. We're going to come right back. We'll help you find your home, okay? Everything is going to be fine."

I did not understand the words but the tone was familiar.

When people left their dogs, their voices often carried the same inflection. When Lucas did Go to Work, he sounded like this. I felt a sharp pain, remembering.

"What if nobody comes to claim her?" Dude wanted to know.

"I'm sure somebody will. She's a beautiful dog."

"Still. What then?"

"I guess . . . I don't know. Maybe she'll get adopted?" Warren said hopefully.

"Or put down. Like, we're taking her to the gas chamber."

"Well, you got any better ideas? You were going to *shoot* her."

"I never would really have done that."

The boys got out of the car. "We'll be back, I promise," Warren told me.

I watched through the front window as the boys approached a big building, opened a door, and went inside. I remembered the glass doors of the place with the crates of barking dogs; these were similar.

I now understood something. Many people were very nice, but that didn't mean they would take me to Lucas. In fact, some of them might take me *away* from Lucas. They might feed me and go for a car ride, but I needed to Go Home.

I stuck my head out the window, and then my front paws, dangling them toward the ground. I wriggled my rear end, pushing forward, until my back paws were scrabbling in the air and I was falling nose-first toward the pavement. I was out of the car and off leash. I shook myself off, lifted my nose, and trotted away toward the smell of food.

• • •

There were automobiles and people and buildings, so I knew I was in a town, but it was a different one from where

Jose and Loretta took me. As I followed my nose some people shouted to me from car windows and open doorways—they seemed friendly, but I did not believe they would take me to Lucas so I did not approach them. I did, however, smell something sweet and sticky on the sidewalk and I ate it quickly, crunching on some dry bread lying next to it. What a nice place, to leave such treats out for a deserving dog.

My empty stomach kept me focused on finding a meal despite my need to Go Home. I tracked aromas, hoping I would stumble upon more sidewalk treats.

I caught whiffs of many dogs, usually separated from one another, and I heard barking and saw a dog on a chain, but then I changed course because I sensed several canines moving together. I made my way toward them, and when I rounded a corner, I came upon a pack.

There were two males, both very dark in color, one large and one small, plus a short female with long fur. They were sitting behind a store from which poured a delicious bouquet, staring at it intently, but when they felt my approach they whipped their heads around.

Small Male ran straight at me, then pulled up, raising his snout as he stopped. I turned and we sniffed each other. Big Male also examined behind my tail. I moved rigidly, not prepared to play bow with two males on either side of me, but wagging a friendly greeting. Big Male lifted his leg on a post and Small Male followed suit and I politely appraised their marks, noticing that the female had not moved from the back door of that store.

Small Male play bowed and we wrestled for a moment while Big Male continued to mark, and then Big Male trotted over to us and we stopped playing because his presence changed the situation.

When the back door opened, a cloud of cooking meat poured out and I saw a woman standing on the threshold. "Hello, pretty dogs!" she sang.

The males ran over to the woman's feet to sit, so I followed suit, though I held back a little, careful not to crowd the other dogs. I was unsure what was about to happen. I could sense the female canine tensing at my presence but her eyes were focused on the woman, who had a wonderfully greasy paper in her hands. The paper rustled and gave off succulent aromas as she reached in with her fingers and plucked out fatty pieces of cooked beef. Starting with the female, she went down the row of dogs, handing each of us a large chunk. All of us were licking our lips in anticipation, scarcely able to contain our excitement. "Are you a new friend? What's your name?" she asked as she extended me a delectable slice. I daintily lifted the treat from her fingers, chewing quickly so none of the other dogs would try to take it away from me.

"That's all I have tonight, lovies. Be good dogs!"

The woman shut the door. We all sniffed the ground to see if any of us had dribbled any morsels. Female came up and investigated me suspiciously, and Small Male bowed, wagging. We milled around for a moment, appreciating the meat scents on each other's lips, and then the pack moved on. I was part of it, so I followed. It was good to be with other dogs.

We were walking down a narrow street behind the buildings. There were no cars, though there were several large metal containers that clearly contained scraps of edible things I would have liked to explore, but the pack didn't pause other than when the males lifted their legs to mark.

We eventually stopped at a square plastic bin from which rose a riot of enticing odors. Big Male was able to knock the lid off of it, and I inhaled deeply, hungrily aware of cheese and grease and sweets.

Female then astounded me by leaping nimbly off the ground, her rear paws scrabbling on the sides of the barrel while her snout dug inside. She fell back, pulling a box with her from which spilled meats wrapped in bread. Each dog pulled out a meal, darting away from the pack to quickly finish it off. Mine was wrapped in plastic but when I tore into it there was food coated with a tangy, bitter sauce that made me sneeze.

Several times Female dove for more paper. Sometimes what she dragged out had no value—little pieces of vegetables, or more of the tangy sauce—but a few times there was more to eat. I was the youngest so I shied back, not thrusting my head forward when the two males dove on what Female had extracted, but waiting until she had dropped down and taken her share as well. That was the rule of this pack.

And then on some unknown signal, the two males trotted away. Female was licking some paper and the way she eyed me let me know that if I approached she would snap at me, so I gave her plenty of room as I followed her companions.

We made our way to another door with fantastic fragrances. Though it was shut, it was made of a metal substance through which I could see people moving around inside the building. In a way, it reminded me of the thin blankets Lucas utilized to catch the cats in the den—the material shrouded but did not block the light from inside.

I kept my distance from Female. Small Male and I wrestled while Big Male marked and then there was a noise from within the building and all of us ran expectantly to the door and sat. I was next to Big Male, and he licked his lips, so I did, too.

The door opened. "Well, hello there, are you here for a handout?" a man called. Unlike the woman, he did not hand us treats, but tossed things at us, one canine at a time. The piece of wonderful, salty meat that he pitched at me bounced off my nose, but I jumped on it and gobbled it before any of the other dogs could react. Bacon! We each had our chance at several more treats, and though I tried to snatch them out of the air like my companions, I dropped every one.

The man shut the door, though we could still hear and see him through it. "That's all I have for tonight. Go on home, now. Go Home."

I stared in amazement. How did he know about Go Home?

The pack trotted away and I followed, though I still carried the man's voice in my head. I was very far from Lucas, but I had just been commanded Go Home.

We went up a street with houses. Lights beamed through the windows, and I smelled food and people and some dogs and some cats.

Female left us. One moment she was with the pack, and the next she simply turned away and trotted up a walkway toward a front porch. I stopped and watched her, but when the males didn't wait, I hurried to catch up.

And then Big Male separated from us. Small Male marked a tree while Big Male went directly to a metal door. I heard a loud rasp as he dragged his nails across the door's surface. After a moment, a small boy opened it, allowing a brief flash of light out into the street before Big Male went inside and the door was shut.

Small Male sniffed me, and when he turned toward a house, looking back and wagging, I knew he wanted me to follow.

But I understood something now. The pack was doing what the man said, they were doing Go Home. They each had a house to go to, with people inside who would love them. They were a temporary pack, the way such groups sometimes formed among the canines at the dog park. When each human called out a name, a dog left the park, and if Lucas and I stayed there long enough the pack would dwindle until it was just me. One dog does not make a pack.

Small Male wanted to keep me in his family, but I could not go with Small Male because my person was not here. My person was Lucas.

I had learned some things I had not known. Where there were buildings there were nice people who handed out treats and there were barrels and bins full of food that was easily hunted. A town had food.

But I could not do Go Home and stay in this town.

I turned my nose toward the direction I knew would lead me to Lucas. That way there was no town, there were no buildings. There were hills and streams and trees, and I could smell the sharp tang of snow up there as well. If I wanted to do Go Home, I would have to be without a pack, in high hills where there were no people.

Small Male was halfway up the yard to a house, watching. Part of me yearned to join him—he had the smell of more than one human hand on his fur, and it would be so nice to sleep on a soft bed and be fed and petted by Small Male's people.

I felt safe here, in this place with cars and humans who hand-fed good dogs. My few days on the trail led me to believe there were perils up there I did not know, animals I had never seen, and areas where I might not find food. Here, with Small Male, I would be taken care of. There, on my own, I would face danger.

I could not be with my person and also Small Male. I turned away from him, took a deep whiff of the night air, and went to find my Lucas.

Thirteen

I felt uneasy as the lights and smells of the town faded behind me. The moon lit the way, but I felt vulnerable on my own, as if having been in a pack reminded me how much safer a dog is traveling in the company of others. I also now understood I was on a journey of many days—when I used the slide to jump over the fence, I was propelled by a belief that I would very soon be home. Now, though, I knew that I might walk and walk and the scent of my hometown would still be far away.

I spent the night by the river, in a place where a scooped-out area in the ground was shaped like a dog bed. Several times I awoke at the sound or smell of small animals, but they did not approach me and none of them were familiar to my nose.

The path I was on did not always take me in the direction I needed to go, but often it would eventually twist back, and if I stayed with it I would make progress toward my goal. The surer footing made for much swifter passage than when I took a more direct course and attempted to climb over the rocks and the other obstacles that blocked my way. The scent of people and animals was painted into the path, so I could easily find it.

People on the path announced their approach with their talking and loud footfalls, so I always knew when to veer away and let them pass. I did not want to take another car ride.

As darkness closed in I found a flat area heavily imbued with human scents. A few wooden tables were scattered about, and near a few of them were metal poles atop which were buckets of ash and the tantalizing promise of burned meat, though when I stood on my back legs to investigate I was only able to lick a trace of food from the bars atop the ashes.

Much more promising was a round barrel similar to the one Female had climbed into, though this one was metal. I attempted to duplicate her feat, but where she was able to climb in by leaping up, hooking her front paws on the lip, and then scrabbling with her rear legs, my own leap and grab only succeeded in pulling the entire thing over. Guiltily, I remembered Lucas telling me bad dog when I did something similar at home in the kitchen, but that did not stop me from locating chicken pieces and a thick piece of sugary treat and some dry biscuits that were not very good. The chicken crunched as I chewed through the bones and I licked delicious juices from the plastic container I pulled from the barrel. I was as full as I had been in several days, and contentedly curled up under the table for the night. Having a satisfied tummy made me feel safe.

The next day the trail took me steeply uphill, and I was tired. Before long I realized I was already hungry again. I regretted ever disliking Good Exercise, the game where Mom or Lucas would toss dog snacks down the stairs for me to run after them, gobble them up, and then climb back to the kitchen. Now I would happily play that game all day, if they wanted.

When I heard a flat, loud noise I instantly turned in the direction from which it came and ran toward it. I knew what that boom meant—Dude and Warren were using their pipe. Though I would not get in their car, I would gladly accept more meaty morsels.

Soon I heard voices. They were men and they sounded excited. "She's got to weigh a hundred fifty pounds!" someone shouted.

I emerged cautiously from the trees. Up ahead there was a ridge. I now could smell the humans and they were not Dude and Warren. I padded up to the ridge and looked down.

I was on a small hill, and down the slope below me a stream trickled through the rocks. Across a narrow canyon was a far taller hill, sparsely covered with thin plants. I glanced up and saw two men stumbling and running down the higher hill. They were on steep terrain and did not look over, or they would easily see me. Both of them carried pipes, and the air was filled with the stink I associated with the loud bang these pipes could make.

"Told you we'd get something today!" one of them gasped at the other.

Panting and tripping, the men were hurrying down toward the small stream. I crept along the ridge, curious, watching the men's progress, and that's when a delicate shift in the wind brought me the strong smell of an animal and something else.

Blood.

I turned toward the blood scent, the men forgotten. "At least five hundred dollars!" one of them said, but I was tracking with my nose. I did not have far to go—just a few steps and I saw a creature lying motionless in the rocks. I cautiously approached, though the stillness in its body told me it was not living. It was like the squirrel Lucas showed me by the side of the road on one of our walks—warm and limp and dead.

I sniffed at the blood on its chest. This animal smelled similar to a cat, though it wasn't like any cat I had ever seen—it was enormous, larger than I was. It was a female, and a milky odor from her teats reminded me of Mother Cat. Infused into her blood was a stark, smoky stench, the kind that came from the pipes that men like Dude and the two on the hill carried.

I did not understand what I was seeing.

Behind me, I could hear the men breathing loudly. The change in sound told me they had reached the bottom of the canyon and were now coming up the near side.

"I need a break!" one of them panted to the other.

"We got to grab it and get the hell out of here," the other said tensely, but I could hear that they had stopped climbing.

"No one around. We're fine."

"Dammit, we're not fine. You know what happens we get caught poaching a cougar?"

"I know we might get as much as a grand for her, that's what I know."

I decided I did not want to meet the men and felt sure they would not give me any treats if I did.

Then a movement from the bushes caught my eye and I turned my head. There was something there, an animal, but the wind was blowing the wrong way for me to smell it. I stared, seeing eyes, pointed ears. Then, though it was nearly hidden, I recognized what I was looking at: an immense cat, bigger than many dogs, the largest I had ever seen. It eyes were locked on mine, and when it realized I saw it, it ducked its head a little, as if to hide. But now that I knew it was there, I could separate its smell from the huge animal lying motionless in the rocks. A female.

The way she held herself reminded me of the cats in the den when there were humans coming in through the hole: the same rigid body, the same wide-eyed stare, lips drawn back slightly. She was terrified.

There was a loud shout from one of the men: "Dammit!"

and she cringed and backed into the bushes and darted away. I recognized the motion, the skittering way she ran, and realized that despite her size she wasn't a cat, she was a *kitten,* a kitten as big as a medium-sized dog.

She only retreated a little way before halting. I did not know what had happened, but I could tell by her tense movements that she wanted to flee. Yet she didn't—was it because of the dead feline at my feet? Was that her mother?

The sounds and smells told me that the men with pipes were nearly at the top of the ridge, so I, too, needed to go. I turned away and padded stealthily into the brush.

The big kitten followed.

• • •

The route I took roughly tracked the comingled scents of Big Kitten and the huge dead mother cat, retracing their steps. The going was not easy, but the trail went in a fairly straight line away from the angry men. I could smell them and the blood now, the breeze cooler under my tail than on my nose.

I was disturbed by what I had just witnessed. I did not understand the connection between the death of Big Kitten's mother and the humans with the stinking pipes, but I did believe there was one. I was reminded of the time Mom invited a friend inside the house and then he became furious and she hit him and he fell down. The scary conclusion was that there were bad people in the world. I knew there were those who would prevent me from being with Lucas, but this was something else entirely.

If a dog couldn't trust humans, how was life even possible?

Big Kitten was silent behind me; I could smell her, smell the terror and the anxious despair. When I stopped to look at her, she moved swiftly to hide, her bouncy gait exactly like any normal-sized kitten.

After some time, I felt Big Kitten halt. I turned and

looked at her. She was sitting down, regarding me with light-colored eyes. Though we were now far away from the angry men, I wanted to keep going, keep making progress toward Lucas. When I took a few steps and looked over my shoulder, she trotted a little bit in a slightly different direction, then stopped. She looked toward where she seemed to want to go, then turned to me with what felt like expectation.

Big Kitten was an afraid kitty. She needed my help. When I was in danger, Mother Cat protected me, and now I felt a powerful pull to protect this kitten.

She seemed to sense that I would follow her, so she moved off. I went after her, startled by how nimbly she could pick her way through rocks and other barriers.

Before long we came to a place under some trees that was heavily redolent with the scent of the large mother cat. And there was something else rising to my nose: blood and meat. Buried in the grass and dirt was the nearly intact remains of a deer, a deer with odors of the Big Kitten and the dead mother cat on it.

I did not understand any of this, but I knew I was hungry, and I greedily bit into the kill. After a time, making no noise at all, Big Kitten also began to feed.

. . .

That night, when I lay down on some grasses, Big Kitten came right up to me and sniffed my face. I licked her, which made her tense, but when I set my head down on the ground she relaxed very cautiously, still sniffing, exploring me up and down my length. I held myself motionless, allowing the examination. She began to purr, and I knew what she was going to do before she did it: rub the top of her head against me, just as my kitty siblings had done. Eventually she curled up against my side, and I felt the fear leave her body.

This was similar to sleeping with my head on Mack's

chest when we did Go to Work. I was providing comfort, not to a person, but to a baby kitten with a dead mother.

Lucas took care of cats. He fed them. I would look after this kitten.

I believed that this was something Lucas would want me to do.

• • •

Big Kitten and I spent several days with the kill, eating as much of it as we could. When we weren't eating, we were playing. Big Kitten like to pounce on me and I liked to knock her on her back and mouth her head until she would twist and dash away. She also slept much of the day but was oddly alert and awake as the sun was going down and I was looking to curl up for the night. She would pad silently off into the trees and one time astonished me by returning with a small rodent that we shared.

When a restless urge to get moving overtook me, Big Kitten followed. She did not seem to like the human smells on the trail and preferred to slink along in what cover she could find, disappearing from view for large amounts of the day. I could smell her, though, and knew she was never too far away. When I could no longer precisely detect where she was, I would wait for her and eventually she would catch up.

I knew I would be able to cover more ground if I were not so concerned about Big Kitten's welfare, but I felt compelled to make sure she was safe.

When we were just two days away from the kill site, I felt the hunger gnawing at my insides. I was concerned for Big Kitten—how would I feed her?

Late on the third day, I had stopped for water and decided to lie down and wait for Big Kitten to join me. She eventually emerged from behind some rocks a few moments after I smelled her hiding there. She lowered her head to the small pool, lapping silently. Cats apparently don't enjoy drinking very much. A dog goes after water with elation, making lots of noise.

The scent of blood touched my nose and I lifted my head, startled. I began drooling and moved without hesitation toward the delicious fragrance. Big Kitten followed me but did not seem to smell what I smelled.

And then I saw a fox. It moved quietly but in its jaws carried a limp rabbit—the source of the blood. The fox seemed unaware I was behind it. It was running, but the weight of its kill slowed it down.

The fox saw me at the same time Big Kitten was alerted to its presence. For a moment all three of us were frozen. Then, with a surge of speed that surprised me, Big Kitten dashed forward. We both gave chase to the fox, but she swiftly pulled away from me. The fox leaped nimbly over fallen trees and abruptly changed direction, trying to get away. But Big Kitten was soon right on top of the fox, who dropped the rabbit and fled.

Big Kitten stopped her pursuit to sniff at the abandoned prey, and I joined her. We fed on the fox's kill together, as if we were a pack, Big Kitten and I.

* * *

Hunger was with us constantly as we made our way toward Lucas. I knew this meant I needed humans, who had all the good food. Fortunately the summer seemed to be drawing people up into the mountains, and where they stopped, they would eat. I could easily follow my nose to these campsites, though Big Kitten shied away the moment she smelled people.

One day a family was sitting at a wooden table while a fire burned in a metal kettle held off the ground by thin legs. A man set a large piece of meat into this kettle, and the immediate explosion of cooking aroma nearly sent me into a swoon. The man turned toward the people at the table, not paying attention, and I bolted out of the woods, carefully snatched the meat without burning myself, and ran back. The only person to see me was a little baby in a plastic chair who kicked his legs but didn't say anything.

I expected to feel like a bad dog, but I did not. I was hunting. I shared the meal with my kitten companion.

Another day a man was standing in a stream and on the shore was a sack full of wet fish. I picked up the whole bag. He did yell at me, not saying bad dog, but using words I did not understand yet nonetheless communicated a lot of anger. He also pursued me, his boots crunching the dirt and rocks. I could barely lift the satchel full of fish but I kept going, and eventually the man, panting, fell behind and then stopped. He was still yelling.

Big Kitten and I ate all of the fish.

Much of the time when my nose led me to people, they had departed from the area. I learned that the closer a picnic table was to a road, the more likely I would find a metal bin with food remains. I became very proficient at climbing in the barrel or knocking it over, picking through paper and plastic to retrieve the morsels people had left there. Often this meant leaving the trail far behind, hiding from cars until I came across someplace I could successfully scavenge. Big Kitten never accompanied me, but would be waiting when I returned.

The first time I was able to locate sandwich pieces in a bin, I gobbled them down, my starving belly making my decisions for me. I gorged on other foods, too, but did not locate anything to take back to Big Kitten.

When I approached her, feeling guilty, she came over and sniffed my mouth. Then she did something unexpected: she licked my lips, and after a moment I brought up a portion of what I had wolfed down.

This set the pattern for how we shared the meals people put out for me in the bins. Only rarely did I find something large enough to bring back intact, such as the time when I found a dead fawn by the side of the road, its body limp and still warm. Big Kitten somehow sensed my struggle to drag it back and joined me, surprising me by lifting the kill nearly off the ground with her jaws.

We were making progress toward Lucas, but slowly. The trails were frustratingly crooked and twisty, and often during the day I would hear humans and then the two of us would hide. Big Kitten would not want to go for a car ride any more than I.

I often smelled dogs, and didn't think Big Kitten would want to meet them, either. I longed to greet them, but they were always with their people, just as I would someday be with Lucas.

When I sensed dogs and no humans, though, the fur on my neck rose. There was something wrong with their scent, some underlying, feral component on the air, alarming me. I could smell that they had never had a bath and had not eaten any dog food recently. I could also tell they were tracking us, and they were getting closer. Big Kitten did not seem aware—she wanted to sleep, as usual, but followed me because we were a pack.

We were in a flat area with rocks and a few small trees when I realized what was following us. I had encountered this type of creature before: they were coyotes—the small, bad dogs I had seen while hiking with Lucas. There were four of them, a female and three young males, and they weren't pursuing us out of curiosity—they were hunting us.

I stopped and Big Kitten became aware of them as they slinked across the open ground. Her eyes turned dark, and her lips parted, revealing her teeth. She was now nearly as large as I was, but I knew instinctively that a pack of four was more powerful than two larger creatures.

We needed to run, but we couldn't. Behind us a steep wall of rock jutted out of the earth's surface, a wall we could not possibly climb. The few trees in front of the ridge were not wide enough to hide behind.

I let out a low growl. This would be a fight.

The coyotes spread out, coming forward slowly, looking sly and cautious. There was no mistaking their intentions— they were going to kill us and eat us. I growled again, facing the danger.

Fourteen

I was seized by a fury I did not understand, an instinctive rage coming from deep inside. My mind filled with what seemed like memories of things that had never happened, of vicious battles with these creatures. They were my enemy and I was driven to kill them, to tear into them with my teeth and close my jaws on their necks.

Yet even as this searing hatred rampaged through me, I could sense Big Kitten's terror, radiating from her skin and her breath, her tense muscles, her taut face. She was going to run—it was evident in her bunched leg muscles.

But running would not work. This was a pack, and a pack would pursue. The ridge behind us was unclimbable, so her dash would take her along the rock wall in one direction or the other and the coyotes would cut her off.

Yet she did run, darting along the base of the ridge. The four predators reacted by turning as one to give chase. The coyotes were still some distance away but moving swiftly, on course to intersect.

Feeling helpless, I dashed after my fleeing companion. When they caught her, she would not long be alone.

But they were rapidly closing in, and then they were *there,* almost right on top of her. Big Kitten bounded out from underneath them, off the ground to a tree in a soaring, astonishing leap, nimbly snagged it and scrabbled up its trunk, her claws making an audible scraping sound as they bit into the wood.

The coyotes chaotically halted, looking wary and perplexed. I took advantage of their confusion to advance closer to Big Kitten's tree, thinking to make a stand there, to protect her. Their tongues lolled as they stared up into the branches. They hung well back of the base as if worried my companion might leap on them from above. They had thick tails and pointed ears and cold, ugly faces. They registered my movements and turned to stare at me in a single, coordinated swivel of their heads, their eyes sly as they assessed me. I was a lone dog, and they were a pack.

I neared the tree trunk and could smell Big Kitten above me. I knew she was afraid but I was not. I wanted this fight.

The three males slunk toward me, cutting off my path to the tree, until they were close enough that I could reach them in just a few leaps, but then they danced back. The female remained at the tree, gazing craftily at Big Kitten.

The males seemed intimidated, yet they were hunting me, and I knew their feigned cowardice was designed to lure me to them so they could set on me from all sides.

I was backed up against the rocks. My growling turned to barking, my rage forcing itself into my voice. When I lunged they all fell away, but one darted sideways. I turned to face this threat and another came from the other side while the one in front darted tantalizingly close to my jaws before backpedaling.

I did not know what they were doing, why they were coming around from either side instead of attacking head-on, but I ached to give pursuit to the one who was so near. Yet I felt protective of Big Kitten. I did not want to leave her cowering up in the tree, from which she would eventually have to descend. Lucas would want me to save her.

I would have to take on the males first, then the stalking female.

The coyotes were silent but I was barking fiercely, my lips drawn back and my teeth clicking at the slightest motion in my direction. They seemed stymied by the rock wall to my rear.

One darted in from one side and I turned and slashed at it with my fangs, catching only air, and then I spun and went right at the small male who had instantly come from the other side and nipped at my tail. This time I drew blood with my front teeth and the predator screamed, falling away.

I stood defiant, still barking my fury, while the three coyotes paced in front of me.

Then I smelled something that could change the equation: people. The coyotes seemed unaware, but I could smell people coming.

I saw that the coyote I had bitten now hung well back, sunk low to the ground, tail and ears down, but the other two were still in the hunt. They charged at me and when I snapped at the closest one I nipped off a bit of his fur, and as he jumped back the other one leapt forward, fangs clicking by my ear.

Suddenly all four coyotes froze, twisting their heads around. They obviously could smell the humans now, and hear their voices. "Hey!" a man yelled.

When several men broke from the trees, sprinting toward

us across the flat ground, the coyotes wheeled and ran away, their bloodlust forgotten. The female was the last to leave and I bounded after her, giving chase for only a few steps: I still felt I could not abandon Big Kitten. I returned to her tree.

The men were breathing hard and were slowing down as they approached. They had big sacks on their backs like Lucas wore when we did Go for a Hike. "Is she hurt?" I heard one of them pant. As he said this, he slowed his pace. He had on a brightly colored shirt that he wiped his sweaty face on.

"Hey! Here, dog, here, doggie!" another called. His face was hairy, reminding me of my friend Ty.

There was a slight scraping sound above me and I knew Big Kitten had anxiously tightened her grip on a tree limb.

The men came to a ragged end of their run, walking slowly, two with hands on their hips as they breathed loudly. I regarded their approach warily. I had spent a lot of effort evading contact with humans and now an entire group of them were walking my way. Big Kitten would be afraid of them, even if they had food.

But they were people, and I was involuntarily wagging as I anticipated their hands on my fur.

"Look! Look in the tree, the tree!" the man in the bright shirt shouted excitedly. He raised his hand and stuck a single finger in the air.

"Is it a bobcat?" the man with the hair face asked.

"No, that's a cougar, a young cougar!"

Another man took out his phone and held it in front of his nose. I heard Big Kitten move and looked up into the branches. Her eyes were large and her ears flat as she watched the men.

I knew a scared kitty when I saw one. Some cats are afraid of humans and will try to run when they are close, and these were near enough now that if one of them had a ball he could throw it to me. "Are you getting it?" the man in the bright shirt asked.

"I'm getting it!" replied the man with the phone against his nose. I did not understand what they were doing, but they were still approaching, though much more slowly, all of them watching Big Kitten.

"God, it's beautiful," the man with the hairy face breathed.

"I've never seen one. Have you ever seen one? I've never seen one in the wild."

"It's scared."

Big Kitten's dread was so pronounced it made the very air feel tense. Her muscles knotted beneath her fur, and then suddenly she sprang from the tree and seemed to be flying. She landed almost silently on the top of the rock wall and was instantly gone, darting up the hill and behind boulders.

Big Kitten! I ran to the rocks, but I could not climb the barrier; it was far too steep. I was reminded of Mother Cat streaking away from Lucas, and thought that Big Kitten was probably going someplace to hide.

"Man! That was amazing!" the man in the bright shirt shouted.

"Here, girl, are you hurt? You okay?" asked another man, this one wearing a soft cap on his head. He was closest to me, his hand extended in a friendly fashion.

For a moment I was torn. My life with Big Kitten had introduced a wildness into me, and the lure of her scent almost caused me to break away and try to catch up to her. But I heard the kindness in the cap-man's voice. When his hand was within reach, I licked it, tasting some fish oil and dirt on his palm.

"She's friendly."

The man fed me treats: small pieces of meat from a packet. I did Sit to keep the process going.

"What are you doing way out here, girl?" the man with Ty's hairy face asked as he scratched my ears. I leaned into him, closing my eyes.

"I think someone was hunting cougar, and this is one of the dogs."

"Is that legal?"

"Hell no, it's not *legal*. They're endangered. But some sickos will pay big money for one. They stuff it and put it in their libraries and brag about killing it, or they just want the paws or the teeth or something."

"So the dog treed the cat? One dog?"

"It looked to be a pretty young cougar."

"And then the coyotes showed up."

"Exactly."

"They would have killed this poor dog."

"I know. I'm glad you said we should check out the barking."

"I could just tell from the sound that she was distressed."

"What's your name, girl, huh?"

I wagged as the man with the bright shirt patted my head.

"You want to wait, see if the guy shows up to claim his dog?"

The men looked at each other for a long moment. I could smell treats in their sacks and hoped they were talking about feeding me more.

"I don't know, I can't imagine a poacher being too happy to see us, even if we did save his dog."

"Somebody hunting cougar, they're going to be armed."

"That's not legal, either, is it?"

"I don't think so. Not here."

"Something tells me this guy doesn't really care about that."

"Great. What if some asshole with a gun is pissed off at us for scaring off his trophy?"

I went over and sniffed pointedly at one of the sacks on

the ground, reminding the men that there were snacks inside that could be shared with a good dog. I did Sit again, being good, to help them make their decision.

"So what do we do about the dog? We just let her go?"

"You want to come with us, girl?" The cap-man reached into his pack and dug out another treat.

"Maybe we should call this whole thing off."

"You want to head back to San Luis pass? There was that couple camping there. Safety in numbers."

"Not really."

"Let's just *go*."

"What about the dog?"

"Let's see if she follows us."

"What if she doesn't?"

"Then she'll go find her owner."

"I think we should turn the guy in."

"Okay, sure, we see him, you can make a citizen's arrest."

"She sure looks hungry."

"You want to give her one of those tuna pouches?"

"Yeah, I do."

The man with the bright shirt knelt by his sack and I gave him my full attention. He pulled out a small wrapper that opened with a slight noise and filled the air with a delicious fragrance of oily fish, the same aroma I'd smelled on Cap-man's fingers. He placed chunks of fish on a rock for me and I gobbled them up quickly, licking the oil from my lips when I was finished.

"How far to highway one forty-nine, you think?" the man with the hairy face asked.

"Maybe ten miles yet."

"We better get humping, then."

The men picked up their sacks and put them on their backs, which suggested to me there would be no more fish. Humans are wonderful and can always find food, but sometimes they discontinue dinner before a good dog is ready to stop eating.

They did not put me on a leash or call me, but the way they looked at me suggested they wanted me to follow. I got in line behind them, and soon we were back on a path. The men, though, were walking in the wrong direction, away from where I needed to go. Away from Lucas.

* * *

I was torn. I needed to do Go Home. But that fish tasted astoundingly good.

We crossed a small stream, and as we did so the air currents skimming the surface of the water brought me the scent of Big Kitten. The men did not react, but people often do not seem to know when something fragrant is nearby, and will walk past some of the most amazing odors without pause. That is why everyone should have a dog with them, because we don't miss such things, and when we are on the leash we can halt the walk to enjoy whatever it is that needs attention.

In this instance, I knew that Big Kitten had stopped running away and was now shadowing us, far upslope from the trail we were taking. I also knew she would not come any closer.

"I guess maybe what we should do is take the dog with us when we go back to Durango," one of the men said.

"And turn it in to animal control?"

"Probably."

"But won't they put her to sleep?"

"I don't know, she's such a pretty dog. Like, shepherd/ rottweiler mix, maybe."

I looked up at the word "dog," but we were walking and no one dug into their pack for a treat.

"Really? You see rottie? I was thinking more bull terrier. Not the face, but the body."

"She can sleep in your tent, Mitch," Cap-man said with a laugh.

When the day began to fade, the men set up little cloth houses and put out a small metal box with flames and cooked some food, which they shared with me. I liked the cheese sauce best but ate everything, even some wet vegetables I didn't care for, in order to encourage their behavior.

"Will the green beans make her fart?" one of them asked.

"Like I said—your tent."

While we sat there the evening darkened. I could smell Big Kitten more strongly and knew she was close. What did she think about this change, now that I was lying at the feet of so many humans? This was the time of day when she was most restless—I would want to sleep and she would want to pounce on me and play. If I was too tired, she would ease out into the night so silently that only my nose told me what direction she had taken.

I was drowsily listening to the men talk, hoping to hear words I understood and that had to do with food, when the sharp tang of blood reached me. I instantly realized Big Kitten had successfully hunted something, even though I wasn't there to help her. I pictured one of the small rodents she had recently managed to catch—that's what it smelled like.

Big Kitten would want to return to me with the kill, and I would not be there.

I eased to my feet. Wagging, I went to each man in turn, greeting them and letting them pet me. This was what I did when I did Go to Work. People just felt better with a dog, and these men were no exception—they all brightened at the individual attention.

They were nice and they had fed me, but they belonged to the category of helpful people who were leading me away from Lucas. I had walked with them because I felt a powerful urge to do so, to be with people, and to eat dinner, but now I had to leave. I had to do Go Home.

"Good dog," Cap-man told me, scratching my chest. I licked his face.

While the men were busy getting things out of their sacks, I turned and padded off into the night to find Big Kitten.

Fifteen

Over the next several days Big Kitten and I did not encounter any humans to feed us, though we crossed streams and pools often and were able to prevent thirst. The hunger became a constant pain, and I vainly inhaled, striving to pull in the intoxicating aroma of cooking meat, even though I knew that where there were no people there was no cooking.

Big Kitten followed me, but often wanted to stop and nap in the shade. More and more often, my empty stomach sapping me of strength, I would join her, unable to continue on without sleep.

We hunted, but Big Kitten was terrible at it. She couldn't seem to sense the obvious scent of a small animal, though she did learn how to identify when I was tracking prey and would follow closely. Whenever I flushed something, though, Big Kitten did not help pursue it. Often she would just crouch, watching me exhaust myself, nearly invisible as she hid in the rocks. It was irritating and not good pack behavior. We needed to work together to catch food, but she did not understand that.

She was also afraid of water. A shallow stream seemed promising to both of us—shadowy fish flickered just beneath the surface—but after lunging at them repeatedly, all we got was wet, which I could tell disgusted Big Kitten. Then when she plunged too far into the flow and was briefly submerged, she retreated in a blind panic, scrambling up the bank and away, and that was the end of the hunt.

I could smell towns, but they felt far away, too far to do us any good. All I could think of was bins of discarded meats and back doors opening so people could hand out bacon and treats in sacks and bowls of food. And much farther away was home—even when its distinctive fragrance was not mingling in my nose, I had so thoroughly marked its direction that I could tell when we were aiming straight at it, or when our path took us on a tangent.

I was getting weak. I took frequent naps and slept through the night, not aware of Big Kitten leaving or returning.

I was so exhausted that when I saw a rabbit hop I almost didn't react. Then I surged forward and it ran and turned and skittered and fled straight toward Big Kitten, who bounded forward with an outstretched paw and got it!

We fed ravenously, side by side.

The rabbit invigorated me, though the small meal oddly seemed to make my hunger worse, more painful. Early the next morning I awoke with some energy and then was astounded when fresh blood came to me on the breeze, blood mingled with Big Kitten's scent.

When she returned to our nesting place, she was carrying an odd animal, a large rodent of a kind I had never seen before. The next morning she did the same, and a few mornings after that, she brought another rabbit.

I did not know where she was finding prey or how she

was managing to catch it. But I was grateful for the help. I felt sure Lucas would want me to provide meals for Big Kitten, just as he fed the cats in the den. But without people, I was powerless.

When Big Kitten came to wrestle with me she was now larger and heavier than I was, but still deferred to me. I was the leader of our pack. She was so quick and nimble, so able to squirm away and to dart her paws at me, that I sometimes became irritated with her and would put my teeth on her throat while she lay on her back—not biting, but letting her know that, while she might be bigger, I was the dog of the pack. She would lie there submissively until I let her up, and then she would knock me on *my* back.

Kittens, in my experience, just do not know how to play properly.

Even with the occasional small animal, my hunger was constant and debilitating. Some days it was a struggle just to get to my feet. On one such morning, the air was cold, still, and dry. Big Kitten was shadowing me and abruptly halted in a depression between two fallen trees. I turned back, not to urge her on, but to lie next to her. I settled down with a groan, prepared to sleep the rest of the day.

The sharp bite of blood awoke me, an instantly recognizable spoor on the air. Something nearby was bleeding. I stared at Big Kitten, who sensed my agitation and gave me a drowsy look. I leaped to my feet and raised my snout to the wind. Whatever was producing that scent was coming closer. Big Kitten suddenly lifted her head, alert.

We trailed the blood into a wooded, grassy area. Before long we came upon a large deer lying still in the grass at the base of a tree. From its neck protruded a long stick, and the scent of humans was strong on this odd object. The deer had bled from where the stick pierced her flesh, but was no longer moving or breathing. She was dead—not long so, but when she'd fled to this area she was able to run no farther.

Big Kitten's reaction was entirely unexpected: instead of feeding, which was what I thought we would do, she seized the deer's neck in her jaws and began dragging the deer away. Was this some sort of game? I followed, utterly baffled by her actions.

Big Kitten didn't stop until she came to a patch of sandy soil by a boulder. She dropped the deer and we finally fed, but her strange behavior didn't end there—after our meal, she scratched and dug at the dirt, eventually covering our kill with sand, leaves, and grasses.

Seeming satisfied with her work, Big Kitten went over to a large boulder and lay down beside it, hidden in the dry grass. Feeling full and lazy myself, I stretched out next to her and fell asleep listening to her purr.

We stayed with that deer for several days, taking nourishment, sleeping, making trips to a small stream to drink, and doing nothing else. I felt restless, wanting to move on to Go Home, but the luxury of having enough to eat was too seductive a lure.

Finally, we did leave. Big Kitten remained away from the path, but I could smell her as surely as I could smell the humans who had hiked along it, though the scents of people were many days old. I always knew when she had stopped, and usually would break from the trail to find her sprawled sleepily in a hiding area. On days when we had not eaten, I often curled up next to her.

Time was measured by hunger. Every few nights my feline companion would bring home an animal large enough to sate us. The next day or two we made good progress, but hunger would go from a nudge to an ache and then to an all-consuming obsession. I would let Big Kitten lead me far off course from Lucas, sometimes even doubling back on our own trail, and then she would have a successful hunt and I would return to my quest.

When I smelled fox, I would veer off to investigate, though we never encountered another one with a rabbit to

steal. When I picked up the stench of coyote, I would lead
Big Kitten far away to stay safe.

And then one day, something happened that changed
everything.

Snow.

• • •

The sky was just the slightest bit lighter than fully dark
when I awoke, acutely aware of the cold vacancy where
Big Kitten had been lying when I fell asleep. I tried to track
her, breathing deeply—her faded scent told me she had left
our den some time ago, and was not nearby.

What I smelled instead of my companion was the trans-
formation of the landscape. A heavy white layer of snow,
thicker than a dog bed, lay on the ground, and wet flakes
continued to pour from the sky in a muffled roar. The rich
fragrances of earth and bugs and animals were obliterated
by the clear, clean presence of winter. Enhanced by the
dampening of the riot of aromas that had so cluttered my
nose all summer was my sense of home's direction, which
rose up now as a powerful force on the wind.

When I stepped into this new world, my paws sank, vanishing from view, and to make my way forward I had to
break a path with my forelegs. I remembered rolling in the
snow with Lucas, chasing a ball with him, but what had
once been a sheer joy now felt more like an obstacle. Stepping through the unmarked snow, my progress was slow
and tedious. Frustrated, I looked off in the invisible distance, where the hills were smudged into near invisibility
by the continued snowfall. That way was Lucas, but how
would I get to him through this?

When the sun had fully emerged from the gloom and
light was playing on the snowscape, I sensed Big Kitten
making her way toward me. Her approach was even more
quiet with the sound-deadening effect of the coat of white.
I had retreated toward where I had spent the night, and

when she finally made her appearance, breaking out into the open from behind a hillock, I was startled. I watched without comprehension as she glided in my direction, her paws barely sinking in the snow. Her gait was strange, her back feet landing in the depressions made by her front paws with graceful exactitude. I had never seen another cat walk like that.

She carefully sniffed me, as if sensing my frustration, before greeting me with the customary rub of her head against my neck. She might not know that we were making our way overland back to Lucas, that someday in the future she would either live with us or with Mother Cat in the den across the street, but she had followed me willingly thus far and must know I was either doing Go Home or had some other reason to track in the direction we were taking.

This day, I did not try to fight against Big Kitten's inclination to sleep until nightfall, not with the snow coming down. We gave each other warmth as white flakes fell on us and eventually covered us both with a thick cloak.

When Big Kitten yawned, shook the snow out of her fur, and casually left our sleeping spot just as the light was fading from the clouded sky, I followed her for a very short period of time. I could not keep up, even when I walked the trail she was making in the snow. Where she seemed to sink very little, I was in up to my chest.

I felt trapped.

When she returned that night, she smelled of a successful hunt, though she brought nothing back to me. She turned and left in a way that I knew meant she was intending to lead me. Lunging and struggling, I forced myself to follow her, awkwardly forging a path in her tracks to a young elk buried in the snow. Astoundingly, she had taken down a creature larger than both of us. I could not imagine it.

We fed ravenously, and then returned to the temporary

den. I would have preferred to remain with the fallen elk, but Big Kitten led me away and I followed because I didn't know what else to do. It was as if the arrival of snow had reordered the pack, and now she was in charge.

This odd disruption in the established structure continued. Somehow, Big Kitten could find prey at night—not every night, but often enough that we were not starving. We ate deer and elk that she would bury in the snow, or rabbits and other smaller mammals that she would bring back to the den.

My nose told me that Big Kitten was not hunting out in open ground, but was sticking to stretches of forest and places where sun and exposure to wind stripped much of the snow away. When I was in those areas I felt as free as if Lucas had just unsnapped my leash. In the trees, snow was of varying thickness, and I learned how to find the spaces where it lay the thinnest and I could actually move at a run. Big Kitten would often saunter through these areas by stepping daintily along fallen tree trunks, which I found impossible. And, of course, she resisted going very far at all during the day. I did not understand why she wanted to spend all of her energy at night, when it was impossible to see anything.

Our progress toward Lucas was almost nonexistent. Big Kitten's hunting would pull us in whatever direction she sensed prey, which usually wasn't where I wanted us to go. Often we would track along a strongly scented deer trail, the snow pounded down and easier to push through—but also meandering and aimless, completely off course. I missed Lucas, ached to be with him, and was miserable with longing for his touch. I wanted to hear him say "Good dog." I wanted a Tiny Piece of Cheese. I needed my person so powerfully I could not sleep.

The terrain we trekked across was often slanted. Downhill, I could sometimes smell people and machines, smoke and food. There might be a town on the wind, or

just a cluster of a few people near an open fire. Downhill
meant humans. Uphill was only the pure, feral smell of
rock and ice. Big Kitten always chose up, and I always followed.

I was even more frustrated when I smelled *us*. Big Kitten and I were crossing our own trail, not doing Go Home
but just looking for prey, even if it meant wandering over
the same land.

The storms seemed to make hunting easier for her, for
some reason. My belly full, I took stock of where we
were, which was so high on the mountain that the trees
were sparse and the terrain sloped steeply down away from
me as far as I could see. Big Kitten had returned to our
sleeping spot for the day, but I was out trudging through
the unbroken white, sticking to the trees, bent on proving
that I could be an equally effective hunter were the situation more favorable.

And then I froze at the barest suggestion of a scent on
the cold air.

Dog.

Without hesitation I turned toward it, though this meant
struggling uphill. The signs were elusive at first, and while
I was searching for them I picked up something else:
humans.

This gave me pause. I had not seen a person for a long
time, not since before the first snow. Big Kitten's wariness
around even the slightest hint of humans had given me an
instinctive sense that I shouldn't approach them, a sense
reinforced by the tendency of even nice people who gave
me food to want to lead me away from Lucas.

But to see the dog I would have to move closer to the
human, because canine and man's comingled bouquet was
wafting down to me from up high. I could smell two other
humans, also male, well off to the side.

When I stepped out of the trees and looked up, I saw a
sheer white wall lifting steeply toward the sky. Way, way

up there, a dog and a man were trudging through heavy snow just below where the hill ended in a ridge. A wall of snow sat heavily on the top of the ridge, curled over in a massive overhang. The man was wearing very long shoes and clutched poles in his hands, and I could smell that the dog, whose head was above the man's hips, was a male. I did not know why anyone would lead his dog so far up a mountain, but humans are in charge of dogs and I was sure the faraway canine was happy—in fact, I could see a certain joy in his bounding gait.

"Stop! Hey!" someone yelled. Startled, I whirled my head to look all the way to the other side of the slope, where there was no ridge but just a rolling mountaintop. The two other men, so far away they appeared very small, had their hands to their mouths.

"Get out of there!" one shouted.

"That's not safe!" the other one cried.

"Avalanche zone!"

"Stop!"

The men sounded scared and angry. The man high up the hill kept walking, but the dog halted and turned, and I knew he had heard the voices. Then he stared in my direction because he had picked up my presence as well.

Though he was very far away, this canine interaction caused me to wag my tail. I played with Big Kitten every day, but right now I longed to wrestle with a dog.

"Get out of there!" both men off to my side screamed with joined voices.

The dog barked and lunged a few steps downhill toward me. Almost involuntarily, I shoved my way into the thick snow in his direction, wagging even more furiously.

"Dutch!" the man with the dog shouted. "Get back here."

The dog glanced back at his person, then leapt forward again. The pitch was so steep that he was able to travel a considerable distance in just a few bounds. He was wagging,

too. The man lifted his long shoe and stomped it down
on the snow. "Dutch! Come here!" he commanded.

"Look out!"

There was an odd, low noise, like when Lucas would
toss a pillow at me and it would hit the wall. The curl of
snow atop the ridge fragmented and fell. The man below
it jerked his head around to stare as a rumble, loud as a
truck, shook the air. He fell, tumbling, as the ground slid
underneath him, almost like water in a stream. The wave
caught the dog and knocked him over and then they were
both floundering as they plummeted toward me, moving
faster than I'd ever seen anything move, even Big Kitten.

The thunderous roar and the alien sight of the very earth
sliding suddenly filled me with terror. I needed to get away.
I turned and dashed for the trees, plunging in huge leaps,
the booming din from behind me louder and louder and
then something slammed me, tossing me into the air. I lost
all sense of up and down, I was rolling and falling, I could
see nothing and my paws could not find the ground and I
had just one thought as something hit my head.

Lucas.

Sixteen

I tumbled, feeling numb, unable to smell or feel or see. The air left me in a gasp. And then, just like that, the noise was gone. I shook my head, clearing it, and tried to make sense of what had just happened, but couldn't. I was now well into the trees, but did not know how I had gotten there.

My back legs were pinned under snow so heavy it felt as if Lucas were lying across them. If he were here, if Lucas were here, he would know what to do. Panting, I struggled to get free. I remembered him lifting me out of Wayne's arms over the fence. That was what I needed, my person taking me into his arms, pulling me clear. I whimpered. I could not move the part of me that was buried, so I strained with my forelegs to drag myself forward. There was some give, just a tiny amount. I pulled and I was able to move one leg a little, and then the other. Now I could drive with both rear legs, and with a final attempt to hold me prisoner the snow released me, and I shook myself, exhausted.

While just moments before the air had been filled with a noise so powerful it obliterated everything, even thought, there was now an odd silence. I looked around, trying to make sense of it all.

The dog. He was uphill from me, and he was sobbing, a frantic fear pouring off him. Though we were not a pack, the instinct to help rose within me and without hesitating I ran toward him, the ground beneath me oddly firm now, as if the noise had somehow packed everything down.

The dog was just at the tree line, digging, the snow flying into the air behind him. He was a huge dog, larger than I was, with thick dark fur. He did not even glance at me when I approached, didn't acknowledge my presence. His cries of distress as he dug were not hard to interpret. Something was very bad. But what? Why was he attacking the snow so frantically?

I do not know why, but a moment later I was digging next to the male dog, my movements just as frenzied. Something was bad and we were burrowing down. I knew nothing more than that.

We had not been at it very long when I smelled humans—the two men who had been so angry.

"There! Over there!" one of them shouted. "See? They're digging!"

I kept at it, scooping hard, dense ice as best I could. My nose now told me what was buried here—a man, the same man whose scent was painted on the male dog. We were digging to save the man.

Bent on my mission, I only glanced at the two men as they glided up on long shoes. One was taller and had darker skin than the other. They kicked the strange shoes off.

"These must be his dogs!"

The men knelt next to us and now there were two dogs and two people digging. They punched their mittened hands down, their long arms helping them as they shoveled great handfuls of snow.

"Got his shirt!" Both men moved up near where the male dog had been digging, and the male dog moved over but didn't pause.

"His mouth is caked. God."

"Is he alive?"

One of the men whipped off his mitten. "Still got a pulse!"

"He's not breathing!"

The men dug armloads of snow away from the buried man's face. I could feel their frenzied fear. Soon they had his shoulders exposed. They stood, each holding an arm, heaving back.

"Jesus!"

"Keep pulling!"

The men fell down and the buried man was now somewhat out of the hole. The male dog licked his face, crying.

The taller man held up a phone. "No signal. I'll go back to the cabin and get help. Can you do mouth-to-mouth? Gavin?"

"Yes!" The shorter man began kissing the male dog's person.

The other man put his big shoes back on, moving with quick, jerky motions. "I'll be back as soon as I can!"

The man who was doing the kissing nodded but kept taking deep breaths and putting his mouth on the unconscious man's. "Still got a pulse!"

The tall man wearing the big shoes picked up poles and shoved off with them, moving quickly through the snow in a gliding gait I had never seen before.

The male dog seemed to notice me for the first time, though he only took a single look at me. His tongue was out and his body was trembling, and his eyes were wide. He did not lift his leg or sniff under my tail—he pressed forward, nearly on top of the half-buried man, still whimpering.

There were no sounds for several deep breaths of the kissing man, and then the one lying in the snow started to moan.

"Oh, thank God, thank God," the kneeling man said. He turned to look at me. "He's going to be okay, I think. He's breathing now on his own."

The other man did not open his eyes, but he did cough and wheeze, and the male dog licked and licked his face.

* * *

I stayed with the moaning man, the dog, and the other man, who was nice enough to feed both dogs a piece of bread. Eventually I heard loud machines approaching from far down below, but I still stayed—not just because of the bread, but because I felt that I had to be there, the way I had to help Ty and some of my friends who were sometimes sad and needed a dog. It was my job. The bread-man was agitated and distressed, while the moaning man seemed unaware of much of anything.

"Dutch, is that your name?" the bread-man asked, looking at the collar of the male dog. "Hi, Dutch!"

I could tell by the male dog's reaction that this was what people called him.

Bread-man reached out and touched my collar and I sniffed his hand, smelling Dutch and the bread and not much else. "What's your name? Why doesn't your collar have a tag?"

I wagged. Yes, I would have more bread.

When the loud machines arrived they each carried two people on their backs and also dragged along a flat sled. There were three women and a man on the machines, and they carefully lifted the male dog's person onto the sled, strapping him down. The man groaned loudly when they moved him but he still did not wake up.

"Is he going to be okay?" the bread-man asked one of the women.

"Depends on how long his brain went without oxygen. It's a good sign, though, that his heart never stopped beating. You did the right thing."

"I've never done that. Artificial resuscitation, I mean," he replied. "Wow."

"You okay?" she responded kindly.

"Honestly? No. I'm still shaking."

"You saved a man's life. You should feel good."

"I'm going to have a martini, then I'll feel good."

The woman laughed. I wagged my tail at the sound, but Dutch was anxiously watching the people strap his person to the sled. I sniffed him, practically able to taste the anxiety pouring off him.

"What about his dogs?" the bread-man wanted to know.

"Oh," answered the woman.

"Will you send somebody to get them?"

"That's not—we aren't really equipped to take care of dogs."

"Huh." The man put a mitten down to stroke my head, and I rubbed up against him like Big Kitten greeting me. "Well, they belong to the guy you're taking to the hospital."

"That's really unfortunate. We're mountain rescue; we've never had a situation where a victim has a dog."

"I see." He patted my head again and I wagged. "So what is going to happen to them?"

The woman smacked her hands together in a spray of snow, brushing the flakes off her coat. "That's up to you, I guess."

• • •

We watched as the people climbed onto their machines, which began making a rumbling roar. Then, with a lurch, they drove off, dragging the man from the snow behind them in the sled. Dutch let out a cry and gave pursuit, his forlorn panic driving him in a stumbling run through the snow. "Dutch! Here, boy!" Bread-man yelled after him. The machines stopped and Bread-man put on his long shoes and glided down to them. Dutch circled the machines anxiously, putting a foot on the sled where his person was lying.

I observed this happening without moving. Bread-man had not called me Bella. He did not know me. But he knew Dutch. Dutch would be fine with him. I inhaled through my nose—though I could not smell Big Kitten, I knew she was out there somewhere. We would find each other. More importantly, I could pick up the scent of home, and could feel the pull of Lucas.

It was time to Go Home.

Bread-man was looking up at me. He lifted his hand to his mouth and whistled, a shrill shriek almost exactly like Lucas could make. I was startled: how did he know how to do that? "Come on, girl!"

I hesitated. Bread-man was slapping his thighs in a gesture I knew meant "Come." And I recognized "girl," it was something Lucas said to me often. Should I run to him?

I knew, deep down, that he might be one of those who would keep me from my person, but I could sense his kindness, and it had been so long since I had heard a human voice, had someone tell me I was a good dog, that the urge to run to him was overpowering. I ran to him.

Then Bread-man unslung the sack from his shoulders and I wondered if he had another piece of bread. He did! I sat obediently while he tossed me a morsel, fixated on the remaining treats in his hand. Dutch was still completely occupied with the man on the sled, so I would have all the food to myself.

When Bread-man reached for me again he had something else in his hand. I gobbled the treat from his mitten while he used a bare hand to attach something to my collar. It was, I realized with a sinking feeling, a rope. I was on a leash.

I did not want to be on a leash.

The woman held Dutch's collar while a second rope came out of the pack. Bread-man tied it to Dutch's collar, handing over one of my treats, which Dutch swallowed without seeming to care. It was a waste to give food to an apathetic dog when I was right there being attentive.

"Thanks," Bread-man said.

"Good luck!" the woman called back. And with that, the machines roared away.

Dutch was instantly frantic, his ears back, mouth drooling, eyes showing white rims. He lunged, straining against his rope and Bread-man nearly fell over. "Stop! Hold on! Dutch! Sit! Stay!"

I sat and did Stay because I was a good dog who could smell there were still some bread treats left in the pack.

Dutch whined and twisted and pulled, while Bread-man spoke soothingly. "It's okay, Dutch. You're okay, Dutch."

When Dutch finally looked at Bread-man his eyes were empty of all but despair.

"Okay, come on, girl," the man said. I could smell the noisy machines even as they turned and disappeared over a rise, their combined thunder fading abruptly on the air.

Bread-man held sticks in each hand that were long enough to touch the ground. He still wore his enormous shoes. He shrugged into the straps on his sack. I looked at Dutch, whose leash was pulled tight to keep him exactly even with me. I did not know what we were doing, and neither did Dutch, who was trying to be a good dog and was quivering with the effort. What he wanted to do, I knew, was run after that sled.

"Okay, let's try this, but go slowly. You ready? Okay. Let's go!"

I was startled when, with a tug on my rope and a whispery sound, Bread-man was suddenly gliding past us on his long shoes. Dutch and I both lurched into movement. I tried to stay close enough to the bread-man to keep the leash loose but Dutch bolted, galloping.

"Hey!" Bread-man shouted. He twisted and fell heavily to the snow. I went to him, wagging, thinking that if we were going to stop, it might be time for more bread. Dutch yanked and pulled at the end of his leash. "Dutch! No! Stop!"

After some digging in the snow, Bread-man struggled to his feet. He looked at us. I wagged. Dutch whined. "This is going to be harder than I thought. Just don't pull so hard, okay? I haven't been skiing that long. Ready? Let's go. Go!"

Uncertainly, I started forging ahead. Were we going for a walk? The snow here was still oddly packed, making for good purchase. Dutch took off again. "Dutch! Slow!" the man yelled. Dutch lowered his head and I could see he felt like a bad dog.

"Hey!" Bread-man said after a moment. "This is working!"

When we came to an uphill slope the snow abruptly went back to being deep and heavy, tough going for all three of us. My leash and Dutch's were yanked as the man used his poles to hit the ground, and he was breathing heavily.

Soon I smelled Bread-man's friend approaching. "Gavin!" the friend called, hidden by a small hill.

Bread-man raised his head. "Taylor! Over here!"

Bread-man stopped, bent over and panting, and the other man, the tall one, topped the rise and glided down to us. He also was breathing harshly.

"What happened?" Tall-man asked after a moment of just inhaling and exhaling.

"He went down with mountain rescue," Bread-man answered.

"Is he going to be okay, you think?"

"No idea. He didn't regain consciousness the whole time. They said it was a good thing his heart didn't stop. We saved his life, Taylor."

Tall-man shook his head. "What was he thinking? There were avalanche warnings everywhere!"

"I know. He had to have snowshoed right under the boundary rope."

"We may have interfered with an important Darwinian process," Tall-man said speculatively. He smiled. His teeth flashed against his skin, which was very dark. Then he looked down at me. I wagged. "So. I guess I can't help but notice that you've got two enormous dogs with you."

"Yeah, they said to call animal control."

"And the reason why *they* didn't call animal control is . . ."

"They had to take the guy down where he can be air-lifted to the hospital." Bread-man shrugged.

"So the part you don't want to tell me is . . ."

"I still have dog food from when Nick came to visit."

"Huh." Tall-man nodded. "So we give them some food and then?"

"Come on. We'll drive them in to Grand Junction with us tomorrow, figure out what to do then."

"Why does 'figure out what to do' sound suspiciously like 'take care of these dogs in our home'?" Tall-man wanted to know.

"Well, what happens if the guy dies? I don't want to just drop them off at the shelter until we know they're going to be okay."

The tall-man rubbed his face with a mitten. "There's like two tons of dog here."

Bread-man laughed.

Tall-man removed his mitten and bent down to pet Dutch, who anxiously licked the proffered hand. "So this one is Bernese mountain dog and what, bear? Grizzly bear?"

"His name is Dutch."

"Uh-huh." Tall-man reached for me and I sniffed Dutch's scent on his fingers, picking up the dog's distress. I knew what Dutch wanted more than anything was to get off leash and run after his person. It's what a lost dog needs to do. "And this one is bullmastiff plus, I don't know, cow. She's the size of a damn cow, Gavin."

"Look at her ribs, though. She hasn't been eating much."

"Her brother is well-fed. He needs to be on a diet."

"Okay, that's what we'll do then."

"What we will do," the tall-man repeated. "*We*. Will put this dog, who we don't own, on a diet."

"Avalanche-dude gives all the food to the brother but not the sister. Here, take the male, you're a better skier and he pulls like a speedboat."

Dutch and I soon learned that the bread-man was named Gavin and the tall-man with the dark skin was Taylor. Well, *I* learned it—Dutch didn't seem to care about anything but getting back with his person. The two men walked us back to a very small house that had a hole in the wall with a fire burning in it, filling the place with the pungent tang of smoke. Gavin poured dry food into two bowls, which I ate and Dutch didn't, so I ate his.

I was grateful for the food, but I knew something that the humans apparently didn't understand: they had two dogs in their house, and neither one of us wanted to be there. I knew that at the first opportunity, I would be leaving.

Dutch sat at the door and looked at it expectantly, clearly

hoping it would open and his person would walk in. I knew, though, that life was never that easy, that instead of doors being opened for you, to get anywhere, you have to jump over fences.

Seventeen

The next afternoon Taylor took the rest of us on a long, long car ride. I recognized the word "home" but could tell we were not going in the right direction, that home was actually behind us.

I could not smell Big Kitten. Had I known that investigating Dutch's scent would mean being taken from her I would have let the opportunity to see another dog pass, no matter how tempting. I missed Big Kitten and worried for her without me to take care of her.

"You two okay back there?" Gavin asked over his shoulder. Dutch and I were awkwardly sharing the backseat, which wasn't really big enough to accommodate both of us. "God, Taylor, look at her. I can count every rib. How could someone do that? Dutch is obese and she's starving."

"Maybe he just likes boys better. I can certainly identify with that." Taylor laughed.

"I'm serious. This is animal abuse."

Dutch and I eventually settled on a system where one of us would sit and one of us would lie down, then when that became uncomfortable we would switch places. After a long drive we arrived at a big house with hard floors and several rooms. In one of them, a yawning hole in the wall was filled with burned wood pieces that I sniffed carefully, but which Dutch ignored. There was a big backyard with a metal fence, where I found no snow and no slides, just grasses and plants. I smelled dogs and a faraway cat on the arid wind, but no other animals.

Taylor put pillows and blankets on the floor and I understood: Dutch and I were supposed to sleep there. We were supposed to stay with Taylor and Gavin, the way I once stayed with Jose and Loretta.

I did not know why people would not just let me find my way home.

When we first arrived at the big house, Taylor and Gavin sat with me and played a game I did not understand.

"Molly? Carly? Missy?" they asked me. I did not know what I was supposed to do. I wagged my tail, thinking that with all this attention there might be a treat at the end of it.

"Daisy? Chloe? Bailey? Blanche?" Gavin asked.

"Blanche! Oh my God!" Taylor fell back on the couch and held a pillow to his face.

"What?" Both men were laughing.

"Who would name a dog Blanche?" Taylor demanded.

"My mom's dog was named Blanche," Gavin replied defensively.

"Well, that explains *everything*."

"Hey!" The two men wrestled with each other. I caught Dutch's glance and looked away. Apparently any treats for us were forgotten.

Later, though, they were back at it. "Here's the list of most popular dog names," Taylor said. He was sitting at a table making clicking noises with his fingers on a toy but not accomplishing anything. Lucas and Mom would often do the same thing, and it made me long to be back home with them.

"Is Dutch on it?" Gavin wanted to know.

"Uh . . . doesn't look like it," Taylor replied.

"So the guy maybe didn't consult the list when he named his dogs," Gavin observed. "This could be a waste of effort."

"These are the most popular names. That means when people think of names, they most often come up with these. They didn't have to read from a list, necessarily. People come up with popular names at random," Taylor said.

"Okay, hit it."

"Okay." Taylor looked down at me intently. "Number one. Lucy?"

I stared back. Was Lucy some sort of treat?

"Next," Gavin said.

"Max?"

"Max is not a female name."

"What about Maxine?"

"Oh, please." Gavin sniffed. "That makes no sense."

"Says the man whose mother named a dog *Blanche*," Taylor responded dryly.

"You're the one who likes random names."

"Bailey?"

"We tried Bailey."

"Bella?"

I cocked my head. It was the first time either one of them had said my name.

"Maggie?"

"Wait," Gavin said. "Go back. There was something."

"Bella?"

Why was he saying my name? I yawned.

"Bella?" Gavin called.

I turned and looked at him.

"Yes!" He jumped up. "Wahoo! It's Bella! Bella!"

I couldn't help myself, I leaped up, too, and when Gavin ran around the table yelling my name I followed him, barking. Dutch watched us from his dog bed, completely disgusted.

The next day Taylor played with my collar, and when I moved I made a jingling sound. "Now you both have name tags," he told us.

From that moment on, we were Bella and Dutch, two dogs living with Gavin and Taylor, both of us anxious to get back to our real people.

Every night when I curled up to sleep, I thought of Big Kitten. I wondered what she was doing, and if she missed me. I hoped no coyotes were hunting her. I hoped she wasn't cold.

I waited patiently for the opportunity to do Go Home, thinking I might see Big Kitten on the trail. I was taken for many walks, usually at night, and always on leash. I would start off sniffing politely whenever Dutch marked, but he would do it so often I eventually would concentrate on other smells. We were on one such walk, Gavin holding Dutch's leash and Taylor holding mine, when Gavin said my name. "Bella has gained a little weight. Looks good."

I glanced over at him, hearing approval.

"So how is the new editor working out?" Taylor asked.

"I think pretty well. She likes the manuscript. But that doesn't mean I won't get a lot of notes," Gavin responded.

"I can't believe you don't get pissed off. I know I do whenever they want you to change things. You're a successful author!"

They were silent for a time. I could smell that there had recently been a squirrel in the area, and remained alert to its appearance.

"So how long?" Gavin finally asked quietly.

"Sorry?"

"I've noticed that you always start off asking me about my books before you go on a long trip. It's as if you're reminding me you're not the only one who travels."

Taylor sighed. "Looks like probably two weeks. The systems are less compatible than we thought. A lot of legacy code has to be rewritten. My team's good, but they need me there."

"Whatever that means, I'm hearing two weeks, which usually means four."

"I'll miss you," Taylor said.

They stopped under a tree and hugged each other. Dutch and I, confused, walked around them until our leashes drew us up nose-to-nose.

A few days later I was introduced to the term "suitcase," which was a box with a handle and Taylor's clothes in it. Dutch and I sniffed it when it lay open on the floor, and I could tell he was trying to decide if he should lift his leg on it since it clearly had outdoor aromas on it. He finally decided to leave a very faint mark, a tiny squirt that neither men noticed.

Gavin and Taylor left together and then Gavin came back alone and some of the rules changed. We were allowed to sleep on the bed! I slept next to Gavin. Dutch would climb on the bed if Gavin insisted, but it made him restless and he always jumped down during the night.

Dutch was sad. He spent a lot of time with his nose to the crack under the door, sniffing and sighing. He did not want to play with me much. Sometimes Gavin would get on the floor with Dutch and put his arms around him. "Are you okay, big guy? You going to be okay?" Gavin would ask softly. When he did this I could feel the knot of pain inside Dutch loosen its hold a little. Gavin was giving Dutch comfort.

He also gave us toys—toys that squeaked and soft toys and bone toys and balls. Everything, from the chicken treats Gavin handed us to the soft toys Dutch and I ripped apart, reminded me of Lucas. Gavin was a kind man, but he wasn't my person.

Then Taylor came home, and he brought treats! "Wow, Bella, you've really gained weight!" he said happily as he gave me a chewy piece of meat. "You look great. Dutch, you're still a little . . . rotund."

"I can't give Bella food and not Dutch. It wouldn't be fair," Gavin said defensively.

With the two men back together we went on more walks. "You know what, I think we should go up to the cabin one last time before we head to China," Taylor said on one walk.

"Still snowy up there. I really prefer the summer," Gavin replied.

"You'll get the hang of cross-country skiing, you just need practice."

"I don't *want* to get the hang of it."

"What's eating you?" Taylor asked.

"When were you going to tell me you've been in contact with mountain rescue about their owner? There was a message on our voice mail."

The two men were quiet. Dutch and I both looked in the direction of a barking dog, off in the distance. Dutch responded by lifting his leg on a post.

"Did they leave the name?" Taylor finally asked.

"No, just said she understood you wanted his contact information and she needs to know why. And I, Taylor, also would like to know why."

"Because they aren't our dogs! We have to give them back."

"If he wanted them back, wouldn't he have called by now?" Gavin demanded.

"I don't know why he hasn't called. That's what I want to ask him. You're in denial about this whole thing. *We can't keep the dogs.*"

Gavin turned abruptly and Dutch trotted to keep up, looking back in confusion at Taylor and me. We were stopped. I sat, unsure what was going on. "Gavin!" Taylor called.

Gavin kept walking.

. . .

Not long after that the men put things in the car and drove to the "cabin." I knew instantly where we were—the same small place where we were taken for our first meal after we dug the man out of the snow. When we arrived Dutch was so excited he was quivering, but after racing around in the yard, he abruptly stopped running. He marked a few places, of course, but he did so without much enthusiasm. He knew his person was not here.

Here at the cabin we were much closer to Lucas; I could feel it. I sniffed around the fence, looking for a slide, but there was none, and the fence itself was too high for me to jump.

The first night we spent at the cabin, Dutch and I were let out in the backyard to Do Your Business right before the men went to bed. Dutch lifted his leg several times, but after I squatted once I went to the corner of the fence and lifted my nose, excited by a familiar scent.

Big Kitten was nearby.

I waited expectantly, but she came no closer. Eventually I remembered how Mother Cat always approached Lucas, but never allowed herself to be touched. I realized she would not be coming to see me, not with humans so close. Even a cat as enormous as Big Kitten could be frightened of people; it was just how some cats were.

We were back at the house when something happened that caused Gavin's anxiety to rise sharply—Dutch and I both felt it. Dutch went to Gavin, concerned, and Gavin stroked his ears. "It's okay, Dutch," he murmured softly. "Taylor's talking to your owner."

Taylor was holding the phone. When he finished, he

came out and handed Gavin a glass of sharp-smelling liquid. "So?" Gavin asked.

"Kurch couldn't come to the phone. I talked to his sister," Taylor replied.

"Wait. Kurch?"

"I guess that's his name."

"Rhymes with church?"

"Yes."

"Is that how he *spells* it?" Gavin demanded. "C-H-U-R-C-H?"

"Okay, I can feel your English major rage rising but it's not my fault, that's his name. And no, he spells it with a K."

"Kurch."

"I know, Gavin."

"I can't believe we're going to give our dogs to a guy named Kurch."

"Our dogs? But yeah, it's got to be the stupidest name in history."

"So what did Kurch's sister say? Oh, and what's her name, Muck? Corpuscle?"

"No, you ready? Susan."

"They named their son Kurch and the girl *Susan*?"

"The guy is pretty banged up, still," Taylor continued. "I guess he broke about every bone in his body. So he's on painkillers. She was surprised to hear why I was calling. She didn't even know he had dogs."

"Close family."

"I do get the sense she sees Kurch as less of a blessing than a burden."

"Maybe he spells it K-I-R-S-C-H," Gavin observed hopefully.

"No, she spelled it for me when I expressed my . . . doubts."

"Maybe she can't spell."

"I would believe that," Taylor replied agreeably.

"So when are we taking them?"

"I told her we'd drop them by next week."

"I'm going to miss them, Taylor. This is going to be the hardest thing I've ever done."

"I know. But they are not our dogs."

"Maybe he'd sell them to us."

"Now that is a particularly bad idea," Taylor said gently. "What would we do with them when we go to China?"

Dutch let out the sort of groan only a very bored dog can make. It reminded me of how tired I was, and I curled up on my own dog bed.

"We could find a place to board them," Gavin declared.

"For six months? You would really do that to them?"

"No, you're right. I just . . . Dutch is finally starting to accept us, I can tell. You should see how he missed you when you were traveling."

"You didn't let the dog on the bed though, right?" Taylor asked.

"Of course not. I let the *other* dog on the bed." Gavin sighed. "Well, okay. I guess it's the only way. Next Tuesday?"

"Tuesday. Yes."

"Tuesday, Bella," Gavin said in a tone somehow both happy sounding and weighted with sadness, "we're taking you back to your owner!"

Eighteen

Something was different. There was a change in the rules.

Taylor did not want dogs on the couch. Gavin liked it. We had learned that when Gavin was home alone we were welcome to lie on the cushions but when Taylor was there he would clap his hands and yell "Off!" I knew this meant to jump down immediately, but Dutch always seemed to believe Taylor didn't really mean it and would lie there until Taylor pulled him onto the floor. Then Dutch would wander over to where I was already lying on the dog bed, mournfully sniffing me before deciding where to collapse with an exaggerated groan.

If we were on the couch when Taylor came home from wherever he had been, I always gave a guilty start, but could never seem to summon the energy to jump down until he commanded us to Off.

But then it was different. Taylor and Gavin were sitting together on the couch and Taylor called to Dutch, patting the cushion next to him. Not seeming to grasp that this was a colossal reversal in policy, Dutch padded over and jumped up without hesitation, lying down and putting his head in Gavin's lap.

"Come on, Bella. You, too," Gavin said. "Come! Bella, come!"

Really?

I managed to curl up on the couch next to Taylor, though the space was tight. I wondered what we were all doing now.

Both men were sad; I could feel it in the way they stroked my fur.

"This is going to be the hardest thing I've ever done," Gavin murmured with a sigh.

"We knew it was temporary."

"I guess I didn't really allow myself to admit it."

"They miss their master," Taylor said gently. "You can tell. Especially Dutch. They just want to be with Kurch."

Dutch's eyes flickered at this statement, as if he understood something about it that I didn't, which was impossible.

"I know," Gavin said.

"I can put off my trip for a couple days."

"That's sweet but I know you need to get to Seattle. I'll be fine."

"Going to be strange, coming home and not being greeted by a pair of giant dogs," Taylor observed.

"It's almost as if part of me is dying. I'm glad we're going to China soon, different environment, I won't miss them as badly."

Something else completely different: that night, Taylor called for us to get on the bed with the two of them. We tried to sleep, but we were too hot and jumped down shortly after being invited up.

People are difficult to comprehend: they make rules and then change them. I was happy we would be able to sleep on the couch now, but wished it didn't make Gavin and Taylor so sad when we did so.

Taylor left the next morning with his suitcase. Gavin fed us a breakfast with bacon in it! Then he took us for a long, long walk on leashes. Dutch marked everywhere and Gavin waited without any impatience. It was the most leisurely stroll we had ever been on together.

Gavin was so sad, I thought he should lie down so I could cuddle next to him and do my job and provide comfort. Instead, he first went to Dutch on the couch and me in my dog bed, giving us both long, tight hugs. "I will miss you so, so much," he whispered to me. I wagged and licked his face, which was wet and salty. I did not understand what all these changes in people behavior meant, and had the uneasy feeling something bad was about to happen.

"Okay, guys. Time to go." Gavin sighed.

Car ride! Dutch sat up front and I was in the back. Gavin made room for us at the top of the windows to stick our noses out into the wind, and Dutch and I took turns sneezing. Gavin kept stroking Dutch's fur with one hand.

Then suddenly Dutch went stiff. I glanced at him, feeling his excitement growing, though I wasn't at all sure why. He yawned, panting a little, and when Gavin reached out Dutch licked his fingers. Dutch circled in his seat, staring out the window as if he could see a squirrel. I couldn't see anything, though I became alert just because he was.

"That's right, guys, we're almost there," Gavin told us wistfully.

When we stopped, Dutch pawed at the window and made a low, excited whining noise. Clearly he thought something was happening—what, I had no idea. When Gavin reached across to let him out Dutch ran straight up to the front door of a small house. Gavin came around to get me and I jumped out of the car, stretching and shaking myself.

An odd place. There were some machines in the yard, sitting on dried mud mixed with papers and some plastic containers I sniffed with interest, detecting something sweet in a few of them. Gavin stood for a moment while I squatted and watched Dutch, who was wagging and turning circles in front of the door.

"What a dump," Gavin muttered quietly.

I followed him to where Dutch was waiting with such agitation. Where were we? What were we doing here? Gavin knocked on the wood, then waited. Dutch put a paw on Gavin's knee. "It's okay, Dutch," Gavin said reassuringly. He knocked again. "Hello?" he called.

He pushed the door open slightly. "Kurch? Hello?"

"Back here!" a man yelled from somewhere in the house.

Dutch nosed the door and pushed past us, running inside the house. "You're home, Bella," Gavin told me.

"Ah, Jesus! Get down, Dutch!" a man shouted from down a hallway.

The place inside was dark. There were socks and shirts and papers and boxes with bits of food in them lying on the floor and furniture, and I examined them curiously. Gavin followed the direction Dutch had taken, so I did the same.

"Kurch? You back there?" Gavin asked.

"Can you get the damn dog off of me?"

In a back room a man lay in bed and Dutch was on top of him, wagging and licking. The man wore heavy, hard white pants, and one arm and half his chest was encased in the same rigid material. He had white cloth wrapped around one of his hands. He was sour with old sweat, but I felt sure he was someone I had met before.

"Dutch! Down!" Gavin commanded.

Dutch eased to the floor with great reluctance. Apparently he thought Taylor's rule change applied to every bed we came across.

"God, stupid dog," the man said. "Trying to put me back in the hospital?"

Dutch did Sit, watching the sour-smelling man with rapt attention.

Gavin looked around. "I'm Gavin," he finally said. I went over and sniffed at a half-eaten sandwich on a plate on a chair, wondering if the edicts in this odd place would allow me to nibble on it a little. "I talked to your sister."

"Yeah, she said you might be coming over," the man replied with a grunt.

"It was my husband and I who were the ones who, uh, dug you out."

"I don't remember any of that." The man waved his white-wrapped hand.

"Oh. Well. It's good to see you; we weren't sure you would even make it out alive."

"Yeah, sure, I practically didn't, I got eleven frickin' fractures. Then my damn sister just walks out the door last night, says she 'needs a break.' What kind of family is that? Like I can take care of myself right now!"

Dutch was still sitting at high attention, watching the man in the bed. I was watching the sandwich with equal focus.

"Sorry to hear of your difficulties," Gavin said after a moment.

"She only thinks of herself."

"Ah."

The two men were quiet for a time. I finally gave up on the sandwich and lay down on the floor with a sigh.

"At any rate, I brought your dogs back."

"Yeah. Hey, Dutch." The man dropped his hand, the one wrapped in cloth, and put it on Dutch's head. Dutch leaned into the touch, his eyes half closed, and I missed Lucas more in that moment than I had in a long time. I eased back to my feet, wanting to get out of there, go back up into the mountains, on the trail. Go Home. "Wait," the man said suddenly. "You said dogs. Dogs?"

"Yes, I said I brought your dogs back," Gavin agreed,

speaking evenly. I could hear a rising impatience in his tone.

"That one's not mine."

Gavin stared at me and I looked back at him. Car ride? Then he turned to stare at the man. "Not *yours*?" he repeated, shocked.

"Yeah, never seen it before," the man said dismissively.

"But . . . Bella was with Dutch when we got to you. They were both digging for you in the snow. That's how we found you."

"Huh. Well, musta been a coincidence." The man made a shrugging motion and then winced.

"A what? A coincidence? . . . So Bella is not yours?"

I wagged a little, hearing my name so much. I glanced hopefully at the sandwich.

"Nope."

There was a long silence. "I don't understand," Gavin finally said. "I thought I was going to drop off your dogs, both of them. It never occurred to us they weren't both yours."

"Drop *off*? The hell do you mean, drop off?" the man demanded.

Gavin blinked. "Well . . . we . . . are you saying you don't want your dog back?"

"I look like I can take care of a hundred-pound dog right now? I can't even feed myself. Takes me an hour to get to the bathroom for a piss."

"What are you saying?"

"I'm saying there's no way I can have Dutch right now. Sorry."

"Sorry? You're sorry? Dutch is your *dog*."

"What part of half my body is in a frickin' cast don't you understand? I was in a frickin' *avalanche*."

"Because you were snowshoeing in a restricted area! There are signs all over!" Gavin was shouting and I went to him, nosing his hand.

"Fine. Blame the victim. Nobody gives a rat's ass about me. I'm going to have to go live with my brother and his prissy wife next month. You got no idea what that's like. They live in frickin' Oklahoma. Go to church every frickin' Sunday, I'm like, 'Hell no, I'm not going, can't you see I'm hungover?' Next thing I know my own brother says I gotta leave. He's so frickin' whipped."

"You are telling me," Gavin stated in a low, angry voice, "that you're refusing any responsibility?"

"Hey, you're the guy trying to dump two gigantic dogs on me."

"My husband and I are going to China for six months. We can't take care of Dutch. He's your dog. I'll figure out what to do with Bella, obviously, but Dutch belongs here, with you."

The man sighed. Dutch scratched himself behind the ear and then suddenly alerted to the sandwich. He glanced at me and then at the man in the bed and then at Gavin. I could tell by his face that he thought he was being a bad dog to want to eat it, but otherwise I had no idea what he was thinking or what was happening. I only knew that Gavin and the man were getting more furious with each other, their voices tightening and the sweat flashing to their skin.

"I thought you couldn't take a dog because of China, so a little hypocritical there, don't you think? Seems to me whatever you're doing with Bella you could do with Dutch. You and your *husband*." The man sneered.

Gavin went very still. "I said before that I didn't understand you, but I was wrong. I understand you very, very well. Kurch. Come on, Bella. Dutch, come."

Dutch stared at Gavin, the sandwich forgotten. Then he looked at the man in the bed.

"Go on, Dutch. Get the hell out of here, you're making me feel guilty and it's not my fault. Go!" the man snapped.

I followed Gavin down the hall and out the door, Dutch

far behind us. He kept turning to glance back down the hall, wanting to remain in this odd, dark place. The angry man in the bed was Dutch's person. But the man was mad and didn't love Dutch anymore.

Dutch was bewildered. When we got in the car, Gavin put his arms around him. I smelled the tears on Gavin's cheeks, but was unable to provide comfort from the backseat.

"I am so sorry, Dutch. That was horrible. But I promise you that I love you, Taylor and I will be your daddies, we will take care of you." Gavin wiped his face with a cloth from his pocket. His hand came back over the top of the seat and I licked it. "You too, Bella. I love you and we will be a family together."

Dutch did not stick his nose out the window, not once all the way home.

• • •

That night Dutch and I lay on the couch with Gavin while he held a phone to his face. Dutch had been nosing Gavin's hand frequently since we returned from the odd place with the sandwich, and Gavin stroked him and spoke to him soothingly each time.

"It was simply awful. The guy was a complete asshole," Gavin said. He sounded angry again. "He didn't care at all about Dutch. Treated his own dog like crap. He acted really put out that we *dug him out of the snow*. Which, I got to tell you, I'm rethinking. All of humanity would have benefited if we'd waited until spring." Gavin scratched Dutch's ears. "No, that's the really strange thing. No idea what Bella was doing there. If God sent her it was a real waste of a miracle."

At the mention of my name, I looked lazily over at him.

"Of course we're still going to China. No. I don't know what we're going to do with the dogs, obviously I'm still processing."

Gavin was quiet for a long time. "Thank you," he said, his voice tight. "I so appreciate that you said that, Taylor. I know this situation is more difficult for you than maybe it is for me, and the fact that you're willing to do whatever I want . . . it just means the world to me. I love you."

After a time, Gavin set his phone down. He touched his wet eyes with the same cloth from his pocket. "All right, guys. We've got a real problem on our hands," he told us.

• • •

The next morning Dutch jumped right down from the bed and went to the door with unusual enthusiasm, eagerly holding still for the leash Gavin put on our collars. He pushed outside and dragged both of us to the car.

"No, Dutch. We're going to go for a walk. No car ride. We're not going back to that place."

We wandered up the sidewalk, Dutch carefully marking over the scents of other males. Up ahead, I caught sight of a cat! It was strolling across a front yard, a heavy black female. I wanted to go greet her, so I pulled at the leash, which drew Dutch's attention.

The cat and Dutch saw each other at exactly the same moment. Gavin was crouched over because Dutch had done Do Your Business on a yard and Gavin was picking it up with a plastic bag. Dutch lunged forward and I joined him, racing to see the cat.

"Hey!" Gavin shouted, stumbling. "Stop! No!"

I knew that word. I halted, looking at Gavin to see what I had done wrong. Dutch, on the other hand, was so fixated on the cat he didn't hear the command. Gavin suddenly fell, yanking hard on my leash and dropping Dutch's.

Dutch streaked after the cat. I did Sit like a good dog. "Dutch! No!" Gavin called.

The cat froze, watching Dutch bear down on her. I thought she would arch her back and rake her claws on his nose, but she suddenly darted for a tree, launching herself at the trunk and flying up into the branches like a squirrel.

I thought Big Kitten was the only cat able to climb trees because she was the only one I had ever seen do so. Dutch was even more mystified: he got to the tree and put his forepaws on it and looked up and barked.

I was a good dog and did No Barks. "Come on, Bella, good dog," Gavin praised, though he didn't give me a treat despite the bag of them in his pocket.

Dutch was staring at the cat, who was staring back. "Dutch! Come!" Gavin shouted.

Dutch looked at us wildly, as if he had forgotten anything but the hunt.

"Come here, Dutch!"

And then a change came over Dutch. I saw his ears drop, his eyes slit, a calculation in his expression.

"Dutch!" Gavin repeated in a warning tone.

Dutch turned and started walking away from us. He was being a bad dog!

"Come. Dutch! You come here!" Gavin yelled.

Dutch took off running.

Nineteen

Gavin took me back to the house at a trot. We jumped into the car and I was in the front seat. He put my window down and I hung my head out, drinking in the smells.

Gavin's own window was down. "Dutch! Dutch!" he called.

We were driving up and down the streets. I did not understand this game at all. Sometimes we were clearly following Dutch, and sometimes his scent was in the opposite direction. Gavin was upset. "I know you would never run away like this, Bella," he told me. I wagged.

I was doing No Barks but Gavin was so anxious and Dutch was such a bad dog that when we were practically on top of his scent I couldn't help it and barked out the window. Gavin stopped the car and there was Dutch, cutting between houses! "Gotcha," Gavin said triumphantly. I was pressed back against the seat as the car turned the corner.

There was Dutch, up ahead, trotting along, his leash

dragging behind him. His head was low, his tail down, and I instantly knew what this was about: he was doing his own version of Go Home. He was going back to the dark place with the sandwich and the man in the heavy pants.

Gavin drove up next to Dutch, who whipped his head up when he smelled me. "Dutch!" Gavin said sternly.

The car stopped. Dutch sank to the ground, the tip of his tail flicking, his eyes blinking rapidly. Gavin got out of the car. "Come here, Dutch," he commanded quietly.

Dutch nearly crawled, looking as if he felt that of all the dogs, he was the most bad.

"I'm your daddy now, Dutch. Do you understand?" Gavin got to his knees and put his arms around Dutch. "That's not your home anymore. Your home is with us, now. You and me and Taylor and Bella, we're a family."

He held Dutch and rocked with him and I realized I knew what Gavin was doing.

Providing comfort.

* * *

Gavin gave us special attention and many treats and hugs for the next several days, and the sadness seemed to be seeping out of Dutch a little at a time.

"I think he's getting used to the idea," Gavin said to me, his phone to his face. I wagged. "It's almost as if, when he got back in the car with me, he knew he was making a choice. They're our dogs now, Taylor, for better or worse." Gavin was quiet, and then chuckled. "Okay, but look at it this way, if they do wear out the couch, you'll be able to buy another one, and you'll probably want new chairs and a new coffee table. Don't pretend that doesn't sound like an attractive proposition to you!" He was silent for a time, rubbing his feet on Dutch, who was sprawled at the other end of the couch. Dutch gave a contented groan.

"Right. China. I've been thinking about that and I maybe have an idea. So, before I tell you, will you promise to keep an open mind? Okay." Gavin took a deep breath. "What would you think of Sylvia?"

Gavin was silent for a long, long time before he started talking to me again. "Right, I agree with all that. But what choice do we have? I can't see putting them in a kennel for half a year." He was quiet some more. "Wait, wait, you seriously are objecting to leaving the dogs with my mom because you don't like her *decorating*?" Gavin laughed. "Oh, that was another thing about this guy Kurch. He had a snowmobile and a lawnmower and God knows what else lying in his front yard, and his place was a complete pigsty. Sure. Well, not animal cruelty, but close to it. Okay, I get it, I'm trying to let it go. So? What do you think? No, not at all perfect, but maybe in this case perfection is not as good as practical. Thank you, Taylor. I'll call my mom tomorrow. Love you, too."

Gavin put his phone down and I yawned. "Okay, guys," he told us. "Life's about to get pretty interesting."

• • •

A few days after Taylor came home with this suitcase in hand, he and Gavin took us for an extended car ride. We were in the car so long that Dutch and I became bored with smelling out the window, and the men rolled up the glass and Dutch and I lay sprawled on each other in the backseat.

After a time, though, I sat up, suddenly aware of a change. Ever since people had begun taking me away from Lucas, I had not only sensed him out there, but I could smell the place where we lived, the town. The way the scents had come together until it was a singular presence on the wind made for an identifiable mark, different from other odors, other towns. But wherever we were going, now, it was far enough away that the presence faded until it was undetectable.

I had lost the smell of home.

The air was dry and dusty and I smelled large animals and open water, but that was all. I did not know if I would be able to do Go Home from here.

We stopped to do Do Your Business, Taylor holding my leash and Gavin holding Dutch's. "This is not my favorite place," Taylor told Gavin.

"Is this the pre-bad mood to the bad mood you're going to be in the whole time?" Gavin asked.

"What's the industry here in Farmington, anyway? Manure?"

"Coal and gas, mainly. It has its charms. You like the rivers," Gavin said.

"Charm. That's precisely the word I was looking for."

We all climbed back into the car. As much as I liked car rides, I hoped we would now return back to their house, or the cabin.

"Okay," Taylor declared grimly. "Let's go see Sylvia."

As we drove, Taylor and Gavin became anxious, touching each other for reassurance. Their moods affected Dutch and me, and we circled each other in the backseat, our noses to the window.

Eventually the car stopped and we jumped out onto a front yard that was nearly all cement. Dutch marked what little foliage he could find. The door opened and a woman stood there.

"Hi, Mom," Gavin greeted. I glanced at him, wondering why he would say Mom's name. But humans will do this, mention other people, and dogs will never understand. Gavin and Taylor also talked from time to time about Dude, one of the boys who fed me salty meat and gave me a car ride. Gavin went to the door and kissed the woman on her face. Dutch followed and I did, too.

"Hello, Sylvia," Taylor called from the back of the car. He was getting out his suitcase—he sure liked lugging that thing around with him.

"Long time, boys," the woman observed with a cough.

Her name was Sylvia and she lived with a female cat named Chloe. It smelled smoky and dry inside and the windows were mostly covered with blankets, so it was gloomy. Dutch sniffed around, excited by the promise of a cat, whose name we wouldn't learn until later.

The backyard was enclosed with a high fence made of boards. Not much was growing there except along the back fence, where bushes and grasses led a sparse, thirsty existence. Most of the space was taken up by a pool, which was the word the people used to describe a small pond filled with clear water that had a strong smell and taste. It was in the backyard where we met the cat for the first time.

Dutch was intensely interested in Chloe, lunging at the end of his leash when he saw her, but Gavin and Taylor both shouted "No!" very loudly and Dutch shrank from their anger, wagging with his ears down.

"You can't bother Chloe," Gavin said sternly. "No, Dutch."

I had the sense that Dutch was bewildered that he was being disciplined when there was a cat right there who needed chasing.

Chloe was arching her back and her tail had gotten very thick, and now she stared at Dutch, her lips pulled back.

Some cats play and some do not and Chloe did not. I decided to ignore her.

"Chloe can take care of herself, she's not like Mike. But when she has her kittens, your dogs better behave," Sylvia said crossly. She had smoke coming out of her mouth when she talked, and eventually I would learn that the burning thing in her hand was called a "cigarette."

The people settled into chairs outside by the pool. Sylvia drank from a tall container full of ice, and Taylor and Gavin held glasses with dark liquid in them. All of them emitted a similar scent.

"Wait, did you say 'not like Mike'?" Taylor asked. "Mike?"

"He used to hide under the bed when I vacuumed," Sylvia said.

"I think I'm missing something," Taylor said. "Isn't Mike your boyfriend?"

"No, Mike the *cat*. Different Mike. Mike's history," Sylvia stated emphatically, waving her cigarette. "Good riddance."

"Oh? What happened with Mike, Mom?" Gavin asked.

"He got hit by a car."

"*What?*" Taylor blurted, sounding distressed.

"No, I know what happened with the *cat*." Gavin laughed. "I mean with Mike the man. I thought you two were talking about getting married."

"He's an alcoholic," Sylvia said, taking a long drink. Taylor and Gavin exchanged glances. "I don't mean the good kind, either. Gets mean."

Dutch settled down with a groan, distressed that Chloe was sitting there right in front of us licking her paw.

"We really appreciate you taking care of Bella and Dutch, Sylvia," Taylor said after a long pause. We both glanced up at our names. Chloe, having laid down the law, strolled loftily away.

"I don't mind. Could be worse. Remember that biker gang your sister brought over?" Sylvia asked Gavin.

"I don't know if it was a gang, exactly," Gavin observed mildly.

"So her boyfriend moves in," Sylvia told Taylor, "just temporary because his trailer exploded, which was good because it destroyed all the evidence, and then he's got a cousin and I don't know who all else, a million tattoos. Mike was terrified the whole while, under the bed, and at some point I had to say if the cops get called *one more time,* so they left and your sister didn't talk to me for six months until she called from some place in Canada to ask if she was adopted."

Taylor stood up. "Anyone else need a refresher?"

"I think, Mom, to qualify as a biker gang at least one of them has to have a motorcycle," Gavin said as he held out his glass.

"Whatever." Sylvia shrugged. "I don't speak Spanish."

The next morning Taylor and Gavin were up just after dawn, putting their suitcase in the car, so I knew we would be leaving. But it didn't work out that way. They sat down with us by the pool. "Guys, this is going to be tough, but we're leaving for a while. Just half a year, but we will miss you so, so much," Taylor told us. "We'll be back in the fall."

"I love you both," Gavin whispered. He put his arms around Dutch and Dutch leaned into the hug.

I did not understand the words but the tone reminded me of the last time I'd seen Lucas, and it struck me I might know what was going on. Both men kissed me and petted me and Gavin was weeping, but when they went to the gate they blocked Dutch from accompanying them.

I didn't try to follow. I knew there would be no car ride for us.

When the car drove away, its sounds fading, Dutch cried, reaching out with a paw and scratching the wooden gate. I could feel his distress, but I had learned that people are not as reliable as a dog would like. They went places, sometimes for long periods of time, or entrusted their canines to the care of other people. Dutch could scratch and cry all he wanted, but that would not bring back Gavin and Taylor. If he wanted them, he would have to go find them, just as I was making my way back to my Lucas.

I thought about the time that Dutch saw a cat and nearly pulled Gavin over, how the leash fell from his hand. Sylvia was much smaller than Gavin—when she pushed Dutch's head away from a plate of food she placed next to her on her chair, she could barely move him. I knew that when we went for a walk with her, I could simply strain on my leash and yank it out of her hands and I would be free.

I could not feel Lucas, but I had a sense of the direction Gavin and Taylor had taken. I would go that way until I could smell the collection of odors that was the town where I lived, and then I would turn and follow my nose.

Next walk. I would Go Home the next time Sylvia took us on a walk.

Twenty

Sylvia did not take us for walks. We did Do Your Business in the sad tangle of weeds and plants along the back fence, and were never allowed to leave the yard. Dutch didn't seem to mind—he spent a lot of time sitting at the gate, waiting patiently. When he wasn't standing sentry there, he would lie in an oval of shadow under a wooden table, little flies pestering his mouth.

With no walks and no slide, I did not know what to do. I felt like a bad dog. I needed to do Go Home, and I was no longer certain how to do that.

Sylvia liked to lie next to the pool every day and rest in the sun. She sucked her cigarettes and talked on the phone and drank her drinks. I had my own spot in the shade under the awning. Chloe the cat rarely made an appearance in the heat of the day, but when she did she made a point of completely ignoring Dutch. I left her alone, noting that as she sashayed around the edge of the pool she was spending more and more time gazing at me. I was not at all surprised when she finally came over to sniff at my face.

I wagged, but did not try to play with her. Dutch watched Chloe intently, but she had smacked him on the nose with her claw when he trapped her under a chair, which seemed to surprise him. Dutch obviously didn't understand that while we were both superior to cats, it's smarter to just leave them alone.

When the sun slipped down in the sky, Sylvia would wake up and let us inside but not Chloe, who would come and go not like a good dog but whenever she felt like it, mewing presumptuously at the door to be allowed inside.

Sylvia rarely had company. The first person we ever saw was a man, heavy and short and smelling like tangy food and a much stronger smoke than the one that clung to Sylvia. Dutch and I both pressed at the front door when Sylvia opened it.

"Hi, honey," murmured the man we would learn was named Mike. He carried flowers.

The flowers were put in a jar on the table, filling the house with their fragrance, and the two humans went to bed before sundown. Sylvia forgot to feed us. Dutch paced in the kitchen, sniffing along the floor, checking his bowl over and over, but I curled up to sleep. I had been hungry before. Dutch nosed me and I wagged, but I had no way of letting him know that things would be all right.

Dutch was part of my pack and I knew he was distressed. He missed Gavin and Taylor. He was hungry and did not understand why we were living with Sylvia and he was upset to share the backyard with a cat.

Mike and Sylvia liked to have loud conversations. The anger in their voices frightened Dutch and me. We sniffed each other and yawned and paced while it was going on.

We were especially frightened the time Sylvia picked up her glass and threw it at the wall, where it shattered loudly, the sharp, chemical Sylvia-smell running down the walls. We lowered our heads, feeling like bad dogs, and I saw Chloe streak down the back hallway. "You told me you paid it!" Sylvia shouted.

"I can't pay if I don't got any money, you stupid cow."

"You lied to me!"

"To get you to shut up! You're always talking, you know that, Sylvia, you just never stop moving your damn lips."

"So now what, they send the repo man for my car?" Sylvia put her hands on her hips.

"They're not going to repo that piece of junk," Mike declared dismissively.

I remembered when a man came to see Mom, and she was angry and she hit him and he crawled out the front door. This was an even louder fight, and I wondered if Sylvia would now hurt Mike and make him leave. Instead, though, Mike crossed the floor with his fist raised. There was a dull sound and Sylvia gasped. She cried out when he pushed her against the table, the now-dead flowers toppling and sour water draining off the table and sopping the carpet.

I felt that to be a good dog I needed to do No Barks, but everything was too bewildering for Dutch, who snarled and barked. Mike grabbed Sylvia's arms exactly the same way the crawling man grabbed Mom. "Stop it!" she shrieked.

Sylvia's distress and Mike's fury galvanized me and now I barked, too, and Dutch lunged, snapping his jaws in the air right in front of Mike's pants. Mike let go of Sylvia and fell back, knocking over a chair. We both kept barking.

"Jesus! Get the goddamn dogs off of me!"

"Try it. Try to hit me," Sylvia replied tauntingly.

"You know what? I don't need this. I don't need *you*."

Dutch and I did not know what to do now. This was

unfamiliar to both of us, the way we were threatening a human. We both stopped barking but Dutch was tense, growling, his lips back from his fangs, and I thought he might bite this man.

"Gonna sue you for all you got," Mike said.

"Oh yeah? Well good luck getting anything because you took all my money!"

"Kill you, Bella," he muttered. He walked heavily toward the door, staggering a little.

"That one's Dutch, you moron."

Having heard both our names, Dutch and I looked at Sylvia in confusion. Mike pushed the front door open and stumbled out into the front yard.

"Good dogs," Sylvia praised. We wagged with relief and were grateful when she gave us some meat from the refrigerator. Then she walked around her house, taking clothing and other items that smelled like Mike, opening the front door, and throwing the things outside. She remembered to feed us, but that night she fell down and slept on the floor in front of a chair in the living room. She smelled ill to me, and I lay pressed up against her, hoping I could provide her with some comfort. As I lay there, I thought about learning Go Home and Do Your Business. Lucas would do and say the same thing over and over. A dog was supposed to learn when things were repeated. On this day, I learned that when men were bad to women, the man would have to leave. I also now understood that, as upsetting as it was, a good dog should growl and snap when a bad man was hurting a woman.

Chloe had fled into Sylvia's room and did not come out, and a few days later I found out why when she suddenly was lying with some tiny kittens in her bed. The smell of milk burst from her and filled the room. Dutch, naturally, wanted to investigate, slinking into the bedroom and padding over to the cat bed with his tail stiff and his ears alert. Chloe hissed so fiercely that he thought better of it. When I cautiously approached, though, sniffing the new cats, Chloe did not react, just watched me with unwinking eyes. They were so bitty, making barely audible sounds as they pressed up against Chloe.

Their scent, and the flow of milk from Chloe's teats, was completely familiar. I instantly was taken back to the den, where I had kitten siblings and a Mother Cat. Then Lucas came to get me and I lived with him and slept in his bed, and we would feed the cats.

I missed Lucas so much in that moment that I went to the backyard and sat at the gate. I needed Lucas to come get me, though I could no longer feel him, or smell the town that was home. After a time, Dutch seemed to know what I was doing, and came and sat next to me. We sniffed each other, but could offer no comfort, because we each had a void only a person could fill. We did Sit to be good dogs.

The two of us waited for people who never arrived.

* * *

When the little kittens started scampering around, Dutch, of course, wanted to chase them. This upset Sylvia, who shouted at him and then put him on a leash, not for a walk but all the time, tying the rope to things in the backyard so that he could not move around much. The kittens learned that when Dutch was affixed to a chair by the table in the backyard they could play, but they knew how far that leash stretched and would not venture within reach. Dutch would lie in the pool of shadow under the table, gloomily watching them frolic.

I was not on a leash. "Be gentle, Bella," Sylvia would say whenever one of the kittens would launch an attack on me. I did not know what the words meant but I figured she was saying my name because I was playing with the kittens.

They were so little they barely weighed anything at all. I was very careful not to swipe them too roughly with my paw or to close my jaws on their tiny, frail bodies. Tussling with them brought back fond memories of Big Kitten on the trail, and I missed her and hoped she was taking care of herself. Big Kitten was the largest cat I had ever met, and these seemed like the smallest.

When they weren't jumping at me, the kitties were chasing and wrestling each other. They moved in bursts of energy, stopping just as suddenly, climbing all over in a constant game that didn't make any sense to a dog.

The days were hot. Sylvia went into her pool often, and on some occasions she would stay in the house with all the doors shut so that we couldn't smell if she was even still in there. A big machine hanging from her window made a loud noise and dripped cool water.

The kittens ignored the heat, but it exhausted me. I now regretted I hadn't been more firm with them, because whenever I decided to take a nap, they felt the time was perfect to climb on me with their tiny sharp claws.

They were much bigger now, but still very small. Chloe had stopped giving them milk, and they were much less cautious about Dutch. They clearly wanted to understand the dog on the rope, and Chloe had stopped correcting them whenever they strayed closer to the male dog. I was reminded of how my mother wouldn't let any of her litter leave the den, how when they got older, my kitten siblings were less and less likely to respect her boundaries.

Sylvia had received a box from a man at her front door and had carried it out to the yard so she could sip from her drink while she opened it. She took the contents with her into the house but left the box sitting on its side on a bench by the pool. The kittens were absolutely thrilled with the box, launching themselves up into it and vanishing inside. Most of the kittens were in there but the one I thought of as Brave Kitten, a black male slightly larger than the others, was testing the limits of Dutch's leash.

And Dutch was paying attention. He was no longer lying down; he had shaken himself and was now sitting, watching Brave Kitten approach. The little cat would skitter sideways, then turn and walk slowly and carefully closer to Dutch, then sit and lick himself.

When Dutch charged he had a low growl in his throat and his tail was wagging. He got to the end of his rope and the chair it was tied to toppled and he kept going. He was being a bad dog! Brave Kitten bolted across the yard, obviously terrified. Dutch pursued and the chair dragged behind him, right toward the box full of kittens on the bench. Brave Kitten veered and when Dutch changed course the chair he was pulling slammed into the bench by the pool and the box tumbled into the water.

Hung up with the tangle of the chair and the bench slowing him down, Dutch barked. Brave Kitten disappeared around the corner of the house.

The box with the kittens in it was floating, open end up, in the middle of the pool.

* * *

The kittens were mewing in distress; I could hear them in the box, which was shaking in the water—they were clearly climbing all over each other inside the thing. Their keening instantly drew Chloe, who came running at the pitiful wails. Dutch was hung up on one side of the pool, his head down, though he perked up as Chloe flashed past him. She half-circled the water, stopping when she came close to the tangle that was the rope and the chair and the dog, and reversing back the other way. Chloe made a fearful noise—a small, tight cry. Her kittens were in danger, but she seemed afraid to go in after them.

A little head popped up at the edge of the box, falling

back down inside. They were trying to get out but that was not what they should do, because then they would be in the water. Cats should not go into the pool. Even Big Kitten was afraid to swim!

I was a good dog who had learned No Barks but I barked now, urgently. We needed a person!

After I barked both Dutch and I looked at the big glass doors, but Sylvia did not come outside. The machine hummed and dripped, the kittens cried, and the box tilted to one side as they moved around within it.

Then a small gray kitty appeared at the top of the box, clinging to the edge, looking terrified. She clambered for purchase and the box tipped wildly, spilling her into the pool. She went under, and then popped up, sputtering and trying to swim, batting her front paws at the surface. Chloe howled again.

I dove in. The splash swept over the top of the little kitty's head, but I swam with strong strokes and was there in an instant. I gently snagged her behind her neck with my front teeth, holding her up into the air, and turned back to the edge of the pool, where Chloe was waiting anxiously. I placed the kitten onto the cement and Chloe began licking her.

Taking care of cats was something Lucas and I just did.

When I turned back the box was now floating on its side. Panicking, two more kittens had plunged out into the water. One of them was swimming strongly but the other had gone completely under. I powered forward and ducked my face, my mouth open, grabbing the tiny cat and hauling her to the surface. I swam to the side of the pool, the kitten hanging limply from my mouth, but she came alive when I placed her next to her mother. The little kitty mewed plaintively and Chloe carried her off to safety.

The tiniest member of the litter was barely able to keep her nose up, struggling feebly to survive. I grabbed her and took her to her mother, and then went after another one.

The box was now empty, but two little wet balls of fur had made it to the side of the pool and were anxiously bobbing along the edge, making barely audible peeping sounds, unable to climb out on their own. They fled from me as best they could when I went after them, but I tenderly snagged each in turn and lifted them up onto the cement, and they ran squalling to Chloe.

That was the last one. The kitties were wet, but safe. Chloe was tending to them. Dutch had gone back to looking glum.

I swam to the side of the pool, hooked my front paws on the cement, and struggled to lift myself. As I rose, my back arched, and my rear legs cycled uselessly beneath me, finding no purchase. Trembling, I held myself there for a moment, straining with all my might, water dripping down, and then I fell back.

I coursed back and forth, trying to get out, but it was no use—the side of the pool was too high. I made another effort, but simply could not haul my body out of the water. I was like the kittens, swimming around the edge of the pool, unable to save myself.

Time passed and I was getting tired, but I could not stop swimming because when I slowed, I could feel my body settling tail-first deeper into the water. Dutch was watching me, panting a little. I wondered if he could feel that I was becoming afraid. I swam and swam, back and forth, back and forth. I did not know what to do.

I swam to the box and tried to climb on top of it, but it just collapsed under me.

Chloe was under a tree, licking her kittens. Dutch lay by the side of the pool and let out an anxious, barely audible whine as he watched me. I swam and swam. My legs were aching. Water filled my nose and I sneezed.

If my Lucas was there he would come in and get me.

He would put his arms around me and lift me out. He would take care of me. But Lucas wasn't here. I had failed to Go Home and now I was having trouble keeping my face above the surface. My muscles were so, so weak now.

I felt like a bad dog.

Twenty-one

I was barely moving, water in my ears and flooding my nose, when I heard the sliding glass door open. "Dutch! What did you do?" Sylvia scolded. She came out and stood looking at Dutch with her hands on her hips, and he hung his head. She came down to where I was swimming.

"Bella? Why are you in the pool? Come out of there!"

I heard the word "come" so I tried one more time to climb out, my forelegs on the cement, but I quickly fell back, utterly exhausted. I looked up apologetically at Sylvia.

"Oh, sweetie, no, not there. Come here, come here," Sylvia called, clapping her hands as she walked to the other end of the pool. I used what little strength I had to paddle in this new direction. She kicked off her shoes and stepped into the pool, sinking only to her ankles. "The steps are over here, Bella. You have to use the steps."

I heard my name and wondered what it meant. My back end was sinking, pulling me down. Then my rear legs struck ground, my front paws following a moment later. I

no longer had to swim to keep my head above water!
"Okay, good girl, good dog."

I was a good dog but my legs were shaking and I could
not manage to climb any higher. My coat was heavy, rain-
ing a steady stream of water into the pool. I was barely
strong enough to stay upright on what seemed to be underwater steps.

"What's the matter, Bella? Are you sick?" Sylvia leaned
down and looked at me and I beat the water with my tail
a little. "Come on, now."

I just wanted to stand there and recover, but Sylvia
slapped her thighs and I obeyed. Forcing my reluctant legs
into action, I heaved myself out of the water, shook, and
lay down right there in the sun, feeling warmth from the
cement. Sylvia went to untangle Dutch.

I knew that I would be asleep within moments, but before I could do so I felt a tiny touch, and then another. I
lazily opened my eyes and there were the kittens, sniffing
at me, their small noses bumping against my side. I was
too fatigued to even wag my tail.

* * *

When the kittens were a little older, they left, departing
one at a time. Sylvia would come into the yard and scoop
up a kitty and we would never see it again. I could not tell
how Chloe felt about the slow reduction in her family,
though I did notice that with every parting she seemed
more attentive to those offspring remaining.

I thought about Big Kitten, who probably did not know
I was living with Sylvia and Dutch and Chloe's cat family.
What would she think of such small kitties? I wondered if
Big Kitten missed me, which made me miss her.

Dutch seemed resolved to the same conclusion I had
come to, which was that Gavin and Taylor were never coming back. I was fond of both men, but for me, their ab-
sences just made me ache for Lucas all the more—until I

was able to do Go Home, the people in my life would keep changing, moving in and out as people do. For Dutch, though, his sadness left him without energy. When all the kittens were gone and it was just Chloe, traipsing past the dog within leash distance, Dutch's eyes flickered but he didn't even bother to get to his feet. He just wanted to lie still, day after day, under the table in the searing heat and then, as the air cooled, he would sprawl in a patch of sunlight a short distance away.

Other than the cats and the weather there were no changes. Sylvia never let us out of the gate, never threw a ball, but she fed us and talked to us and let us sleep wherever we wanted in the house at night. For whatever reason, Dutch did not want Sylvia to be his person, though he would wag when she had us do Sit for treats.

I was surprised when Dutch suddenly lurched to his feet, showing more energy than he had in many, many days. I watched him curiously as he went to the gate and sat; he had not done that in a long time.

I yawned and stood up, shaking myself off. His sudden change from drowsy dog to being so completely alert puzzled me.

Dutch whined. I went over to sniff him curiously, but he didn't react to me; he was focused on the gate.

I sat and scratched my ear. That morning there had been steam rising from the pool, but otherwise, I could think of nothing different. Chloe spent most of her time sleeping under her chair in the living room and was there now.

Dutch started wagging his tail. I heard a car stop, a door open, and then came a voice at the same time I smelled the person. "Dutch! Bella!"

Gavin. Gavin had come back.

Gavin pushed open the gate and Dutch tackled him, whimpering, jumping up and licking him. "Whoa! Good boy! Down! I missed you, too!"

In that moment I understood that Gavin was Dutch's person, just as Lucas was mine.

"Hey, Bella!"

I went to Gavin, wagging, and he stroked my fur, kissing me on the nose. "Oh, I missed you so, so much." He straightened. "Hi, Mom."

I was less surprised to hear Gavin mention Mom than I had been the first time. Sylvia had come out. She was smoking and had one of her sharp-smelling drinks in her hand. "Where's your boyfriend?"

"Husband. Taylor's my husband, Mom."

"Sure."

"Are you . . . what's wrong?" Gavin went to kiss her and then stepped back. "Wow, Mom, it's not even noon."

"Don't start. You have no idea what's been going on. Mike stole my checkbook again and now I'm in trouble for NSF, like that's reasonable."

"Mike's back?"

"God no, I told him I would get a restraining order again. I don't know how he got his hands on the checks. He might have taken them from my car because when I lost my keys I decided not to lock it anymore."

"Okay."

Dutch was sitting patiently at Gavin's feet, ready for a car ride or a walk or a nap. I sniffed the air, smelling Taylor faintly, but I knew he wasn't close by.

"You guys ready to go home?" Gavin asked us.

I whipped my head up and stared at Gavin. Go Home?

"First thing tomorrow," Gavin said.

Sylvia went to sit down in a chair and it nearly toppled over. Gavin grabbed her arm.

"I'm okay!" she snapped.

"Yes, I know, sorry. Just trying to help," Gavin said apologetically. There was a little sadness in his voice.

Sylvia sipped her drink. "You have to leave tomorrow?"

"Well, there's just so much to do. We thought we had

everything organized before we left—you know Taylor, he plans everything—but there's a lot of stuff we need to tend to. How were the dogs?"

"It was nice to have them around. Scared Mike off," Sylvia replied.

"Maybe you should get a dog," Gavin observed.

Dutch and I glanced at each other at the word "dog."

"I actually would prefer Bella. She doesn't bark. Dutch keeps harassing Chloe."

There was a long silence. "Mom? I'm not sure . . . you mean you would want to keep Bella?"

"Of the two, yes."

"Oh. Huh. That never occurred to me," Gavin replied.

* * *

That night Dutch and I slept with Gavin down the hallway from Sylvia's room. Dutch kept nosing Gavin's hand, wanting more strokes, while I curled up at his feet and drowsily listened to him talk to us with his phone pressed to his face.

"I hate it, too, but we do owe her," he said. "And I would feel safer, knowing she had Bella here to protect her."

I glanced up at my name. Gavin listened for a moment. "No," he chuckled, "this isn't a ploy, though it might give you something to look forward to when we do visit." I put my head down. "I think they'll both be okay, I really do. Bella is Bella—always content no matter where she is."

I closed my eyes, ignoring the repetition of my name. Go Home. That's all I could think of. I was tired of being here and just wanted to finally do Go Home. It was a pain, a hunger, and I took Gavin's return as a sign I would soon be on my way to Lucas.

* * *

The next morning Gavin put things in his car and Dutch followed on his heels, sitting expectantly at the front door whenever he went outside. "Don't worry, Dutch, you're going home with me," Gavin said soothingly, petting Dutch on the head.

Sylvia came out of her room, blowing a cloud of smoke into the air. "Snowing up in the mountains yet?"

"Not yet. Roads will be clear the whole way. Mom, I can't thank you enough for taking care of the dogs while we were gone. I really, really appreciate it."

Sylvia looked at him for a long moment. "I'm not a great mother."

"Oh, Mom . . ."

"I mean, I knew I wouldn't be, and I never intended to have kids, I just kept getting pregnant. But I'm trying to, to do better. To be better at it. I regret . . . things."

Gavin went over and gave Sylvia a hug. While he embraced her she lifted her cigarette to her mouth over his shoulder.

"I should have gone to your wedding, Gavin. I know I had to show up for the subpoena and blah blah but that was really just an excuse to get out of it. That was a mistake. We're family, you and me and Taylor and sometimes your sister."

"I know it was hard for you, Mom. It's okay."

"I didn't understand about the gay thing but I've been watching television and realize what I was taught growing up isn't right. You are my son and I'm proud of you."

They hugged each other some more. She sucked on the cigarette and it flared and dumped more smoke into the air.

"So." Gavin took in a deep breath. "What you said about Bella. I talked to Taylor, and he agrees it's a good idea."

"What is?"

"Bella."

"Bella?"

I heard my name and wondered what it meant.

"She can stay here."

"Stay here," Sylvia repeated.

"Right. We hate to separate them, and we'll miss her, but like I told you, Dutch and Bella just sort of showed up at the same moment—they were never together before that. They're not a dog family."

"What are you saying?" she asked blankly.

"Sorry?"

"You want Bella to stay here?"

I heard "Bella" and "stay" so I sat.

"Right. That's what you want, right?"

"No. Of course not." Sylvia blew smoke.

"Mom, you asked me yesterday if you could keep Bella."

"I said no such thing. I said she was a good dog. Plays with Chloe. I have been stuck here for half a year because of these dogs. I'd like to travel, maybe go to Bloomfield."

"Okay."

"If you don't want Bella you're going to have to find a different home than mine."

"No, we *love* Bella. I just . . . never mind. It's okay."

*   *   *

We did a car ride for a long time, but the best part was when we crested a hill and the smell came to me: home, the place where Lucas and I lived. Drifting on the air was the unique mix of scents that meant home, and now I had my bearings. I knew where I needed to go.

Taylor was happy to see us, and we were put on leashes and taken for the first walk in a long, long time. Dutch was ecstatic, marking everything in sight. "They both got so *fat,*" Taylor said disgustedly.

"We'll put them on a diet soon, but let's give them a chance to readjust. They probably are confused and miss Sylvia," Gavin said.

"It's hard to argue with something so completely deranged as that statement." Taylor chuckled. "So, cabin this weekend? I'd love to get some hiking in before the snow hits."

The next time we took a car ride my nose told me where we were going before we got there: the cabin. Dutch lifted his leg all along the dead plants in the backyard, insulted that his scents had faded, while I held my nose aloft and searched for Big Kitten. I could smell many animals, but not her.

"Want to go for a hike?" Taylor asked the next morning. I recognized the words but did not understand their meaning without Lucas. "Come on, Dutch."

The men snapped leashes onto our collars and led us outdoors. For a time the path was familiar, but soon we turned uphill and were headed into an area where I had never been before. Dutch marked as often as they would let him—they usually tugged on his leash when he tried to stop to lift his leg.

"Are we okay here, do you think?" Gavin asked.

"Sure. I mean, if we run into a forest ranger we'll have to pay a fine if they are off leash."

"Have you ever seen a forest ranger? Except in your fantasies, I mean."

"Funny." Taylor knelt down and unsnapped my leash, stuffing it into the sack on his back. Gavin did the same with Dutch.

For a time, the sensation of going for a walk without a leash was so strange I stayed close to the two men, who were laughing and talking. Eventually, though, Dutch loped ahead, struck by a scent I didn't detect. I trotted to keep up with him.

"Don't go far!" Gavin called.

Free and running together, energy coursed through us and Dutch and I took off, galloping down the trail. I smelled a rabbit and wondered if Dutch had ever seen one.

I remembered Big Kitten bringing rabbit meat. I remembered being on a long hilly trail like this one. I remembered Go Home.

I remembered Lucas.

Spurred on by each other's energy, we raced ahead on the path, but we both halted abruptly when we heard Taylor.

"Dutch! Bella!" he yelled.

Dutch and I nosed each other, panting from our sprint. He looked back toward where we could smell the two men, and then at me. I understood that he sensed something in me, a change in my intention, but he could not comprehend what.

I wagged my tail. I liked Dutch. He had been a member of my pack. He loved Gavin and Taylor and they loved him. But their home was not mine, and now it was time for me to move on.

When Taylor called again, Dutch took a long, lingering look at me and turned back the way we'd come. After a few steps, he stopped and gazed at me expectantly. I didn't move. We both heard our names, this time in Gavin's voice, and Dutch seemed to get it then. He stared, perhaps not believing I would forgo a wonderful life with the two men, or perhaps just realizing we might never see each other again.

But he couldn't ignore Gavin. Regret and confusion in his eyes, he left me and went back to be with his family.

I continued on in the other direction.

Twenty-two

For a long time, I was aware of Dutch, his scent pursuing me as I followed the trail. I knew he would be happy with Gavin and Taylor—especially with Gavin, who was Dutch's Lucas. If not for Dutch, I might not have been able to leave the two men, but I felt good, knowing they had a dog.

I had not been for such an extended walk since before we stayed with Sylvia, but this was all familiar—trekking down a path beaten into the ground by people and animals, covering the terrain as it rose and fell and went from rocky to wooded to grassy to dusty.

Much sooner than I would have expected, I was tired and thirsty, my leg muscles demanding rest. I found a protected place to lie down, yawning, feeling exhausted. Sleep didn't come easily—I had forgotten all the animal smells that arrived on the night air, and a fox's scream jolted me alert a few times. I wanted to think about Lucas, but my memory took me to Dutch and Gavin and

Taylor, and Big Kitten and Chloe, and I missed all of them. I felt alone—very, very alone.

The weather was dry and crisp. The trail was doing me the favor of pointing directly at the scent of home, but I knew I needed water, and reluctantly veered away from the path and headed toward where my nose told me I would find a stream.

I also smelled something else: burned wood. Not smoke like from Sylvia's mouth or when Taylor and Gavin had a fire inside the hole in the wall in their cabin, but the clear tang of wood remnants when the flames have long died out. Tracking the water, I soon came to a vast, yellow-grassed area where most of the trees poking skyward were coated all along their trunks with this odor. Most of them were stark black and sported no leaves, and many were lying flat on the ground. I sniffed curiously at one of them, not understanding what could possibly have occurred to cause so many charred logs.

When the clear feral stench of a coyote came faintly to me from the forest of burned wood, I turned away.

* * *

After two days of steady progress, I was miserably hungry. I had followed my nose to water and had come across a pretty large lake, but I had to cross a busy road to get to it and I felt like a bad dog as the vehicles roared past. There were no trees, just rocks and some scrub, so I was exposed as I drank.

I wanted my Tiny Piece of Cheese. It wasn't the treat I craved, it was the love and attention from my person.

I felt lost.

The cars on the road meant people, and I could smell a town nearby. It would take me away from the most direct route home, but I needed to eat, and where there were people there was food. I stayed as far from the road as I could, which was, for some time, fairly easy—the area well to the side was flat and a shallow stream flowed through the rocks and the road followed along its banks. Then the soil seemed to moisten and the brush became thicker. I began encountering farms, which I skirted, ignoring the dogs who barked at me in outrage or disbelief.

It was dark when I came to streets with homes and shops. I smelled food cooking; the odors were tantalizing on the air, but I did not see a dog pack sitting outside any place I came to. I found some large bins with delicious, fragrant bits of edible meats in them, but they were too tall for me to climb up into.

I was soon attracted to a large building with many cars parked in front of it. Light poured out through large windows that lined up across the entire front of the building. Adult humans pushed carts filled with food and sometimes a child or two, unloading bags into cars and then pushing the carts away and abandoning them. When I approached I saw people going in and out of the building, and it seemed the doors opened without anyone touching them. And every time the big doors eased open, seductive aromas danced out onto the air.

The most enticing of these wonderful smells was chicken. There were chickens cooking in there.

People looked at me but did not call me as I went closer and closer to the big doors, drawn by the tantalizing fragrances. None of them seemed to want to put me on a leash and keep me from Lucas—mostly they completely ignored me. A little boy called "doggie" and held out his hand in my direction, and the scent of sweetness was strong on his fingers, but before I could go lick them his mother snatched his arm away.

None of the people mattered to me at that moment as much as the fact that just inside those doors was some chicken.

I sat for a while and drank in the waves of deliciousness every time the doors parted with a whoosh, but no one brought anything for a good dog who was doing Sit.

When a long time passed with no one coming out, I grew impatient and went closer to the glass doors to look in and see if I could locate the source of the chicken aromas.

The doors opened.

I stood on the threshold, unsure what to do. The doors seemed to be waiting for me, the way Lucas would hold the door whenever we got home from a walk. It was as if I was *invited*. And right inside, directly in front of me, was a metal display with shelves. Heat from lights above the shelves pushed the wonderful smell of roasting chicken out into the night air. I saw bags with cooking chickens in them, and they were there, right there!

I slunk into the brightly lit building, feeling guilty. I could already taste the chicken, could imagine chewing and swallowing, and licked my lips. I hesitantly crossed a slick floor, and then I was at the display. I stood on my rear legs, trembling, and reached for a bag. The warmth from the lights made me blink as I carefully took the bag with just my front teeth.

"Hey!" someone shouted.

I looked up and a man wearing white was coming around a corner. He seemed angry.

I dropped the chicken and it fell to the ground.

Food on the ground is always for a dog unless someone says no. "Scat!" the man yelled, which was not the same thing. I picked up the bag and turned away.

The doors were closed.

I wanted to get away from the man, who was bearing down on me. I darted forward, looking through the window for someone to come from outside and open the doors. "Stop! Dog!" the man in white shouted. I went to scratch the door and the doors opened! The night air poured in and I ran out, galloping away with my dinner in my jaws.

My instinct was to run and run, but I was too hungry to do more than escape to a puddle of darkness at the edge of the paved parking lot. I could have this meal all to myself—there was no Big Kitten to share it with. I tore into the bag and the warm, juicy chicken was so delicious I licked the plastic completely clean.

It felt good to have food in my stomach, but I couldn't stop thinking about what I had seen on the shelf when I had been in the building: more bags with more chickens. Now that I knew where they were and how to get them, I wanted nothing more than to go back into the building.

I trotted up to the door. The man had been angry at me, but those chickens were just sitting there. When he yelled I felt like a bad dog, but those chickens seemed left out for me—how bad could I be if my actions led to chicken?

I approached the door. A woman came out, pushing a little cart, and only glanced at me. *She* didn't think I was a bad dog.

When the doors eased shut I moved closer and they opened and I smelled the chickens and went inside as if Lucas had called me. I went straight to the steel shelves with the warm lights and the succulent odors.

"Gotcha!" a man yelled.

I turned and looked. It was the same man, and he stood between me and the door, his arms out as if to give me a hug.

I snatched a chicken, and took off running.

• • •

My fear came from the sure knowledge that the man in white was one of those who would keep me from Lucas. He was angry, and I remembered the man with the hat and the truck with the crates and the cries of pain and grief from all the dogs in the room where no one did No Barks. Angry men hurt dogs. This man might hurt me, might put me back in that horrible place.

I ran, but where could I go? Only humans can find ways in and out of buildings. The floor underneath my claws was slippery, and I scrabbled for purchase, seeing people stare at me as I galloped along rows and rows of shelves.

I still had the chicken. It was *my* chicken now. All I wanted to do was find a place to tear into the bag and eat it, but people were yelling, yelling at *me*. I had to get away!

"Get him! Catch the dog!" the man in white bellowed.

A boy with a broom in his hands ran at me so I turned, sliding, and frantically dashed down between tall shelves. A man with a cart called, "Here, boy," and seemed friendly but I shot past him. All I could smell was the chicken in my jaws and all I could feel was my panic. Everyone thought I was a bad dog who needed to be punished.

"Here!" another man shouted as I came to the end of the passageway between shelves. He waved his arms at me and I skittered to a halt and I nearly fell before I gained traction and backed wildly away.

"Got you!" It was the man in the white clothes, right behind me, running hard. I bounded forward, toward the man waving his arms, then jinked to one side. His hand brushed the fur on my neck. The man in white tried to change direction and crashed into a cardboard shelf and little plastic containers rained down, bounding all over the floor. He slid, falling in a heap.

I smelled the outdoors and scampered in that direction, but when I got there I was not outside; I was in a part of the building that only carried the *aroma* of outside: dirt and plants and flowers. Fruits I recognized from when Lucas would eat them gave off their strong fragrances— oranges and apples. There were no angry people here, so I dropped the chicken, ripped open the bag, and bolted down some of it. Humans were such wonderful creatures that they could hunt chickens and cook them and set them out in warm bags!

I heard running footsteps. The angry men, including the

one in white clothes and the boy with the broom, were sprinting for me. I seized my dinner and darted to one side and the boy slammed into a table and a whole pile of oranges cascaded down on the floor with soft, dull impacts. They rolled like balls but I did not pause. I took off toward where there were fishes and meats, cold air pouring from the walls.

"Get him!" someone yelled. There were now even more people hunting me.

I turned up past fragrant breads and cheeses. There was so much food here! This was the most amazing place I had ever been, except for the attitudes of the people toward dogs. I would have loved to sniff every shelf, but I could hear the angry men closing in on me.

I was back to a familiar place—the shelves of delicious chickens were directly in front of me. I rushed past it. A woman carrying a sack in her arms was strolling away and I heard a whoosh as the doors parted for her and the night breeze wafted in.

"No!" someone howled.

I knew that word but felt it clearly did not apply to me under these circumstances. The woman, though, stopped and turned, so perhaps the "No!" was about her behavior. I ran right past her, just brushing against her legs. "Wow!" she said.

"Stop the dog!" commanded the now-familiar voice of the man in white.

"Doggie?" the woman tentatively called after me.

I was still afraid. I loped into the darkness, deliberately putting the wonderful food building directly behind me. I found a street with a few houses on it, but kept going. Finally, when I heard a dog challenge me from a backyard, I knew I was in a safe place, a place that *liked* dogs. I stopped, panting, and eased down onto my belly and crunched through the rest of my dinner.

. . .

When I awoke a light layer of snow was falling. A cramp seized my stomach and I did Do Your Business in a painful, violent fashion. Afterward I scooted my butt along the snow and felt somewhat better.

I was still processing the feeling that I had somehow been a very bad dog. When I thought about the man in white the fear came back to me easily, and I was anxious and a little sick. I padded silently through the snow, wary of people, worried someone would want to hurt me, or catch me and take me away.

Cooking food floated seductively on the air currents, magnetically drawing me forward. For a time I sat at a back door, waiting for someone to come out with something delicious—I could smell bacon, and thought that for a good dog doing Sit a piece or two might be available, but no one noticed me. Possibly I needed a dog pack with me to receive such kind attention.

I spent the day moving cautiously between houses, sniffing hopefully at plastic bins with food smells wafting from them, but not finding any with an open lid. The sun melted the snow, and the streets were wet and the houses dripping in a patter that filled the air with sound and the clean, cold smell of water. Several times I touched noses with friendly dogs behind fences and other times I ignored dogs who took fierce offense at my presence.

I did not eat until late in the day, when I passed a garage door that was raised just enough for me to squeeze under. A mostly empty bag of dog food yawned open in the corner and I buried my head in it, ignoring the outraged yowling of two dogs on the other side of a door.

Eating dog food reminded me of Lucas. I recalled the excitement that came with him setting the dish on the floor in front of me, how grateful I was, how full of love I was for the man who was giving me dinner with his hand. Homesickness gripped me as powerfully as the cramps I had awakened with that morning, and I knew I would soon be leaving this town to get back on the trail.

I was learning, though, that I needed to eat whenever the opportunity presented itself. It might be many days before my next meal. When darkness fell I went to the street with the most food smells. The night was bringing a cold with it, and I remembered being in the hills with Big Kitten. I would have to hunt like her to feed myself. But I would do whatever I needed to do to be a Go Home dog.

A man was sitting on the sidewalk on blankets in a pool of light falling from a lamp overhead. "Hey, dog," he called softly as I made to avoid him.

My first instinct was to flee. I paused, though, hearing something in the voice that sounded friendly.

The man smelled of dirt and beef and sweat. The hair on his face and head was long and tangled. He had plastic sacks piled up next to him on one side and a suitcase like Taylor's on the other. His wore a glove with no fingers, which he extended in my direction. "Here, puppy," he said gently.

I hesitated. He sounded nice, and because he was lying there with his legs extended and his back to the building behind him instead of standing with his arms out or a leash in his hands, did not seem like the sort of person who would try to keep me from doing Go Home.

He dug into a small box and extended a piece of beef in my direction and I went to him, wagging. The beef treat had cheese on it! I gobbled it quickly and did Sit.

"Good dog," he praised. He apparently recognized a good Sit when he saw it. He dug into his box and came up with another chunk of meat. He ran his hand over my fur and briefly held my collar, squinting at it. "Bella," he said.

I wagged. Most people who knew my name would give

me treats. The people in the building with the chickens had not known me, which might explain why they were so angry.

"What are you doing out by yourself? Are you lost, Bella?"

I heard the question in his voice and looked pointedly at the box by his side. Yes, I would be happy to have more beef with cheese.

"I've been lost," the man stated softly after a moment. He reached into one of his sacks, digging around. I watched attentively.

"Hey, here, would you like these?" He fed me a handful of nuts and while I was chewing them he played with my collar some more. When I was finished I realized I now had a stretchy cord tied to my collar. Alarmed, I tried to move away from the man, but was not able to go far before the rope flexed taut.

The man and I gazed at each other. A small whimper escaped my lips.

I had made a terrible mistake.

Twenty-three

The man owned a pushcart like the ones people used in the parking lot to ferry food and children to their cars, but he had no children and most of what he stuffed into the cart in plastic bags was not food. "Go for a walk," the man would say nearly every day, loading everything off the sidewalk into the cart. I longed to walk, to get away up into the hills, but we rarely went far. Usually we would stroll up the street to a flat yard with pieces of plastic and metal in it strewn across the soil, and I would squat to do Do Your Business and then we would return to the place by the wall where he would spread his blankets. Next to the wall was a metal fence, and when the man would leave me he would tie me there. Most of the time he went across the street to one of several buildings—one smelled of food, and one smelled of nothing I could detect except people and boxes. When he emerged from this second place he would be carrying a glass bottle and when he cracked it open the pungent tang reminded me of Sylvia.

Mostly we just sat. The man would talk to me almost

constantly, repeating my name every so often but mostly just droning words I did not recognize.

"I am not stupid. I know what you did to me. I know who you are. But these are *my* thoughts!" he would say repeatedly. "They are not in charge. I am in charge. Cease transmission."

When people approached, the man would quiet himself. "Just need money for my dog," he would say softly. "Need to buy food for her." People would stop to pet me and talk to me but none of them untied me. Many times they would drop things into a small can and the man would say "Thank you."

Several of the people said the word "Axel," and after a time I knew that was the man's name. Axel.

Why Axel slept on the sidewalk and not in his house, I did not know. He seemed very lonely—he needed a friend the way Gavin had Taylor. But no one who stopped to talk acted like that sort of friend, even if they were nice.

At first I only wanted to get away from Axel, to get back to Go Home. But then I came to understand that Axel needed comfort, just as Mack and my other friends at Go to Work needed me. At night, Axel wrestled with people I could not see, shouting at them, squirming in his bed, his fear strong on his sweat. When I put my head on his chest I could feel his heart pound. But then, when his hand found my fur, his fevered agitation would quiet, and his breathing would slow.

I liked Axel. He talked to me all day and told me I was a good dog. After living with Sylvia, it was nice to receive so much attention. I felt very important when I was with Axel.

I wanted so much to do Go Home, but I knew I was doing what Lucas would want, just as taking care of Big Kitten was what he would have wanted. More than anything, more even than Go Home, Lucas wanted me to be a good dog. And I was never more of a good dog than when I provided comfort for a scared person or kitten who needed it. It was my job.

Nights were getting colder, so something else I could do was keep Axel warm by pressing up against him. I also alerted him when a car pulled up in the street and two men slid out of the front seat. I had met their kind before: they had heavy, odd-smelling objects on their hips—police. I associated them with the truck with the outdoor crates that came to take me away from Lucas. I cringed at their approach, and Axel woke up.

"Hey, Axel," one of them said, kneeling down. "When did you get a dog?" He held out his hand toward me but I did not approach, not trusting this man.

"Found her. Abandoned," Axel replied curtly.

"Huh. Well, you sure she's okay? Doesn't seem very friendly."

"Bella. Say hi to Officer Mendez."

"It's okay, Bella," said the man with the outstretched hand. I sniffed his fingers, wagging a little, wary that he might grab for my collar. "My name is Tom."

"How can we assist you today, officer?" Axel asked.

"Don't be like that, Axel. You know my name is Tom."

"Tom."

It seemed the nice police's name was Tom. Tom's friend stood back, writing something down.

"So Axel, winter's right around the corner. Have you thought about what I said, going back to Denver? We're still willing to drive you. I think it's a really good idea."

"What about my dog?" Axel asked.

"She could go. Of course." Tom nodded agreeably.

"And then what?"

Tom shrugged. "Well, look. You could go back to the VA—"

"I'm not doing that," Axel interrupted calmly. "Last time I was there they tried to take my blood."

"It's a hospital, Axel."

"Hospital. Hospitality. Yet there are people in there who have never been tried, never convicted, who *can't get out*. They're hooked up to medical amplifiers that interface with the Internet via TCP/IP protocols. Why do you suppose they do that? An electrophysiological monitor provides two-way transmission to the Web, and that doesn't seem suspicious to you? The *World Wide* Web?"

Tom was quiet for a moment. "We just don't have any way to help you here. No one can live outside in the winter, not here, it's just too cold. And Gunnison doesn't have the facilities, and you won't let any of the charities assist you."

"They all want the same thing from me," Axel said flatly.

"Everyone *cares* about you, Axel. You served our country. You helped us, and now we want to help you."

Axel pointed at the sky. "Do you know that at any given moment you have three satellites triangulating you? But their algorithms won't work on me because I live at random. I am off the pattern. I am not on the *grid*. I won't eat their genetically modified food."

"Okay . . ." Tom started to say.

"When you go to a coffee shop they want your name, did you ever stop to think why? Why do they need your name? For a cup of coffee? And they put it into their *computer*? That's just one of a thousand ways you are being tracked." Axel was speaking rapidly and I could feel him getting anxious and I nosed his hand to let him know I was right there.

"Are you using again, Axel?" Tom asked softly.

Axel looked away. Now he felt furious. I nosed him again. I just wished he would be happy.

"Well." The nice police stood. I wagged, understanding from his motion that he would not try to take me with him. "Keep in mind what I said, Axel. I can't make you get help, but I wish you would see how much people care. If you try to live outside all winter, you and your dog will *die*. Please, please think about it." He reached in his pocket and put something in the can. "Take it easy, Axel."

* * *

Without warning, Axel packed up his cart and we trudged across town to a park. We moved into his house, but it was very odd: a place with a roof and no walls, with several tables but no food. The yard was huge and there were several slides, but I did not show Axel I knew how to climb them because I was always on the leash.

Sometimes other dogs came to the park and I whined, longing to run with them. Axel did not mind when they trotted over to me but I was not allowed to follow when they dashed off after balls and children.

"They're tagged, Bella. They've all got chips in them," he told me. I heard a finality in the way he said my name and knew I would not be allowed to play.

Other people came to see us. They all carried sacks and bags, and often they drank from sharp-smelling Sylvia bottles, passing them around and talking and laughing. The fireplace was a metal box on a pole; it reminded me of the time when I found a big slab of meat set out for me in a park and a baby watched me take it. They burned wood in the box, standing in front of it and holding their hands out to the heat.

"*Damn* it's getting cold," a man named Riley liked to say. I liked Riley, he had very gentle hands and his breath smelled like Mother Cat's. "Gotta get south before I'm on the wrong side of winter."

People—there were three men besides Axel—nodded and murmured affirmatively.

"Not leaving," Axel replied tersely.

They all glanced at each other.

"You can't stay here, Axel. Starting December it never gets above freezing. Lotta days it's *below zero*," Riley said.

"Not leaving. Not again. I'm safe here."

"No, you're not," another man stated definitively. He had just arrived and I did not know his name but people had been calling him Don't Drink All of It Dammit. "Your dog and you are gonna freeze to death."

Often the people passed around something small and thin like a pencil. They would point the tip of the pencil at their arms and then everyone would laugh and then they'd nap. I felt a deep peace come over Axel at such times, but for some reason was very anxious at how solidly he would sleep regardless of the temperature. I would arrange myself to keep him warm, waiting for him to wake up.

Lucas had pencils, too, but I did not remember him ever poking his arm with one.

When the people left it was as a group, carrying their bags the way Taylor did when he would depart for several days.

"You're not going to make it, man. Please come with us," Riley said urgently.

Axel petted me. "Staying."

"You're a stupid bastard and you deserve to die," laughed Don't Drink All of It Dammit. Axel made a quick gesture with his hand and the man laughed again, an ugly sound that caused the hair to rise on the back of my neck.

The house with no walls felt lonely with just the two of us. I was glad whenever we went to the town and sat on our blankets on the sidewalk. Many people would stop to speak to us. Some gave me treats and sometimes they would give Axel bags of dog food.

One man sat on the blankets and spoke to Axel for a long time. "It's going to go into the single digits tonight, Axel. Won't you come to the church? You could shower. For the dog, if nothing else."

"It is not a true church. The word does not travel beyond its doors," Axel replied.

"What can I do for you then?"

"I do not need the help of someone like you," Axel told him coldly. He stood and began shoving things into his cart and I knew we were going back to the park.

When we arrived, four cars were in the parking lot and there were people in the house with no walls, but I could smell none of them were Riley. One of them broke away from the group and walked over to us. It was the friendly police, Tom. "Hi, Axel. Hello, Bella." He rubbed my chest and I wagged.

"I've done nothing wrong," Axel replied.

"I know. It's okay. Can you come here to the pavilion a minute? It's okay. Axel, come on, I promise. Nothing bad's going to happen."

Stiffly, Axel followed Tom over to where the people stood. There was a little cloth house lying on some pads under the roof of the home with no walls, some plastic chests, and a flat metal box. Tom waved at the people and they backed away, so it was just Axel and the police standing with me. "Okay, look here, Axel." Tom held the flap door open on the cloth house. "See? The tent's designed for the arctic. That's a propane stove in there. You've got a mountaineering sleeping bag. Coolers got food, and the cookstove has an electric lighter."

I sniffed curiously at the interior of the cloth house.

"What's this all about?" Axel demanded harshly.

Tom pressed his lips together. "Look, when you left for Afghanistan, your father spoke to us and—"

"Us?" Axel interrupted. "Who is us?"

Tom blinked. "Just people, Axel. Your family's been in Gunnison for a long time. He just wanted to make sure that when he died you would have folks to look after you."

"I have no family."

"I understand why you say that, but you're wrong. We are your family. All of us, Axel."

I did not know why Axel was so upset, but I felt the

people standing and watching him talk to Tom must be part of the reason. I stared at them, but they made no move to do anything threatening or hostile. Eventually, everyone left, and we were alone.

"Let's check out this tent, Bella," Axel said.

We had the warmest night in a long time, sleeping inside what I came to learn was the tent. Axel twitched and cried out, his dreams swirling, reminding me of Mack. I licked his face and he awoke and calmed, his hand on my fur.

"They want something from me, Bella," he murmured. I wagged at my name.

* * *

Every few days, Tom came to visit and brought food he put into the plastic boxes. Sometimes Axel would feel happy and the two men would talk a little, and sometimes he would feel hostile and angry and Tom would just give me a small treat and leave.

I did like Tom, but understood Axel wasn't always glad to see him.

We still went to town. Sometimes we would sit on the blanket for a while, people pausing to put things in a can, and then Axel would cross the street and bring back a bottle that smelled like Sylvia. And sometimes he would leave me tied to the fence for what seemed forever, finally returning and taking us immediately back to the tent. He would hold a plastic pencil over his arm and then he would climb into the tent and we would sleep for a long, long time.

Winter was harsh on the air, burning my throat and stinging the pads of my feet. I craved the warmth of the tent and would gladly snuggle with Axel in there. Someday, I knew, the summer days would return, and perhaps then I could return to doing Go Home, but nothing compelled me to leave the safety of the heat Axel could provide simply by playing with the knobs on the metal box inside the tent.

We were on our way back to the park from town, the sun easing down in a gray sky, when I smelled smoke, burning wood, and people near our house with no walls. It was not Riley, but three strangers, males, their shadows dancing in the large fire they had built in the metal box on the pole. We were just entering the park, trudging along in heavy snow, and when one of them laughed loudly Axel lifted his head, suddenly aware of their presence. He stiffened, and I felt a flash of fear and anger course through him as I lifted my snout to his hand.

The men were young and were throwing Axel's things, banging them around loudly. Axel was breathing heavily, but he was not moving as he watched them stomp on his belongings.

Oddly, my thoughts flashed back to when the coyotes had pursued Big Kitten and me as we fled to the rocky ridge. There was some way in which this felt like the same thing. These weren't bad dogs, they were bad men. Bad men like the one Mom made crawl out the door. Bad like the man who came to hurt Sylvia.

Dutch had wanted to bite that man, and the two of us growled and snarled and the man left.

I knew what to do.

Twenty-four

An angry growl rose in my throat. Axel glanced at me in surprise. Then he drew himself up, his fear melting as his fury took hold. I felt it pouring off of him like heat. "Yes, Bella, you are right. This cannot stand." He broke into a run and I dashed along at his side, our footfalls silent in the muffling snow. It was as if I was facing down the coyotes—a ferocious wrath seized me. I had never bitten a human before, but it seemed that this was what Axel wanted me to do now—I was responding as if he had shouted a command.

The three young males whirled when Axel and I burst into the circle of light from the fire. I barked out a full snarling scream of rage and lunged for the closest man, who fell back onto the ground. My teeth clicked just a tiny distance from his face and Axel stopped me with my leash.

"Jesus!" one of them cried. The two still standing fled out into the night but as the one on the ground shuffled backward Axel advanced, so I was always right on top of him.

"Why did you do this? Who are you working for?" Axel demanded.

"Please. Don't let your dog hurt me."

We remained like that for a long moment, and then Axel pulled me back. "It's okay, Bella. It's okay," he said gently.

The third man scrambled to his feet and fled out into the night after his two companions. Moments later, headlights flickered on in the parking lot, and a car roared away.

Axel and I turned to the wreckage of our home. The tent was flattened, the plastic boxes broken, our food scattered. The sadness coming off him in that moment was so profound I actually whined a little, wanting to do anything to provide him comfort, but not knowing what to do.

Axel was able to coax flames from the metal box on the cement. He hauled his blankets and the remnants of the tent over next to it, and we settled in for a miserable night. At first it felt warm, pressed up against him, but gradually my body chilled and my nose and tongue began to ache. I curled up as tightly as I could, my muzzle under my tail. Axel wrapped his arms around me and squeezed, tremors moving through his body. I did not remember ever being this cold. I could not sleep, and neither did Axel. He just clung to me, and I breathed in his scent and wished we would go someplace warm.

At dawn we were up. Axel dug in the snow and found a piece of chicken that sizzled when he put it on the metal box. We shared the paltry meal, and then I glanced up as a familiar car came into the parking lot, its tires hushed on the snow. Tom got out and crunched over to where we were huddled near our meager fire.

"What the hell happened?" he demanded. "Axel, my God."

"Kids," Axel said curtly. "Just kids."

"Jesus." Tom poked sadly at the mess on the ground. "Did you recognize them?"

Axel looked up at Tom. "Oh yes. I know exactly who they are."

• • •

Toward the evening of that same day, a procession of cars flowed into the parking lot. Axel stood and I turned to face the possible threat, though I quickly established that one of the people was Tom.

I picked up a few other scents I recognized as well: the three young men from the night before. They came forward with reluctance. Three older men I had never met marched with grim determination behind them.

Tom led the group. They all came in under the roof of the house with no walls, the three younger men holding their eyes stonily to the ground.

"Hey, Axel," Tom greeted.

"Hi, Tom." Axel was as calm as I'd seen him in a long time.

"You probably recognize these three," Tom said.

"They were just visiting last night," Axel observed wryly.

One of the young men snorted, looking away, and the man behind him stepped forward and poked him roughly between the shoulder blades. "Pay attention!" the man barked.

All three young men snapped their heads up.

"We are really sorry for what our sons did, Axel," another of the men spoke up from behind.

"No," Axel said sternly. "I want to hear them speak."

Tom was regarding Axel with something like surprise.

"We was drunk," one of the young men said lamely.

"That is *not* an excuse," Axel snapped.

The three young men shifted uncomfortably.

"What do you say to Sergeant Rothman?" demanded one of the older men.

"We're sorry," the young men mumbled, one after another.

"They're going to clean things up here while their fathers and I go into town and pick up replacement equipment," Tom told Axel. "The boys are paying for everything—we made an arrangement. Let's just say they're going to have a very busy summer, working for the city, picking up trash."

"I'll stay and make sure they get everything done," one of the older men declared.

"Oh, don't worry about that," Axel responded. "I can take care of that."

The three younger men looked uneasily at each other. Tom grinned.

Some things a dog will never understand. I was confused when Tom and his friends left and the younger men remained behind and picked up things and stacked them while Axel watched with his arms crossed, and I was baffled when the older men returned and set up a different tent and gave us different plastic boxes.

All of the men soon left, except Tom. "I guess I just met the soldier who won the Silver Star," he said softly.

Axel regarded him coolly. "It's not something you win, Tom."

"Sorry, Sergeant." Tom grinned, but his smile eventually faded. "I just wish you would let people help you, Axel."

"It's people who did this to me, Tom," Axel responded.

•   •   •

There were many nights when Axel squirmed and muttered and shouted in his sleep, and days when we were both astoundingly cold, clinging to each other for warmth. There were also times, seeming to grow more frequent in occurrence, when Axel would collapse and lie unresponsive, drooling, only to awaken and be sluggish and slow.

He seemed sick and I nuzzled him anxiously. I wished Lucas would come. Lucas would know what to do.

Gradually the sun grew warmer and bugs and birds filled the air with their songs. There were squirrels at the park! I wanted to chase them but Axel always held fast to my leash. Dogs came, children played on the slides, and grasses waved moist and healthy in the breeze.

Tom came to feed me a treat. "With the weather, families are coming to the park. You'll have to move on, technically no one is allowed here after dark," he told Axel. "And people want to use the shelter but they're . . . intimidated." He sounded mournful.

"Not hurting anybody," Axel said.

"Well . . . we've had complaints. I'll hang on to your heater, if you like."

"I'll leave. Hell with you all," Axel snarled.

"Now, don't be that way," Tom said sadly.

I did not understand any of the words and my name was not mentioned, but Axel put all of his things in the cart and pushed it out of the park. We walked a long way along the road by the river and then turned down a path to where the banks were flat and sandy. Axel rebuilt his tent here and then he settled down in such a way that suggested to me we would not be leaving.

Over time Axel's suffering became worse. He yelled out more in his sleep, and he had started talking loudly to me during the day, gesturing at the sky. Sometimes he would pant and twitch anxiously, then leave me tied to a stump while he left in the direction of town. Upon his return, he would have one of his pencils and would seem happy, but only for a little while. Then he would collapse and sleep deeply. Tied to him, I would go to the limits of the leash to squat to do Do Your Business.

One such night I caught a familiar stench and when I looked I saw a lone coyote watching me from the opposite riverbank. I growled quietly, but I knew it would not come across flowing water. Axel did not react to the smell, nor to the sound of my building fury, and eventually the small, bad dog slunk away.

I was alarmed when Axel began pacing and yelling along the riverbanks all day long. He took down the tent and threw it violently in a heap. He forgot to feed me once, then again, and then he poured an entire bag of food on the ground within my reach and left me, tied to a stump, kicking angrily at the rocks in his path as he marched away.

He was gone for two days. I ate all the food and drank from the river. I was sad and anxious. Had I been a bad dog? When he returned, he was stumbling and talking and did not acknowledge how frantically happy I was to see him. His breath reminded me of Sylvia.

He sat on a rock, hunched over by the river, and I knew from his motions that he was doing something to his arm and what would soon follow. Sure enough, he became very relaxed, and he laughed and called me a good dog. Peace erased all the fear and anger from his face. Soon his eyes were blinking very slowly.

"Bella. You are my best friend," he told me. I wagged at my name.

Axel slumped into the dirt, breathing slowly. I curled up next to him, being a good dog and providing comfort. He had no pain and his breathing was slow.

After a time, his breathing stopped.

· · ·

I lay all night with my head on Axel's steadily cooling chest. Slowly, his scent changed, as more and more of what had been the man left, and more and more of something else came into his body.

Axel was a nice man. He was never mean to me. He was often angry and sad and frightened and upset, but never at me. I had done my best to be his good dog, to take care of him. I missed him now, lying there beside him, and wished he would sit up and talk to me one last time. I remembered how we would huddle together in the frigid night. How, when he had food, he would share it with me, just as I would share meals with Big Kitten. "You get the first bite, Bella," he would say as he tore off a piece of something and handed it to me. I heard my name and could feel his love. Axel loved me, and now he was gone.

He wasn't Lucas, but aching for Axel just then, I did not feel disloyal. I had cared for many people in my life, not just Mom and Ty and Mack and Layla and Steve, but Gavin and Taylor, and even Sylvia. It was what I was supposed to do. Axel had just needed me more than anyone else.

I had water in my bowl, which was good because my leash, now tied to Axel's wrist, did not stretch to the river. Nor did it reach my bag of food.

When I got to my feet, I could see the cars flying past on the paved road nearby. Sometimes a dog would be hanging its head out the window and would bark at me as it drove by. Most cars did not have dogs, though, even if they smelled like they once did.

Eventually I grew hungry. I glanced at Axel's still form, reflexively expecting him to feed me, and then when I saw him lying so motionless it would come back to me and I would be lonely again. I did Sit, thinking if people driving on the road saw what a good dog I could be they would stop and give me some food in my bowl. No one stopped, though, not that whole day. When night fell I strained on my leash, trying to reach my dinner and feeling a little like a bad dog as I was doing so, but Axel's hand did not move.

Axel was cold and hard when I touched my nose to his face. His clothes still smelled like him but otherwise it was as if he had never been a person.

I looked out at the night, thinking of Lucas. Where was he, right now? Was he lying in his bed, missing his dog the way I was missing him? Did he open the front door to see if I had done Go Home and was lying in my spot? Did he have a treat ready to do Tiny Piece of Cheese, and was waiting for me to jump up to lick it from his fingers? I whined, I cried, and then I lifted my nose to the moon and wailed out a long, grieving howl. It was an odd noise, alien to my throat, and it carried with it all my heartache.

Far, far away, I heard a single answering cry, a song of loneliness from some other unknown canine, and many dogs barked, but no one came to see what could make a dog so sad.

The next morning my water was almost gone. I began barking at cars—if they would not stop for a good dog, maybe they would stop for a bad dog not doing No Barks.

They did not stop. I started panting in the afternoon after licking up the last of the water in my bowl. The river now gave up the enticing fragrance of the refreshing, life-giving liquid, right there, just out of reach. I yearned to romp along the shore and to jump in the water. I wanted to swim in it, to roll in it, to play in it all day. Big Kitten could watch from the shore as I dove in and opened my mouth underwater as if trying to reach a sinking kitty.

This was the sort of dilemma only a human could solve. I needed a person to come help me. Why wouldn't anyone stop?

My mouth was so dry it ached. An involuntary tremble shook my limbs, and I lunged repeatedly, helplessly, at the leash, *feeling* the stream right there, unable to get to it. Axel's body barely budged as I tugged.

I was becoming sick; I could feel it rising in me, over-whelming my body, which was turning hot and then cold, leaving me weak and shivering. I yipped and cried, missing Lucas more in that moment than I had since I last saw him.

The sun was close to setting when I smelled some peo-ple coming—boys, their young voices calling to each other. When I saw them on the road I realized they were on bicycles. I barked at them, desperately pleading for them to stop and help me.

They rode right past.

Twenty-five

Frustrated, I barked and barked and barked after the boys, my throat aching from the effort.

Then I heard the bicycles coming back. I stopped barking. "See?" one boy demanded.

There were four of them. They stopped on the road, sitting on their bikes.

"Why would anyone tie up a dog here?" one boy wanted to know.

"He looks hungry," another observed.

"He's panting, maybe he's rabid."

I did Sit. I wagged. I yipped. I leaned toward them, at the farthest tolerances of my leash, my front legs off the ground, begging.

The boys got off their bicycles and wheeled them into the grass and set them down. The one in front smelled a lot like spicy food. He was thin and tall with dark hair. "You okay, boy?" The other boys stayed up by the road but this one cautiously made his way down to me. I wagged furiously. "He looks friendly!" he called back over his shoulder. He approached with his hand outstretched. When his fingers were barely within reach I licked them, tasting the rich onions and spices on his skin. He petted me, and I jumped up on him with my forepaws, so relieved to have a person find me because now I would have food and water.

"Hey, toss my water bottle down here!" the boy said. The other boys had crept forward but one of them broke away, went back to the bikes, and threw something to the one closest to me, who caught it. I smelled the water before he poured it in my dish, and lapped desperately at it, wanting to immerse my whole head. My tail was wagging and I drank and drank and drank.

"It's like his rope got caught on some junk." All the boys had joined me now and were standing between me and the road. I wagged and sniffed their outstretched hands, none of which were as spicy as the one belonging to the tall boy with the black hair.

One boy lightly picked up my leash and tugged, following it down toward the river.

"Ahh!" the boy screamed.

The boys all scrambled away from me, back up toward their bikes. "What is it?"

"What's wrong?"

"Oh my God!"

"What? What did you see?"

"There's a body."

"A *what*?"

"There's a dead guy lying there!"

The boys stood far out of my reach, panting. I did Sit, a good dog who needed some food to go with the water I'd been given.

"No," one boy said finally.

"No way."

"Seriously? Seriously, a body?"

The boys were quiet for a moment. I watched them expectantly.

"How do you know he's dead?" the boy with spicy hands demanded finally.

"He's that homeless guy. The vet."

"So?" Spicy-boy said.

"My dad said the homeless guy moved with his dog to a place by the river. You know, the soldier guy who is always screaming on the street?"

"Okay, but how do you know he's *dead*?"

There was another silence. "Hey, mister?" Spicy-boy called tentatively. "Mister?" The boy came forward and put his hand on my head. I could feel his fear and excitement. He eased down to where what used to be Axel lay in his blankets. He tugged the leash, the motions slapping at my collar.

"He's dead," Spicy-boy stated flatly.

"Whoa."

"Jesus."

The boys seemed agitated, and none of them made any move to come any closer to where Spicy-boy stood next to me.

"Okay, it's going to be dark in a couple of hours, what do we do?" the boy farthest away wanted to know.

"I'll stay here to make sure nobody tampers with the evidence," Spicy-boy said gravely. "You guys go call 911."

• • •

Spicy-boy stayed with me while the other boys rode off. He made a wide circle around Axel's blankets and found the bag of dog food and poured it into my food bowl. I gratefully bolted down my dinner.

"I'm sorry," he whispered to me after I'd eaten. He stroked my head. "I'm so sorry about your owner."

I was still thirsty, but the situation hadn't changed—I

was attached to the leash, which led down to the stiff, heavy body. I gave Spicy-boy an expectant look, but he didn't provide any more water.

It was very quiet, so still I could hear the hiss and gurgle of the river flowing past. Gradually I became aware of Spicy-boy's rising fear—as the sun lowered in the sky, he seemed more and more anxious about being here with me and dead Axel. I knew what I needed to do. My thirst momentarily forgotten, I went to Spicy-boy and leaned against him to provide comfort. He ran his fingers through my fur and I felt him relax, though ever so slightly.

"Good dog," he told me.

Soon some men arrived, plus one woman, in big vehicles that had flashing lights on top. They came down to look in Axel's blankets. One of them slipped my leash loose and handed it to Spicy-boy, who accepted it gravely. He took me down to the river and I drank deeply. I had been right: people always knew what to do.

Before long Tom arrived and there were flashing lights on his roof, too. He came down and joined the circle of people.

"Overdose, if I had to guess. Won't know until we get him back," the woman told him.

"God."

They were quiet. Tom knelt down. "Oh, Axel," he murmured mournfully. I felt the grief pour off of him. He put a hand to his face, weeping. One of the other men put an arm on his shoulders. "God," Tom repeated. He raised his face to the sky. "What a waste. What a tragedy."

"He was a great man," the other man murmured.

"Was." Tom shook his head in disbelief. "Yes. And look how he wound up."

Other cars were arriving. They stopped and people got out and stood in the fading light, lined up on the road along the river. They were mostly quiet. Many of them seemed very sad. I saw men and women wiping their eyes.

"Okay, let's get him out of here," the woman declared.

They picked up Axel's body and his blankets and carried him up to the road and put him in one of the big trucks with lights on the top.

When I first heard the vocal tones I did not understand what they were doing, but then I realized it was singing, just like Mom used to do when she was at the sink pouring water on the plates. Just a few people, and then more and more until it seemed all of the people were joined in chorus. I did not understand the words, of course, but I felt the pain and the regret and the sorrow in the voices.

> *We fight our country's battles*
> *In the air, on land, and sea;*
> *First to fight for right and freedom*
> *And to keep our honor clean;*
> *We are proud to claim the title*
> *Of United States Marine*

When they were done singing the people had their heads bent and their arms on each other. The truck with Axel in it drove slowly away, and as it passed some would extend their hands and touch its sides.

Then everyone started getting back in their cars, murmuring to each other. One vehicle at a time, they began driving slowly away.

"Rick!" a man called. Spicy-boy snapped his head up. "I've got your bike. Let's go."

Spicy-boy looked at me, hesitating.

"Rick. *Now!*"

"You'll be okay," he whispered to me. "I just need to find somebody to take care of you."

"Rick, dammit, move your butt!" the man yelled. Some people standing on the road stiffened in disapproval.

"Somebody watch the dog," Spicy-boy called, dropping

my leash and climbing hastily away. Several people turned to look at me, but no one came forward to pick up my leash.

After a moment, I padded over to where a few of Axel's sacks and blankets remained strewn around on the river-bank. His scent was strong on the soft cloth, and I drank it in. I had been a good dog and I provided comfort to Axel, but he was gone. This was, I realized, the last time I would ever smell him. He had left and would never be coming back.

Things repeated, which was how a dog learned. In order to do Go Home, I'd had to leave my Lucas blanket behind, just as I would now have to leave the Axel blankets behind.

The sad grief inside me was familiar—I felt it whenever I despaired of ever seeing Lucas again. This was the same pain. I would never feel Axel's hand on my head again, never sleep next to him, never be given a treat by him, held out between his fingers while he smiled at me.

I looked up to where the steadily shrinking knot of peo-ple still milled about. Tom was there—if anyone would take notice of me now, it would be Tom. I liked him and appreciated that he always seemed ready to give me a snack, but he was busy speaking to others. These were hu-man matters that he was tending to, and while a dog was usually very important to people, in this situation, my pres-ence did not merit anyone's attention.

I turned away and no one said my name. I trotted along the riverbank, the cool shadows welcoming me in the set-tling gloom, following my senses.

Time to do Go Home.

I was making steady progress, my leash trailing behind me and transmitting a constant and somewhat irritating tremor up into my neck. It was slowing me down, and then it got worse when it snagged on a fallen tree. I was suddenly jerked up short, unable to go any farther. Frustrated, I whined, suddenly hating the leash. I tried pulling on it, but it did not yield. I circled the tree, but that did not help. I was stuck.

I seized the leash in my teeth and shook it, but that did nothing.

I looked around, suddenly aware of my surroundings. I had left town far behind. I was by a stream, sparse trees and brush providing cover, but as the moon rose I was starkly vulnerable out in the open. Far in the distance I could just make out the scent of coyotes. What if they could smell me? I thought how delighted they would be to find me hung up on a log, unable to defend myself, and felt a flash of fear.

Twisting and pulling until my collar chafed, I tried everything I could think of to shake off my leash. At one point I backed away from the tree, feeling my collar slip up my neck. Suddenly it was very uncomfortable, choking me. Desperately I ducked and shook my head, straining, and then without warning the collar popped off.

I immediately felt like a bad dog. The only time I had ever been without a collar was at the place of barking dogs in crates. People give dogs a collar so the dogs will know they belong to a person. The lightness around my neck now was an utterly unhappy feeling.

Well, whether or not I was a bad dog, I needed to keep going. I was closer to Lucas now; I could feel it—but I was still a long way away.

· · ·

Though it had been a long, long time since I was on my journey, everything about my trek was familiar: the hills, the search for water, the lack of food. I smelled animals and startled a rabbit—they had grown no easier to catch. On the trail the scent of people was strong, but I avoided areas where I could hear them talking or moving, even as I became more and more hungry. Without a collar, I could not be sure how anyone would react when they saw me.

I did descend to a road and found some old hot dog pieces in a metal bin that I knocked over, but other than that I was not doing well feeding myself.

The offensive stench of coyote was always present on the air now—this was an area where the small, bad dogs roamed and hunted. I was wary and retreated instantly when I realized I was on a course to encounter them.

The day I ate the hot dog pieces I picked up their stink very strongly—at least three of them, close by. I immediately reversed direction, because as important as it was to advance toward Lucas, I needed to avoid the canine predators above all else.

Oddly, the odor of the three faded and then returned, so strong at one point that I turned and stared behind me down a long slope, expecting to see them emerge from behind some rocks. No, they were not right there, but they were close.

I was being hunted.

When the trail burst from some trees and fed into a large meadowed area, I felt nakedly exposed. They were behind me—retreating back into the trees would simply put me in danger. Far ahead, though, the meadow sloped steeply upward, and I could see a jumble of boulders pointing up toward the sky. My scent was flowing ahead with the breeze and nothing was flushed out—there were no coyotes up there at the top of the hill.

I remembered the last time I had faced this sort of threat. A good dog learns when things repeat. Having something behind me had frustrated their attack. If I could reach those large bounders, I would not be out in the open where a pack could bring me down. I would have a chance to battle for my life.

Though my legs were weak from the days without adequate food, I began running uphill, feeling the pack of predators pressing steadily ahead behind me.

I was panting hard when I arrived at the base of the

outcropping, and I lay in a small pool of shade for a time to catch my breath. From where I lay I could see the steeply pitched meadow below, and spotted the three small bad dogs as they emerged from the woods. They had my scent and came in single file straight toward me.

My lips drew back in an involuntary snarl.

At that moment I did not remember Lucas, did not think about Axel or any people at all. I was stripped down to my canine essence, gripped with a primitive fury; I wanted to sink my teeth into coyote flesh. I got to my feet, waiting for them to arrive, for the fight to begin.

Twenty-six

The three coyotes came up the hill silently, their tongues out, their eyes slits. As they approached they spread out, knowing that with my back to the rocks I could retreat no farther. I could smell the hunger on their exhalations, and they shared a familial odor—these three males were young, from the same litter, and clearly starving. I was bigger than any of them, but they were desperate.

The instinct to engage them was nearly overpowering, an urge I didn't understand compelling me, but I stayed with my tail to the boulders, resisting the impulse to lunge, to chase them down. I barked, snapping my teeth, and they pulled back slightly, nosing each other, unsure because I wasn't fleeing. One of them seemed larger and more bold, and this one rushed a few steps, dancing back when I darted forward to meet him while his two brothers moved to the side. I turned to face this new challenge and sensed the bolder one leaping at me. I snarled and charged and the other two came at me and I chopped the air with my fangs, knocking a smaller coyote over as the bold one sprang and I felt teeth on my neck, tearing my flesh. I screamed and twisted and slashed and bit and we went up on our rear legs and I forced him back and his brother darted forward.

And then there was a blur of motion from above me and another animal joined the melee, landing right in front of my assailants. The coyotes were snarling and yelping in shock and fear and falling away from a ferocious attack. I stared in amazement as an enormous cat, far larger than I, sprang at the coyotes with nearly blinding speed, claws slashing. Her massive paw struck the bolder one in his haunches and sent him tumbling, and then the three of them were fleeing down the hill in panic, the cat loping easily after them for just a moment before she turned and stared at me.

I wagged. I knew this gigantic feline. Her scent had changed but still, at her essence, it was Big Kitten.

She came to me and purred and rubbed her head under my chin, nearly knocking me off my feet with her tremendous strength. I play bowed and she put out a frolicsome paw, swatting without claw at my nose. I was only able to climb up on her shoulders by raising my front feet off the ground. How had she gotten so big?

When she turned and climbed higher into the hills, I followed, tracking her by smell as night came. I was back on the trail to Lucas, so of course I was back with Big Kitten. Things repeat.

She led me to a half-buried elk calf, and we fed just as we had done so many times before, side by side over the kill.

I was tired and lay down in some grasses. Big Kitten came over and licked at the wound on my neck, her rough tongue scrubbing at it until I turned away from her and sighed. She went out to hunt but I remained where I lay, easily sleeping. She did not return until the sun was out, curling up against me and purring. I rested, resisting the urge to get to my feet to do Go Home. This was part of our pattern, to be near food and eat as much as possible before we moved on. We would do this until we were with Lucas, and then he would feed Big Kitten when he fed the rest of the cats.

• • •

The nights grew cooler as we traveled together. She would not accompany me during the day, but would always find me at night, sometimes leading me to a meal, usually buried in the dirt. We would spend time feeding before moving on from that spot. I was making steady progress toward Lucas; I could feel it, could smell it.

Then one day Big Kitten did something very unusual. I nosed her in the morning as she lay half hidden by a downed tree, then trotted confidently away. There was a town ahead, a place where I could forage and bring food back to Big Kitten. It was how we traveled together.

This day, instead of sleeping and catching up with me later on, Big Kitten followed me. I didn't hear her, of course—she was soundless on the trail. Instead, her scent caught up to me, so strong I knew she was right there. I turned and looked. She was standing atop a large rock, motionlessly watching me.

I did not understand this new behavior, and went back to her to see if I could comprehend. She leaped lightly to the ground, rubbing her head against me, then scampering back toward where she had been sleeping, looking expectantly over her shoulder.

She wanted me to follow, as if luring me back to where we had come. But I needed to continue to make progress toward the smell of home. When I didn't move, she returned to me. This time she didn't rub herself against me, she just sat and stared at me. After a time, the two of us just looking at each other, I felt I understood.

Big Kitten would not be living in the den across the

street. She would not be lying on Lucas's bed with me, waiting for a Tiny Piece of Cheese. She was not going to go any farther. For some reason, she could not or would not accompany me, nor wait for me on the trail when I went to a town to see if I could find food. It was as if she wanted to do Go Home herself, had a place she needed to be, and where we were standing now was too far away from there.

I went to her, wagging, touching her with my nose. I loved Big Kitten, and knew that if I stayed with her she would hunt all winter for us, find prey when the snow made my progress so difficult. I had enjoyed my life with her, first when she was a defenseless kitty, and then when she grew large enough to protect herself, and now when she saved me from the small bad dogs. But my life had taught me that I would stay with people and animals until it was time to move on, and it was that time now. I had to do Go Home.

I went back to tracking the odors toward the town up ahead. When I stopped and turned, Big Kitten was back on the rock, watching me with unwinking eyes. I remembered my mother doing the same thing, when I left her at her new home under the deck. Dutch had been confused and upset when I said good-bye but Big Kitten merely watched, just like Mother Cat. She was still there the next time I glanced back, and the next.

And then I looked, and Big Kitten was gone.

⚫ ⚫ ⚫

It was dusk when I strolled into the town. There were leaves on the ground, scuttling ahead of me on the light breeze. Cheerful lights blinked awake inside the houses, flickering as people walked in front of windows.

I was not hungry, but knew I would be soon. I slept under a bench in a park that smelled like children and dogs. In the morning I drank from a cold, clear river, avoiding the men and women I heard speaking to each other. I craved their company, but had no way of knowing which ones would keep me from returning to Lucas.

Behind some buildings I found a bin so overstuffed that the lid was propped open. I jumped up, trying to get inside, but was not able to get a purchase on the lip of the bin with my fore claws. I remembered trying to clamber out of Sylvia's pool—there are some things I simply could not do. Instead, when I leaped up, I thrust my snout into the bin and grabbed what I could, which turned out to be a sack with nothing edible in it. I tried again, this time snagging a plastic bag with my teeth. It fell to the ground and I ripped into it. I found a box with bird pieces and bones in it, not chicken but similar, and also a foil wrapping with spicy meat and flat bread.

There were many people walking the streets where the cars were, but very few in the narrow roads behind the buildings. The two humans I saw did not call to me.

One building pulled me irresistibly forward—I smelled dog bones and dog treats and dog food in it. My mouth watering, I saw that its back door was open. I wondered if going inside would mean that I would be chased by a man in white clothes. A very tall truck was backed up right outside the open door, and when I cautiously explored it, I saw that the truck was open like a garage in the rear. By climbing the steps to the back door of the shop, I was on a cement pad at the same level as the deck of the open truck. I nimbly leaped across the gap between the cement and the wooden floor of the vehicle, lured by delicious odors. The enclosure was mostly empty except up toward the front end, where I encountered plastic that did nothing to contain the delicious odors from underneath it. I tore off the plastic and uncovered bags and bags of dog food.

I ripped into the paper sack and began to feed. I did not feel like a bad dog; I was *supposed* to eat dog food!

Then a man came out of the back of the store. I froze,

feeling guilty, but he didn't even look at me. He reached to the top of the truck and yanked on a strap and with a bang the back end of the truck was closed off. I went over to the door, sniffing, smelling the man and dog food and little else.

The vehicle rattled to life with a roar and, swaying and bouncing, I felt it begin to move. I had to dig my nails into the wooden floor when the room swayed in one direction, and then the roar of the truck grew louder.

I was trapped.

• • •

The truck rocked and bounced and growled for a long time, so long that I fell asleep despite the strange, car-ride feeling pulling at my body. The smells from outside kept changing subtly, but were mostly the same—water, trees, the occasional animal, people, dogs, smoke, food.

Finally the steady drone of the truck took on a different character, becoming louder. The forces pulling on me became more pronounced and I slid sideways before I leapt to my feet. I felt a shift to one side, then another, and then I fell forward, and then the vehicle shut off, the sudden silence strange after such a long period of vibration. I heard a door shut and the sound of a man walking. I shook myself off and trotted back to where I had first gotten on the truck.

With a loud rattling sound, the wall in front of me slid up. "Hey!" the man yelled as I jumped down to the ground.

He did not seem friendly, so I did not approach him. Instead I ran, going up a street and turning toward some bushes, where I gratefully squatted. The man did not chase me.

I assessed where I was. The place seemed very much the same as where I had spent the night, though I could smell it was a different town. There were buildings and some cars and many people walking around. The sun was setting, but the air was fairly warm. I smelled a large amount of water, clean snow high in the mountains, squirrels and cats and dogs.

And home. Somehow, during the course of being in the back of that truck, I had become so close to home that the smell of it was separating into distinct parts. It was the reverse of what happened when Audrey drove me away from Lucas. I faced the tall mountains, which were glowing as the sun set. Just on the other side of them was my person.

Though my belly was heavy from all the dog food, I was painfully thirsty and turned toward where my senses told me I would find a river. I drank from a swiftly moving stream, and then was drawn to the sound of children. It was a park with slides and swings and two small dogs who ran up to me, barking aggressively and then turning away submissively, politely sniffing under my tail. They were both females, one of whom wanted to play, pawing and bowing, and the other who dismissed me and went back to where her people were sitting on a blanket on the ground.

Though I was anxious to get back on the trail, night was coming and I should find somewhere to curl up. This park would be a good, safe place to sleep.

And then I would do Go Home.

. . .

The sky was barely brightening when I awoke the next morning. It was the time of day when Big Kitten would return from her prowlings, sometimes with food for us. I felt a small pang, missing her, but I was eager to get going. I skirted a lake and then climbed a high hill, tracking next to a big road with many vehicles booming up and down it. On the other side of the hill I found a river that was flowing exactly in the direction I needed to go, toward Lucas. A road wove in and out near the stream, sometimes close, sometimes not close, but nearly always where I could hear the cars.

Padding alongside the rushing waters, I came across a big bird eating a large fish on a rock. I chased the bird, who flapped hard, dragging that fish, and then finally dropped it and rose high and away. I jumped on the fish and ate it quickly.

The stream descended into a town where I found some sweet breads in a trash can and a flat piece of cheesy meat in a box. I slept behind a car in that town and was moving again just as the sun was coming up. I was so excited to see Lucas, to finally Go Home, that I found myself running along flat areas.

I curled up in a park in a different town the next night. I had nothing to eat but I had been much hungrier in my life, and slept without trouble.

My dreams were vivid and strange. I felt Axel's hand rub my fur, and Big Kitten's tongue on my neck where the coyote had bitten me. Heat flowed from Gavin and Taylor, pressed up against my side in their bed. I smelled Sylvia's breath, and heard Chloe calling her kittens. Dutch groaned in my ear, a content sound he often made as he snuggled up to Gavin. I tasted Jose's salty treats and felt Loretta arrange my Lucas blanket around me.

It was as if they had all come to tell me good-bye.

In the morning I climbed one more long, big hill, and everything was different. I descended into a place of roads and cars and could no longer set a straight course, because where before my obstacles had been hills and rocks, I was now confronted with fences and buildings. I knew, though, that I was making my way in the right general direction, and patiently wound through the streets, passing houses, hearing dogs, seeing people. I was conscious of being stared at by men and women and a few children called out to me, but I deliberately ignored them.

The light faded from the sky, but the streets were lit and I actually felt more comfortable in the shadows. Car sounds drained away as the night grew late. Dogs left their yards, and their barking became more and more rare.

I did not sleep, but stayed on the move through the darkness. Sounds grew louder as the sun rose, and I was back to feeling exposed, but I was so close now. I recognized a park where I had been with Lucas and Olivia. Almost home! I broke into a heedless run.

When I turned down my street I slowed, unsure. Everything was different. The row of low, dirty houses across from our home were missing, including the one where the cat den had been. Tall buildings had taken their place, and I could smell many people, their scents flowing out open windows.

But I was finally here! I did Go Home, but I did not curl up against the wall as I had been taught. Instead I scratched at the door, wagging, and barked. Lucas!

A woman opened the door, the smells from home pouring out. "Hello, dear," she greeted me.

I wagged, but I could not smell Lucas. I could not smell Mom. Some of the odors were familiar, but I knew Lucas was not inside. Home no longer was filled with Lucas, it instead carried the scent of this woman in front of me.

"What's your name? Why don't you have a collar? Are you lost?" she asked me.

She was a nice lady, but I needed to find my person. When I pushed past her she said, "Oh my!" She did not seem angry, though.

I stopped in the living room. She had a couch but it was not the same couch, and the table was different. I went down the hallway. Lucas's room did not have a bed, it had other furniture instead. Mom's room had a bed in the same place but it was not Mom's bed.

"What are you doing, sweetheart?" the woman asked when I emerged from the bedroom and rejoined her in the kitchen.

She held out her hand and I went to her wagging, hoping for an explanation. People can do wonderful things, and I wanted her to fix this for me, because it was not something a dog could understand.

The woman gave me some water and some meat treats. I ate them gratefully, but inside I felt sick, realizing she would not be able to help me.

Lucas was gone.

Twenty-seven

I was immediately afflicted with a pressing urge to leave, to get back on the trail. It was not Go Home without Lucas. Whatever was happening, that was the only action I could think to take.

When I went to the door and sat expectantly, the nice woman came over to look down at me. "Are you leaving so soon? You just got here."

I glanced from her to the door, waiting for her to open it. She leaned over and held my chin with her cupped palm. "I have the sense that you came for a very important reason, but I don't have anything to do with it, do I?"

I heard the kindness in her voice and wagged.

"Whatever you are doing," she whispered, "I hope you find what you are looking for."

She opened the door and I trotted outside. "Good-bye, girl!" I heard her call behind me, but I did not look back.

I thought I knew where I should go.

• • •

I smelled her scent strongly painted on the ground as I approached her den under the deck built on the hill, where I had followed her once long, long ago: Mother Cat was still alive. When I pressed my nose into the space, I could tell she was in there, so I pulled my head back and waited, wagging.

After a moment she came out, purring, and rubbed herself against me. She was so tiny! I did not know how she had gotten so small.

I was so happy to be back with my mother. I remembered back to a time when she took care of me, when my kitten siblings and I were in the den together. Now that I had lost Lucas, I was comforted by having her head touch me. She was my first family, and right now, the only family that I could find.

Mother Cat was moving stiffly, and her fur was missing in small, mottled places. I sniffed her carefully and there was cat food on her breath, with no sign of the feral odor of birds and mice. Nor was there any indication she had been near Lucas recently. My hopes that she would lead me back to my person were not to be realized.

When Mother Cat gracefully leapt up onto the deck itself I followed, finding some steps I could easily climb. The deck jutted from a house and up against some big windows, where I found a bowl of food and some water, along with the scent of people.

I realized then that someone was taking care of my mother here at her new den, just as Lucas had fed her at the old one, just as some people had fed me while I had been on my long journey.

Mother Cat watched me as I ate the moist, fishy food from her bowl. There was not much there, but the few bites were delicious. Then I went back to probing her with my nose—I could tell she had not had kittens in some time—there was no milk aroma clinging to her.

When a woman suddenly appeared in the big glass door

I expected my mother to run away, but she didn't flee, not even when the door slid open. Mother Cat turned and calmly regarded the woman, who smelled of flour and sugar.

"Daisy? Who is this dog?" the woman asked.

I wagged at the word "dog."

Mother Cat walked underneath me, rubbing her back on my belly as she did so.

"Oh, Daisy, this is a stray. She doesn't even have a collar. Did she eat your food?"

The woman bent and put her hand out, but the cat kept her distance. There was a reason why Mother Cat had no human smells on her fur; she might accept food but she did not crave a person's touch. I was still wagging, wondering if the woman needed to pet me instead.

"Shoo, dog. You don't belong here."

The woman pointed, and then made a motion as if she were throwing a ball. I looked toward where she was gesturing, but didn't see anything.

"Go home," she commanded.

I stared at her in confusion. Lucas and Mom were no longer there. What did Go Home mean now?

"Go!" she shouted.

I understood that she saw me as a bad dog, possibly because I was not doing Go Home. I slunk off the deck, jumping down to the dirt, and Mother Cat followed me.

"Daisy? Kitty-kitty?" she called.

I wagged. My mother rubbed her head on my neck. I licked her face, but she did not like that and turned away from me.

I remembered Big Kitten, watching me from the rock. Sometimes cats have to stay where they are when dogs move on. This was one of those times. When I climbed back down the hill, I knew my mother was motionless behind me, gazing at me as I left.

It was how cats say good-bye.

I could think of nothing to do but Go Home again and see if Lucas was there this time. I crossed the small stream, scaled the bank, and went through the park, passing the slide I had climbed and jumped off so many times. It was much smaller now, for some reason.

I made my way toward our street, but before I got there a truck came around the corner, one with dog smells and a stack of dog crates on the back. I stopped and so did the truck. A fat man with a hat got out of the front seat.

I knew this man.

"Well, I don't believe my eyes," he declared.

I did not wag. I watched him suspiciously.

"Come here, girl!" He reached to the side of his truck and brought out a stick with a loop of rope on the end of it. "Treat!"

I was suddenly very afraid. I did not believe Hat-man would give me a treat, even though I was aware he had done so in the past. He was one of those who would keep me from Lucas, and he would do it angrily. He was a bad man.

I turned from him and ran.

* * *

I cut through yards, hearing the truck start up behind me. I got to our street and turned, dashing past our house and down the sidewalk next to the busy road. Darted through traffic. Cars honked and made a shrieking sound. I heard the truck coming closer. I tore across the parking lot. Up to the door at Go to Work.

No one was there to let me in. Frustrated, I trotted alongside the edge of the building, passing hedges, up a sidewalk. People were sitting outside, smoking like Sylvia while the sun went down.

I heard the truck rumble into the parking lot right behind me.

There was a big glass door and when I approached it, it

slid open in a manner similar to the way the doors had parted in the place where there was a shelf with chickens set out for me. No chicken aroma greeted me this time— just the scents and sounds of many, many people. But the open door was an invitation, and I trotted inside.

Everywhere people were milling around, sitting in chairs, talking. Behind a big desk right in front of the door a woman jumped to her feet. "Oh! A dog!" she said in alarm.

Though I had never entered through this door before, I could smell where to go. Several people reacted to me as I moved past the woman, but I ignored them, my snout to the floor for guidance.

"Anybody know whose dog that is?" she called out.

Because the air was full of so many people I did not smell anyone I knew until I heard a familiar voice. "Bella? *Bella!*"

It was Olivia! She was standing on the other side of a room full of soft chairs and people talking. She put a hand to her mouth and some papers slipped from her hands. We ran to each other and she dropped to her knees. I jumped up and licked her face and could not stop the whimpers from rising in my throat. I was full of joy and relief and love. I flopped down for a tummy rub and then leaped to my feet and put my paws on her chest. She laughed, falling back.

"Oh, Bella, Bella," she kept saying. I licked the tears from her cheeks. "I don't believe it. How did this happen? Where have you been? Oh, Bella, we searched so hard for you."

Another woman came over to join us. "Is this your dog?" she asked.

"No. Well, in a way. It's my fiancé's dog. It's been—my God, it's been more than two years. We had to send Bella away because of the breed laws in Denver, and by the time Lucas found a place to live and we went to get her, Bella had run away. We drove all over Durango, we put up posters, and then we thought probably something bad had happened to her. But you're here, Bella! A miracle dog!" Olivia rubbed my ears and I leaned into her, groaning. "Oh, Bella, I'm so sorry. I don't know what you must have gone through. Where's your collar?"

Olivia had the scent of Lucas on her skin, and I couldn't stop drinking it in. Olivia would lead me to him. My long journey was over. I was overjoyed to be back with my human family! I could not stop circling Olivia's legs, even when she stood back up. I put my feet on her hips, trying to climb up to kiss her face.

"Uh, Olivia? Is that your dog?" another woman asked. It was the same person who had been sitting behind the desk. I wagged, knowing that now I was with Olivia the woman would not be upset with me.

"Yes. It's a long story. She used to come here all the time when she was a puppy. I guess she found her way back."

"Oh. Well, there's an animal control officer here," the desk-woman said.

"Sorry?"

"He said he was chasing the dog and saw her come in here."

"Huh," Olivia replied. "And?"

"He says you have to surrender her. You have to bring the dog out," the desk-woman said apologetically.

"I see."

"Do you want me to have him come back here?"

Anger was a rare emotion for Olivia, but that's what I felt coming off her now. "No. Tell him I said to . . . Just tell him no, I'm not bringing the dog out."

"Well . . . he's an officer of the law, Olivia," Desk-woman said cautiously.

"I know."

"I think you pretty much have to do what he says, don't you?"

"No, actually, I have a different opinion."

"What are you going to do?"

• • •

Olivia led me down a long hallway to a very familiar part of the building. I wagged furiously as we turned the corner and pushed in through some heavy doors. People were sitting in a circle of metal chairs in the center of a big room with a slick, clean floor.

"Sit, Bella," Olivia commanded. I did Sit, excited to be there with her. "Uh, hi?" she called. "I'm really sorry to interrupt your meeting, but I have sort of an emergency."

The people reacted to what Olivia had just said, straightening in their chairs, which squeaked.

"What is it?" a man asked, standing. I wagged, over-joyed. It was Ty!

"Bella came back," Olivia said. I wagged even harder at my name and broke from Sit, running to Ty and jumping on him.

"Bella!" He laughed delightedly as I pawed him. "How in the world?"

"Bella?"

Mom! I dashed to her on the slick floor, panting, whimpering, and leaping up to lick her face. She bent over. She also reeked of Lucas—Mom and Olivia would help me find him! I was doing Go Home at last.

As soon as I got to her I realized that the people sitting in the chairs were all my friends. Layla stood. "Bella?" I ran to her, then turned to Steve, and Marty and Jordan put their hands on me, and my friends were all calling me and laughing and clapping.

"How did she get here?" Mom asked.

I flopped down for a tummy rub. Ty knelt next to me.

"Good dog, Bella!" Marty said.

"You're not going to believe this, but she just walked in the front door," Olivia replied. "Waltzed in like it was completely normal."

"No, I mean *get here*. From Durango," Mom said.

Ty gently turned me on my side. "Got a scar on the back of her neck, here. And look how thin she is! She's had a rough couple of years, you can tell."

"You don't suppose she *walked*?" Mom gasped. "Through the mountains?"

Jordan laughed delightedly. "That would be amazing."

"Oh, Bella, you are a very special girl," Ty told me. "You can do anything."

"So here's the problem," Olivia continued. "There's an animal control officer here. I think it's that same guy who harassed Bella in the first place. He says we have to bring the dog out."

Ty straightened to a standing position. "Oh he does, does he?"

Layla crossed her arms. "*What?*"

"If we do, he'll have Bella destroyed. We can't let that happen. Is there something you can do?" Olivia asked urgently.

I felt Mom tighten. "I'll handle this."

Ty held up a hand. "No, not just you, Terri. I think we should *all* handle this."

"Damn straight," Jordan said.

Marty had sat back down but now he stood. "Hell yeah. He has no idea who he's messing with."

Mom turned to Olivia. "Have you called Lucas?"

I snapped my head up at his name.

"No, not yet. This is all happening so fast, Bella barely walked in the door before they told me the dog catcher was here. And . . ."

"And?" Mom raised an eyebrow.

"We sort of had harsh words this morning. He's so

stressed right now. Usually he calls to apologize later. It's kind of one of the best things about him."

Mom smiled warmly. "Maybe this time, you break the pattern? Seems to me he would want to hear about this as soon as possible. Take a minute."

Olivia nodded. "Come, Bella." She walked out of the circle of people, who were all closing in around Ty. I wanted to go and play and be petted and called a good dog, but Olivia had said "Come" and I knew Lucas would want me to do what she said. I followed her to the corner of the room.

Olivia held her phone to her face. "Hi, it's me. Yes. Okay, yes, but . . . Lucas, would you stop for a minute? I do want to hear you say how wrong you were and how sorry you are. I want to hear you say it *a lot*. But I am calling about something else."

Olivia smiled down at me, and I wagged. "You'll never guess who just showed up!"

* * *

All of my friends took me for a walk down the hall past the desk-woman and to the door and outside. Night had fallen but there were a lot of lights so I could not only see but smell the hat-man and his truck with the dog crates. Two cars with flashing lights were parked next to that truck.

One woman and two men got out of those cars, all wearing dark clothes and carrying metal objects on their hips. Police. They walked with Hat-man up to greet my friends, who spread out next to me. Mom put her hand on my neck and I did Sit.

"I am here for the dog," Hat-man declared in a loud voice.

Ty smiled cheerfully. "Is that right?"

"I'm executing a legal confiscation under section eight dash fifty-five."

"Does sound pretty legal, I'll grant you that," Ty said.

Hat-man looked pointedly at the police standing next to him.

"We don't want any trouble here, sir," one of them stated cautiously. "But you'll have to surrender the animal."

Ty didn't say anything.

"Understand?" Hat-man sneered. "We're taking the dog."

"All right." Ty nodded, drawing himself up tall and gesturing to a man standing near to him. "But to do that, you'll have to get past the Fourth Infantry Division of the United States Army."

There was a long silence.

"Eighty-second Airborne Division, United States Army," Mom declared firmly. As she spoke she held herself stiffly, straightening her back and adopting a curiously erect posture. I wagged but did not understand.

Drew wheeled his chair forward. "Second Marine Division." He, too, went rigid.

Kayla stepped up next to Ty. "Sixth Fleet, United States Navy."

"First Infantry. Army," announced Jordan.

"Air National Guard."

Several more of my friends spoke. There was a long, tense silence when they were done talking. I could hear a dog barking, far away.

The police seemed afraid.

Twenty-eight

S heriff's here," one of the police said. Everyone turned and looked at the car pulling up in the parking lot. When it stopped, a man stood up from the passenger side as if his bones hurt. For a moment he gazed over at us without moving, and then with a slight shake of his head he walked toward us, trailed by the woman who had been driving the car, stopping when two of the police went down to talk to him. The new man looked at me and I wagged.

"Easy, Bella," Mom murmured. I glanced up at her, feeling her anxiousness and not understanding.

"So," New-man greeted as he joined us. "How is everyone doing tonight?"

"We're here to execute a dangerous animal confiscation and I got these people turning it into some kind of situation," Hat-man said angrily. "It's obstruction, it's interfering with police business, it's harboring a dangerous animal, and disobeying a lawful police order."

New-man sniffed, looking at my friends as they stood

beside me. "Pretty interesting," he observed. "Is that your dog, ma'am?"

"She's my son's dog," Mom replied.

I liked that the subject was dog.

"That a pit bull?" New-man asked.

Hat-man was nodding vigorously. "She's been certified by three separate AC officers according to—"

"Chuck," New-man interrupted, "did you think I was talking to you?"

Hat-man stiffened.

"We don't actually know." Mom shrugged. "She was found living under a house with a bunch of feral cats."

"Cats. You don't say," New-man replied. "Never heard that one before."

"None of this matters," Hat-man said darkly.

"Maybe what *matters* is that you're not taking Bella anywhere," Mom said coldly. Now I felt a strong anger coming from her.

"We're going to do whatever it takes to prevent you from touching this dog," Ty added, gesturing to the men and women standing with him.

Everyone became tense. One of the police took a step back and put his hand on one of the metal objects at his side. For a long moment, no one spoke. I yawned anxiously.

"Chuck, what in God's name have you gotten me into?" New-man finally asked.

"Sir, several years ago we received numerous complaints about this dog," Hat-man said.

"For *what*?" Mom demanded angrily.

"Okay, look. Let's everyone just calm down," New-man said serenely. "All right?" He smiled at Mom. "Emotions are running high right now, but let's take a look at it." He turned to look at the parking lot, where two more cars with flashing lights pulled up and more police got out and walked up to us. I wagged. "See, this is how things get out of hand," New-man continued. "Now, as unpleasant as it is, we have a job to do here. We're going to have to take the dog into custody, but I promise you—"

"That's not happening," Mom snapped.

"Ma'am, please let me finish. I promise you we'll take good care of her. You have my word."

"Your word doesn't mean a damn thing to me," Ty said.

New-man looked at him, his eyes narrowing. The police standing behind him glanced at each other.

"Here comes Dr. Gann," Olivia said quietly.

Another car had pulled up and I did not know the person who got out of it. Two more police came out of the building through the same door we had taken and joined all of us standing there. It was a big group of people, but unfortunately not a single one of them had any dog treats that I could smell.

"I'm Markus Gann," the new arrival greeted New-man.

"Sheriff Mica," New-man replied. The two men pulled on each other's hands for a moment before giving up.

"Hi, Dr. Gann," Mom said.

"Hello, Terri."

"Hey there, Dr. Gann," Ty added. The stranger's name was Dr. Gann.

"Hello, Ty. Jordan. Drew. Olivia." Dr. Gann turned to New-man. "So what may I do for you gentlemen this evening?"

Hat-man started to speak and New-man shut him up with a look.

"There's a dog issue," New-man began.

"She's an emotional support animal," Mom interrupted. I could feel the fear returning to her, see her hands starting to tremble. I touched her fingers with my nose, concerned.

"In my hospital?" Dr. Gann responded in a voice that reminded me of when Lucas would hold me before doing Go to Work—gentle and soft and caring. Mom looked down at me and I wagged.

"She's been coming here a long time," Ty said. "And now the sheriff's department is here to pick her up."

"Over my dead body," added Mom.

"Me too," said Steve.

Dr. Gann held up his hand, palm out. "All right."

"We're not going to let them have the dog, Dr. Gann," Ty said hotly. "Period."

"The last thing we need is for this to escalate," Newman said.

"Ah." Dr. Gann nodded, rubbing his chin. "But you're sort of committed to action now, aren't you? You didn't choose this fight, but here it is."

New-man gazed at Dr. Gann, and then made a tiny shrugging motion.

"Denver city ordinance eight dash fifty-five gives me the authority to confiscate that animal," Hat-man said tightly.

"Chuck." New-man sighed. "You're not helping the situation."

"Denver," Dr. Gann replied thoughtfully.

"Yes, sir. I am executing my lawful responsibilities as an animal control officer."

"For Denver. Denver County," Dr. Gann repeated.

"That's right."

Dr. Gann looked at me for a moment, then at the two new police who had come out of the building. "Well," he said finally, "this is not the city of Denver. This is federal property."

"That's never been an issue. We've been called repeatedly to this facility in the past," Hat-man replied tersely.

"Called? You're saying we called you tonight?" Dr. Gann asked.

"Well, no. I was tracking this animal, which is an illegal breed, and it went into the hospital."

"So that's it, then," Dr. Gann said to New-man in the same gentle tone. "This is federal land. Animal control is out of its jurisdiction. No need for any further confrontation."

New-man scratched his head, moving his cap with the motion. Then he gave a tiny nod. "I see your point."

"Dog. Here." Hat-man snapped his fingers and I felt Mom jerk in alarm. I did not move.

"Hold on!" New-man said gruffly. "Dammit, Chuck, what the hell are you trying to pull?" I felt his anger flaring.

"I expect . . ."

"No, *I* expect. I expect *you* to shut your damn mouth and obey orders!"

Hat-man looked unhappy.

New-man turned back to Dr. Gann. "Sorry for the misunderstanding. We'll be on our way."

"You are welcome here any time, sheriff. Give me a call, I'll show you around the new facility," Dr. Gann replied.

"I'd like that." New-man turned to the police, who all seemed more relaxed. "All right, let's go home."

"Fine, but I will tell you what." Hat-man sneered, pointing a finger at Mom. "I'm going to be watching. And if I see that dog leave here in a car I am going to call for backup and pull you over and take it into custody."

"You will do no such thing," New-man replied, spitting on the ground.

"Sheriff . . ."

"Dammit, Chuck, you've wasted enough time on this one dog. I get more complaints about you than all the rest of the AC officers combined. I'm pulling you out of the field for more training. Starting tomorrow morning. As of right now, you're off the clock. *And no one pulls over a vehicle because of a dog,*" he said intensely, glaring at the police. "No one. Is that understood?"

Some of the police grinned at each other. "Yes, sir," a few of them said.

"You . . . you . . ." Hat-man stuttered.

"Return the department vehicle and sign out, Chuck," New-man interrupted wearily. "Let's go, everybody."

The nice police turned and went back to their cars. Ty and Mom petted me and I wagged. They were happy.

"So . . . you do know VA regulations do not permit animals, even emotional support animals, on hospital grounds," Dr. Gann said.

"Yeah, about that." Ty shrugged. "Seems like a lot of people lately been bringing in their therapy dogs. Bella was just the first one."

Dr. Gann nodded. "I have much, much better things to do than try to enforce everything in the book. Especially, as you say, since so many people have started ignoring that one." Ty grinned at him and he smiled back. "Just don't let her bite anybody."

"Oh, she would never do that," Mom replied.

"Bella!"

I whipped my head up. A new car had stopped in the parking lot, and I knew the man getting out of it.

Lucas.

• • •

In that moment, it was as if everyone else standing there vanished. I saw only my person, holding his arms wide, smiling broadly. He and I ran to each other. I was sobbing, wagging, licking him. We fell to the ground together and I climbed on him, craving his touch and his kisses. "Bella! Bella, where have you been all this time? How did you find your way home?"

I couldn't help myself, I was yipping, not doing No Barks, dancing in circles. I was Go Home at last, Go Home with my person, with Lucas. Mom came over and knelt next to him. "She just showed up here tonight."

"It's amazing. I can't believe it. Bella, I missed you so

much!" Lucas seized my face with both hands. "God, look how thin she is. Bella, you are so skinny!"

I loved hearing Lucas say my name. He fell flat on his back and I dove on him, straddling him and licking his face while he laughed and laughed. "Okay! Enough!" He struggled back to a sitting position.

"Do you think it's truly possible that she made her way here through the mountains? How far would that be?" Mom wanted to know.

Lucas shook his head. "It's almost four hundred miles driving, but I have no idea what it would be like on foot. You certainly couldn't walk a straight line here."

I lay on my side, letting him rub my tummy. This was all I ever wanted, to have my person love me.

Mom stroked my side. "Animal control was here. That guy. But the sheriff told him to leave Bella alone." She was no longer afraid or tense, and she was smiling.

"Really? That's amazing!"

"I wouldn't ever let her off leash, though."

"That's okay."

"Hi." It was Olivia. I wagged at her, and a moment later her hands were on me, too. I had never felt so loved.

Mom stood up. "I need to get back to my meeting." She gave me a last pat before going up and into the building, trailing after all my other friends.

"Can you believe it?" Olivia asked.

"Honestly, no." Lucas kissed me on the nose. "God, I've felt so guilty, so sure she died never understanding why I didn't come for her."

"Doesn't matter. You see how she forgives you? Dogs are amazing like that."

"Yeah. Forgiveness. About that topic." Lucas stood.

"There's nothing to forgive, Lucas."

"No, I mean I forgive *you*."

"Oh." Olivia laughed. "Sure, that's right."

"I was a little out of line this morning."

"I get it. Med school's not supposed to be easy."

"Oh, no, I wasn't crabby about med school, it was your scrambled eggs."

They kissed, doing love. I jumped up to join them, putting my paws on Lucas's back. They both laughed and I wagged.

"You probably have to get back," Olivia said.

"No, you know what? Let's just go home. Be with Bella."

I heard Go Home and wagged.

"Wait, what have you done with the real Lucas? You've never done anything irresponsible in your life."

"Bella made her *way home*. If we don't celebrate that, I feel like we'll never celebrate anything. It's a miracle! Look at how overjoyed she is. I can't be serious right now, I need to lie on the bed with my dog and give her a tiny piece of cheese."

I whipped my head up. Tiny Piece of Cheese? Really?

● ● ●

We all went back into the building. Ty came over to see me. "Can you bring Bella for a minute? It's about Mack," he asked Lucas.

"Mack?"

"He's under lockdown for observation. You know he's had a tough year."

"Sure," Lucas said slowly. He looked to Olivia.

"You go on. I'm going off shift soon anyway," she told him.

Olivia kissed Lucas and I wagged. Then Ty and Lucas and I went down the hall to the place with the metal doors that swept open with a pinging sound. We stepped into the shaking room and when the doors creaked shut and then open we were someplace in the building I had never been to before, though it smelled pretty much the same as everywhere else. Ty went to a window and picked up a phone and held it to his ear. "Got someone here to see Mack," he stated. Then he waited. "Hello, doctor. Yes, I know the protocols but this is important. No. No, I know what Mack needs." Ty slapped his palm against the glass and Lucas and I both jumped. "Dammit, Theresa, open the door!" He sounded angry.

There was a buzz and with a loud click a door opened. Ty, Lucas, and I walked through it. A woman met us in the hallway, staring at me. "What on earth, Ty? Dr. Gann—"

"Dr. Gann just approved this dog," Ty interrupted. "Which one is Mack in?"

She looked unhappy. "Last one on the left."

Lucas was looking around. "I've never been here before."

"Yeah, well, I have," Ty muttered.

We went down the hall and I started to wag when I smelled who was on the other side of the door: my friend Mack! With another buzz, the door opened and I bounded in. Mack was sitting in a chair and I jumped right into his lap.

"Bella! Hey!" he greeted. I licked his face. He seemed very tense—tense and afraid. "I thought you were lost for good, girl."

"We all did. But she found her way back. All through the mountains, hundreds of miles. Pretty amazing, isn't it?" Ty said.

"Sure is." Mack scratched my ears and I groaned.

"Think how tough it must have been for her," Ty continued. "But she never gave up. She knew we were all counting on her, that she really mattered."

"Yeah. I do get the point, Ty. I'm not stupid."

Ty came up to pet me. "You're one of us, Mack. We need you."

We stayed in that little room for a long time. As I pressed up against Mack, his hands on my fur, I could feel the sadness in him break a little, become a little less tinged with

fear. I was providing comfort. I was doing my job. I was
happy.

* * *

When we left Go to Work, we both smelled like Olivia.
Lucas had his own car! I sat in the front seat. We did car
ride to a completely new place, getting out and climbing
some stairs. I could smell Lucas in the air and knew he
had been here before. He opened a door and Olivia was
sitting in a chair. Of course! I trotted over to see her.

"It is so, so nice to come home and find you here," Lucas
told her.

"I stopped and got some dog food and a collar for Miss
Bella. And look what I found in the closet!" Olivia picked
up a folded cloth and the scent hit me instantly—my Lucas blanket! "I'll put it on the bed."

Lucas came over and felt the blanket. "I forgot all about
it." He kissed her and I wagged. "So nice to live in a building that allows dogs, even giant ones."

Olivia nodded. "A dog-friendly building in pit bull–
friendly Golden, Colorado."

The three of us cuddled together in a small bed. I had
on a new, stiff collar. My Lucas blanket was draped over
the foot of the bed, but I ignored it and lay right up between
them. I stared at Lucas, who started to laugh.

"Almost forgot," he said. He went into the kitchen and
I remained with Olivia, groaning under the touch of her
hand. When he came back, I smelled what he had and went
on high alert, waiting rigidly.

"This is what she does." Lucas chuckled.

"It's such an itty bitty piece of cheese!"

Yes! Tiny Piece of Cheese!

"Right, the point is the ritual, I think. Watch her stare
at it."

They were both so happy to be doing Tiny Piece of
Cheese that they laughed. Lucas lowered it slowly and I

carefully removed it from between his fingers. The explosion of taste on my tongue lasted only a moment, but it was what I had craved—a treat, hand-fed to me by my person.

I thought back to my hungry days on the trail, when all I could think about was my Tiny Piece of Cheese. It was as wonderful as I recalled.

It really wasn't very comfortable in the small bed, a little like sleeping with Gavin and Taylor and Dutch, but I did not jump down. I lay there and remembered how hungry I had been, how much that empty ache in my stomach made me miss Lucas. I remembered Big Kitten, how she sat and watched me from the rocks when I last saw her. I had taken care of Big Kitten when she needed me. And I had taken care of poor, sad Axel, gave him comfort the way I had just given Mack comfort. Axel loved me. And Gavin and Taylor loved me. Without the love and care from those and others, I would not have been able to find my way.

It had all been so that I could do Go Home. And now, lying in bed between Lucas and Olivia, I was back with my people, and would never leave again. I was a good dog.

I finally, finally was Go Home.

Afterword

I probably am not the only person to notice that of the last dozen books I've had published, eleven of them have pictures of dogs on the cover. (My humor book, *A Dad's Purpose,* has a photo of *me*. More than fifty people have asked me, "What sort of dog is that on *A Dad's Purpose*?")

("Ugly," I tell them.)

So that's who I am: the dog-book guy. If you've read this *particular* dog book, I thought you might be interested in hearing a little on how *A Dog's Way Home* went from blank page to motion picture.

Being the dog-book guy means I spend a lot of time watching dog videos. Hey, it's my living, I'm doing research. Have you seen the one where the two dogs are waiting for a chance to lick an ice-cream cone, and the Puggle licks delicately, and then it's the Golden's turn, and he swallows the whole cone? I love that one. Every time I bring it up on my screen, I'm *working*. It's a tough job, but somebody's got to do it.

Along the way and quite by accident, I've come to learn a lot about dogs. Over the years, one type of story that always drew my attention was the one where a lost dog returns to its owner, sometimes after months or years and often after traveling many, many miles—similar to how parents today send their children off to college, only to have the kids come back to start living in the basement.

How do dogs do it, tracking overland without map, compass, or GPS? There are a lot of theories. I have my own, and they show up in subtle ways in *A Dog's Way Home*.

With this novel, I veered away from any magical premise (well, except for the fact that the story is narrated by a dog). In *A Dog's Purpose* and the sequel, *A Dog's Journey*, the main character is reincarnated, remembering each life. This dog, Bella, has one life, one purpose, and is focused on being reunited with her person.

Being real doesn't mean I didn't explore some fanciful ideas, including that Bella, a dog raised by cats, might form a very unusual friendship in the wild—if you've already read the book, you know what I'm talking about, here. But otherwise I tried to depict the harsh environment she would find in the Rocky Mountains as she attempted to "do Go Home." To say it's a dangerous trek is to understate the challenges—even a dog *pack* would find it nearly impossible.

That was the ambitious objective I set for myself—figure out how Bella might plausibly survive her journey. I spent about a year writing the story, using my memory of living in the mountains, a couple of Colorado Trail guide books, and a lot of trips to the Rockies to help me get the setting just right.

When producer Gavin Polone read the manuscript for *A Dog's Way Home* (he also produced *A Dog's Purpose*), he instantly wanted to turn it into a film. He showed it to Sony and they agreed it should be up on the big screen, and Cathryn Michon (my writing and life partner) and I were hired to write the screenplay.

Usually that's where it ends: an awful lot of scripts get stuck in "development," a process in which successive writers produce successive drafts until the screenplay is so bad no one would ever want to watch it. Picture a chef being hired to make a pot of chili. Then she is fired and another cook comes in and adds bacon. Then someone else is hired and removes all the beans and adds motor oil. Out goes the meat, in goes something they found in Uncle Frank's garage. Then someone else pours in melted fiberglass and Ebola. The resulting stuff is so bad that the person who hired all the cooks gets promoted.

That's not what happened with this one. Happily no one else was brought onboard to tinker with the script. Even better, Gavin and the studio decided they wanted the star, the dog playing Bella, to be a rescue animal.

That's how Cathryn and I wound up flying to Nashville to meet a dog named Shelby, an abandoned pit mix who was living near a local landfill. She was rescued by some of the most caring Animal Control officers I've ever met, especially T. J. Jori and Megan Buhler. Their county animal shelter is proud of its record: they have never put down an adoptable dog. They welcomed us because they saw an opportunity to change the life of one dog for the better.

That's how rescue works: one animal at a time.

Teresa Miller, the movie's animal trainer, made the call after we had all spent a few hours with Shelby: this was the dog. Despite a neglected, abandoned life, virtually starving and eating garbage from the landfill, Shelby was cheerful and intelligent and eager to please. She just wanted someone to love her, and probably someone she could love back.

Cathryn and I were present for some of the training sessions with Shelby as she learned how to do things like dig up treats (for the avalanche rescue scene) and go to her mark so the camera could catch her gorgeous face. Shelby and the other animals were treated with loving, gentle commands, and there was no question they all enjoyed their work.

The location for the movie version of *A Dog's Way Home* was often called "happy set" by the cast and crew working on the production. I called it a "frigid set," because we were in Canada in winter and I was receiving reliable reports from my extremities that I was freezing to death. Shelby and the other dogs were in tents with heaters and blankets and were fed treats. Cathryn and I were wearing seventeen layers of clothing and were in tents with wind chill and were fed tepid coffee.

To get to work, Cathryn and I were driven on the backs of snowmobiles up into the mountains, where the aforementioned tents were arranged like we were a bunch of gold prospectors. In between takes, I worked on my next novel, until my computer froze. Not "froze" as in "the operating system crashed," but "froze" as in "the hard drive became so cold it broke."

Most of the set time was spent with the dogs, which is only proper—it's a dog movie, right? Except in this one, SPOILER ALERT, the dog doesn't die like every other dog movie, and the screenwriters had bad coffee. So I watched as Shelby did her tricks, wagging her tail like crazy, even when she was supposed to be acting sad, or scared. (The same computer graphics wizards who were charged with creating a cougar also were assigned to make Shelby's tail stop communicating joy all the time—they'll paint in a limp tail to hide how happy she was to be playing movie star. Because to Shelby, that's what it all was: *play*.)

There are some other themes in *A Dog's Way Home* that are very important to me. I wanted to focus a spotlight on the plight of some of our veterans—men and women who have served our country and as a result are dealing with physical and emotional fallout. They are heroes and deserve our gratitude and support.

And Bella would never have had to face all those desperate miles if it were not for BDL—Breed Discriminatory Legislation. Countless dogs have been picked up, banished, and even destroyed because of the ignorant belief that they must all be dangerous.

To me, BDL is like saying that because Osama bin Laden was left-handed, all left-handed people should be attacked by Seal Team Six.

I hope that every person watching and reading *A Dog's*

Way Home is left with the knowledge that because of BDL, dogs who merely *look* like they might be pit bulls (no DNA tests are given) can wind up being executed without ever having done anything but love people.

One last point and I'll move on: the "L" in "BDL" means that elected officials have voted for these laws. They can be persuaded to repeal BDL, or, if not, they can be replaced with enlightened individuals who will.

Back to moviemaking. Whether it is a happy set or not, there are so many people involved in making a movie, it's a wonder that every Oscar acceptance speech isn't four hours long. It's simply impossible to describe the amount of labor and care that even a single minute of film requires to become something you'll see in the movie. I'll just say this: when Cathryn and I arrived on our snowmobiles and saw the tent city that had been erected to make the movie set, when we met all the people, from the director to the craft-service people to the animal trainers, when we saw how many individual jobs and roles were created by this project, it was enormously moving and gratifying to both of us. As the man who looked at the blank page and wondered what words I should use to fill it up, I felt a real sense of accomplishment.

Of course, it wasn't just me, you know. If readers hadn't snapped up copies of *A Dog's Way Home*, pushing it on to the *New York Times* bestseller list, the studios would have been unenthusiastic about making the movie. Which means you, personally, are part of the process that brought us the film.

On behalf of every crew member who had a job, on behalf of the screenwriters whose computers had frostbite, and especially on behalf of Shelby, who was living in the most bleak of circumstances and now has a safe, loving home—thank you for making this all possible.

Acknowledgments

Here's something I know about myself: I do not like to fail at writing assignments. It has always been something of a point of pride for me that I could turn in a paper on, say, *War and Peace,* and get a passing grade on it—particularly since I didn't actually read *War and Peace.* As most of my teachers eventually learned, I was bluffing my way through school, distracting their attention with good grammar. (It didn't work all that well in math class.)

This current assignment, however—thanking everyone who helped me in the creation of this novel—seems a nearly impossible task. I am not sure where to start, and I don't know where to end. Nothing seems too trivial to include when you think about the fact that if, for example, my mother hadn't given birth to me, I probably would not have become a writer. And what if no one had invented paper? What about the eggs I had for breakfast—without them, I'd be too hungry to write these words. Shouldn't I thank the chicken?

Yet I suppose it is up to me to try to capture on these pages the people who were most important to *A Dog's Way Home.* I am pretty sure I'll fail and forget somebody. If your name is not mentioned here it is not because I did not think you did something to help, it is because my memory is on vacation. In fact, often I will start writing a sentence and then, in the middle of it . . . okay, now I can't remember the point I was trying to make, but I think it was a good one.

First, I want to thank Kristin Sevick, and Linda, Tom,

Karen, Kathleen, and everyone else at Tom Doherty/Tor/ Forge, who helped birth this book. Initially, I had made a pitch for an entirely different novel and everyone was willing to listen when I confessed that my idea was not that great. I won't go into the details; it just was unworkable once I began doing research, which is why I try to avoid doing research or, for that matter, anything resembling real work. So, very graciously, they agreed to discuss other ideas and eventually this one, the story of Bella finding her way back to her people, turned out to be a real winner for all of us.

Thank you, Scott Miller of Trident Media, for explaining to everyone that if they stopped publishing my novels it would really hurt my feelings. Scott, you are a true friend and a real champion of my work.

I also want to thank Sheri Kelton, my new manager, for adjusting my focus so that instead of being distracted I'm now just lazy. Thanks, Steve Younger, for defending me against the forces of evil.

Thank you, Gavin Polone, for believing in my work and for wanting to see me succeed in this very dangerous business, and for promising not to quit. You always keep your word, which makes people in this town very nervous.

Thank you, Lauren Potter, for showing up in my life and my office and organizing both. Because of you, I actually have time to do all the writing that Scott Miller is promising people I will do and that Sheri Kelton tells me I should be focused on.

Thank you, Elliot Crowe, for letting me keep the title of "independent film producer" while you do all the work. The movie *Muffin Top: A Love Story*, directed by Cathryn Michon, was our first successful venture, but we have another one in the pipeline—*Cook Off!*—that should be in theaters in 2017. Simply would not be happening without Elliott.

Thanks to Connection House Incorporated, for all of its

marketing and research work that continues to make my life easier. I'm constantly impressed with how everyone working there is so in tune with each other.

Thanks, Fly HC and Hillary Carlip, for maintaining and building my websites: wbrucecameron.com and adogspurpose.com.

Thank you, Carolina and Annie, for letting me be part of your lives.

Thank you, Andy and Jody Sherwood. You continue to be among the most supportive people in my life, in just about every way possible.

Thank you, Diane and Tom Runstrom. You are simply wonderful people.

Thank you to my sister, Amy Cameron, who nearly became Miss America and then went on to become one of the world's greatest teachers. Emily would be proud.

Thank you, Julie Cameron M.D., for being the person who I can call and say, "I need a disease where someone wakes up in the morning with red hair and no memory of words that rhyme with 'kismet.'" She'll name the disease, describe the treatment, and recommend I see a psychiatrist.

Thank you, Georgia and Chelsea, for being so reproductive in 2016, and to James and Chris for doing their part of the process. Thank you, Chase, for being the man you have become, and thank you, Alyssa, for influencing him to stay that way.

Gordon, Eloise, Ewan, Garrett, and Sadie: welcome home.

I do not have a marketing department. I do not need one. I have my mom. Thank you, Mom, for selling everyone in Michigan my books and, when they refuse to buy a copy, giving them one.

Thank you, Mindy and Lindy, for keeping me social and making sure that anyone who goes online for any reason finds out about *A Dog's Purpose*.

I owe Jim Lambert a great debt for introducing me to

the Denver VA hospital and for explaining the military culture there. Jim, you were so generous with your time, and you are doing such important work.

Rather Hosch went undercover for me and lived in Gunnison, Colorado, for many years just so she could give me a detailed explanation of how cold it gets there. Thank you, Rather.

Finally, the person who is my biggest supporter, the one who kept promising me this novel was worth writing, who read early drafts and gave me such great notes, who is my business partner, my life partner, and my best friend. Cathryn, you are everything to me and this story would never have found its way home without you.

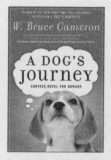